Praise for TEXAS THUNDER

"Fast-paced and smoothly plotted, Raye's light-hearted series starter deftly evokes a variety of emotions while building multifaceted characters."
—*Publishers Weekly*

"A sweet, passionate story that captures the heart and provides a thrilling happily-ever-after."
—*Night Owl Reviews*

"Love and moonshine blend well in Raye's latest novel set in Texas, with her modern, amusing storytelling and strong, lively characters. Callie's sassiness is the perfect complement to Brett's toughness, and their tension is just as fiery and intense as their chemistry, which will appeal to readers. Raye gives us a well-crafted, down-home romance."
—*RT Book Reviews*

"A sizzling tale that features some hot sex, but it's the plentiful laugh-out-loud scenes that will pull readers in. A passionate and enjoyable read from beginning to end."
—*Romance Reviews Today*

Also by Kimberly Raye

TEXAS THUNDER

RED-HOT TEXAS NIGHTS

KIMBERLY RAYE

St. Martin's Paperbacks

This is a work of fiction. All of the characters, organizations, and events portrayed in this novel are either products of the author's imagination or are used fictitiously.

RED-HOT TEXAS NIGHTS

For information address St. Martin's Press, 175 Fifth Avenue, New York, NY 10010.

ISBN: 978-1-250-06396-0

Printed in the United States of America

St. Martin's Paperbacks edition / March 2016

St. Martin's Paperbacks are published by St. Martin's Press, 175 Fifth Avenue, New York, NY 10010.

10 9 8 7 6 5 4 3 2 1

This book is dedicated to my beautiful daughter, Brenna Evelyn Groff.
It seems like just yesterday you were crawling out of your playpen and now you're in high school. Where has the time gone?
You've turned into a kind, thoughtful young woman and I couldn't be more proud!
I am truly blessed.

ACKNOWLEDGMENTS

Being a writer is the best job in the world. It's scary at times and lonely more often than not, but the reward is well worth it. Who else gets to go to work in their PJs and spend all day with some really hot heroes? But there's more to a great book than me and my computer. I would like to say a special thank-you to those special individuals who help breathe life into my books. To the best agent in the business, Natasha Kern, for always giving me solid advice and an understanding ear. To my editor, Holly Ingraham, who goes above and beyond the call of duty to help the story be the best that it can be. And to my family, who put up with take-out and mismatched socks when I'm too busy to leave my fictitious world.

Much love from deep in the heart!

CHAPTER 1

It was the moment of truth.

Brandy Louise Tucker switched off the neon-pink OPEN sign that hummed in the window of her bakery, Sweet Somethings. Pulling down the hot-pink scalloped shades that spanned the storefront windows, she blocked out the rapidly setting sun and a small town full of prying eyes.

The last thing she needed was an audience.

Throwing the dead bolt on the front door, she double-checked to make sure the ruffled curtains were pulled, too, and then walked behind the main display case filled with what was left of today's freshly made cakes and breads.

Her heart beating ninety-to-nothing, she leaned down behind the cash register and pulled out a small pint-sized Mason jar filled with a pale gold liquid.

It wasn't even close to her specialty—chocolate nirvana cake with marshmallow fluff frosting and rich ganache drizzle—but it was just as addictive.

More so if the rumors floating around Rebel, Texas, were even close to the truth.

She could only pray that they were.

Shaking the jar, she watched the bubbles swirl into a telltale funnel that, as her late granddaddy used to say, was the sign of a damn powerful mix. Judging by the speed of the popping and whirling, the alcohol was well over 160 proof.

But potency was just the half the magic when it came to good moonshine.

Not that Brandy knew all the ins and outs of the stuff. Sure, she was a direct descendant of *the* Archibald Tucker, half of the legendary duo responsible for the infamous Texas Thunder—the best bootleg ever made in the Lone Star State. But Brandy made her living baking cakes and pies. Her claim to fame? Mixing up a light and fluffy buttercream, not stirring together a batch of mash.

Until now.

Her finely tuned taste buds had paid off and she'd done it. She'd supposedly mixed up something better than the original she'd been trying so hard to duplicate. Forget Texas Thunder. This stuff was pure lightning in a jar. A raging tornado.

Texas Tornado.

Her heart pounded at the thought and she drew a deep breath. She was getting way ahead of herself. Yes, she'd tweaked the original recipe, but who knew if it was that much better than Archibald's claim to fame? All she had was the word of a few local bootleggers who'd taken her mash and turned it into an actual brew.

She had no idea if they'd added something to it or altered it during the process. There was no way to be sure that it was 100 percent hers without seeing the process through—from start to finish.

Which was why she needed to come up with another batch of mash and get it to a professional. Someone who could run the mix in a safe, controlled, *legal* environment. Someone who could tell her if she had, indeed, found her own version of liquid gold.

But first she had to taste this jar and see if it truly was all that.

"Don't you think you're going overboard?" Ellie, her baking assistant, asked as she emerged from the storage area and noted the tightly drawn curtains. The woman was in her early twenties, tall and thin, with her long red hair pulled back into a ponytail. She wore a SWEET SOMETHINGS pink apron tied around her narrow waist and a matching T-shirt that read GO ON . . . WHISPER SWEET SOMETHINGS TO ME. "It's not like *we* did anything wrong," she added. "I just handed the mash to a friend who handed it to a friend who handed it to another friend who just so happened to have a hidden still."

"We've still got a jar of illegal moonshine in our possession."

"True, but that's also the case for half the people in this town. I'm talking about the processing. *We* didn't brew anything."

"No, but we might as well have." Brandy

paced the length of the counter and fought down a wave of worry. "What if Sheriff DeMassi knocks on that door right now?"

"Sheriff DeMassi is up in Austin at a law enforcement convention for the next two days. There's just Deputy Marty on duty and I've gotten to know that man really well since I rolled into this town"—she winked—"if you know what I mean. And he's gotten to know me. And, well, he's still hooked even though I made it perfectly clear that one night together doesn't make us a thing. He wouldn't bother us even if he had the time, which he doesn't. He's got his hands full with the Ladies Rotary Bunko Night going on over at the senior center. You know how those women get when the stakes are high."

Since Ellie had moved to Rebel only a few short years ago, she'd not only slept with most of the available men but had become *the* source for local gossip.

"*Better to get ahead of it,*" she'd told Brandy more than once. "*I know people are gonna talk about me and mine, so I make sure I do the talking first.*"

"Hear tell," she went on, "Laverne Shipley donated a full spa day at the Hair Saloon as a grand prize. I'll bet those old busybodies are practically pulling each other's hair out by now. You know Sally Goodwin lost her weave during the last poker tournament they hosted, don't you?"

"Seriously?"

Ellie nodded. "Cara Donnelly pulled it out in

one handful after Sally laid down a flush. It wasn't pretty." Ellie's gaze went to the jar sitting on the counter. "Not nearly as pretty as this." Her eyes twinkled. "I'm telling you, this right here is the golden goose."

Brandy could only hope.

While the original Texas Thunder recipe had finally been found, Brandy had no clue if her older sister Callie and Callie's fiancé Brett were still in the market to sell it. The two had solved most of their own financial problems for the interim, which meant they weren't in any hurry to make a deal.

Perhaps they'd hold on to the recipe. Or auction it off. Hell, maybe they'd frame it and keep it for sentimental reasons. Brandy didn't know, and she certainly wasn't asking.

Callie Tucker had given up a scholarship to the University of Texas School of Journalism and forfeited her dreams to stay right here in Rebel and raise her two younger siblings when their parents had passed away. Ten years later, she was finally making her own dreams come true with a job at the local newspaper. Even more, she'd found her own happily-ever-after with the love of her life and once-upon-a-time enemy, Brett Sawyer.

The Sawyers and the Tuckers had been feuding harder and longer than any Hatfield and McCoy, but Callie and Brett were doing their damndest to mend the riff. They were getting married next month, much to the shock and dismay of an entire town still divided, but neither cared about public opinion.

They were in love. Happy.

Brandy certainly wasn't going to fudge that up by dumping a load of problems at Callie's feet.

Big problems.

Namely, Brandy needed to get out from under the loan she'd taken out a few months back to help pay the overdue property taxes left behind after her grandfather's death.

She'd been more than eager to put up her equipment for the secure note to help Callie, who'd been under pressure to save the Tucker family home. But Brandy hadn't counted on the new doughnut shop that moved in down the street from her bakery just a few weeks after she'd signed on the dotted line.

A mom-and-pop endeavor, like most places in Rebel, that had taken a bite out of Brandy's early-morning rush. Sure, she was still the only spot for cakes and pies and other custom-baked goods, but her morning muffin rush had brought in a healthy dime, too. With a fledgling business barely six months old, she had to put every available penny back into her bakery if she wanted it to grow. Chop off a chunk for lost income courtesy of Susie Mae's habanero-jelly-filled doughnuts—the new *it* breakfast in Rebel—and the substantial loan repayment, and she'd barely broken even this past month. Forget growing and nurturing Sweet Somethings into the go-to destination for all things sugar in Rebel and the surrounding counties. Particularly among the special-occasion crowd.

At her current size, she could barely produce one wedding cake per week in addition to her regular offerings. To really make a name for herself and get her bakery featured on the go-to website for Hill Country weddings—www.Heart ofTexasHappilyEverAfters.com—she needed to crank out at least three to four custom orders. That meant hiring another cake decorator and bringing in a massive second oven.

And that meant she needed more cash.

She reached for the jar. Drawing a deep breath, she willed her hands to steady. Her fingertips caught the edge of the metal and she unscrewed the lid.

A soft *poppp!* sounded as the pressure released. In that next instant, the scent of warm strawberries and something much more potent filled the air and teased her nostrils.

"Go on," Ellie said when Brandy hesitated. "Do it."

"I will. Just keep your apron on." She tamped down on her reservations, summoned her courage, and touched her lips to the thick rim of the glass.

A quick tilt and the first drop hit her tongue. Sizzled its way down her throat. Burned a path between her breastbone and . . . *Shazam!*

Heat rolled through her and firebombed in the pit of her stomach. The floor trembled. The walls blurred. A ringing echoed in her ears.

Holy guacamole. The taste packed more of a punch than she'd expected. While she'd never been much of a drinker and she had no intention of turning into one, suddenly she could at least understand why, even in this day and age, there were still men willing to risk life and livelihood to take to the woods and brew up their own hooch.

There was nothing like it.

Like *this*.

The blaze had subsided into a vibrating warmth that bubbled through her and soothed her insides. The sweet, succulent flavor of strawberries danced on her lips. The rich buzz of alcohol filled her head. Dollar signs danced in front of her eyes.

"I think I might be on to something," she gasped, taking another sip just to be sure. Another punch of heat, an echoing hum, and a full-blown smile split her lips. "It's definitely good. *Really* good."

But was it the best?

Drawing a deep, calming breath, she handed over the jar to an eager Ellie. Another quick check of the locks to ease her paranoia, and she started for the back room and the plastic five-gallon tub sitting next to the pile of ingredients she'd assembled for another batch.

Because there was only one way to find out.

CHAPTER 2

"This is highly illegal. You know that, right?"

"Depends on how you look at it." Tyler Mc-Call stood on the rickety front porch and slipped his hand inside the three-inch gap in the weathered screen door. His fingers brushed peeling wood before he finally felt cold metal. He flipped the lock on the inside and the latch groaned.

"I'm looking at breaking and entering," came the nervous male voice behind Tyler. "And trespassing. And maybe even a destruction-of-property charge because you ran over that cactus when you pulled into the driveway and totally ruined any curb appeal."

"First off, that prickly pear grows wild and judging by the knee-high grass, I'm banking nobody in this house gives a shit about aesthetics. Number two, I'm not breaking in. This screen was already cut. I'm just making use of a preexisting breach. As for entering, well, that's more of a gray area." He turned the knob. Joints moaned and the door creaked open. "See? Wide open and welcoming."

"Is this your house?"

"No."

"You're sure? You didn't get kicked in the head during your last ride and lose your memory?"

"Hell, no." There'd been no eating dust during his most recent run. Ball Buster had been one vicious mother of a bull, but Tyler had managed to tighten his grip and hang on anyway to give eight of the best seconds of his entire life. A performance worthy of the highest score of his career, and the very reason he'd inched his way into the top thirty-five in contention for the coveted Professional Bull Riders championship in Vegas in October. Provided he could do a rinse and repeat in Cheyenne in just a few short weeks. Everything hinged on Wyoming. If he busted his ass there, he would slide back down the board and be out of the running, and shit out of luck.

And if he nailed one beauty of a ride?

He'd be set, headed to Vegas, ready for his shot at the big time.

For his chance to finally be something more than the black sheep of the uppity Sawyer clan.

If he nailed it.

He stiffened against the doubt and focused on the dim interior of the shabby blue house that sat on the outskirts of town near the railroad tracks.

It was the old Grainger place. Once the pride and joy of Ken and Mimi, who'd settled down fifty-plus years ago to raise a family and grow their own vegetables. Ken had keeled over from a heart attack fifteen years ago and Mimi had followed not long after, and so the place had been left in limbo while their three kids fought it out. The winner? Ken Jr., who'd eventually moved to Texas City to work in one of the refineries and left the place to his only son, Kenny Roy.

Kenny Roy was just a few years younger than Tyler and about as useless as a screen door on a submarine.

He'd never held a job. Instead, he scraped by running a little local hooch, betting on football pots, and selling his own homegrown marijuana.

Tyler took a whiff and grimaced. Apparently Kenny Roy wasn't just selling. He was also sampling the goods.

"There's no gray involved," Duffy West said. Duff was Tyler's oldest friend and his traveling partner. Not that Duff would dare climb onto the back of a bull. He made up half of one of the best calf-roping teams in the state and while he was usually up for whatever trouble Tyler dragged him into, this was different. This didn't involve either of the two B's—buckle bunnies or booze—and so Duff wasn't nearly as pumped.

"It's black and white," the calf roper went on. "This isn't your house, dude. You don't have a key. Translation? You're breaking in."

Tyler shrugged and ducked his head inside the now open doorway. "It's not like I'm doing it with malicious intent."

"So you admit it? You *are* breaking in?"

"I'm not going to steal anything." He blinked, adjusting his eyes to the dim, musty interior. "I just want to talk to him."

"So pick up a phone and let's get the hell out of here."

"I did that already. Twelve times in the past six hours, as a matter of fact."

"Then take a hint and give up. Cooper obviously doesn't want to talk to you."

"Maybe he doesn't want to, but he needs to." That, and Tyler McCall didn't just give up. Not when his father had packed his bags and hauled ass when Tyler had been only twelve and he'd had to step up and take care of his mother and younger brother, and not now when that brother was about to piss away his entire future.

"He's a grown man now," Duff reminded him. "He can fend for himself."

"Coop's barely nineteen and, trust me, he doesn't know the first thing about fending for himself. He needs to get his act together. He *will* get it together just as soon as I get ahold of him."

"And bully him the way you do everyone?"

But Tyler wasn't a bully. He was just a determined sonofabitch. He'd had to be in order to keep what was left of his family together and make a name for himself on the circuit. He sure as hell had no intention of stopping now when everything was on the line.

His brother had a big, fat juicy scholarship waiting on him. A free ride out of the broken-down two-room trailer that held so many crappy memories. A chance to really make something of himself.

Tyler wasn't letting him fuck it up by falling in with the wrong crowd just to make a few quick bucks to satisfy their mother's selfish habits.

That was Tyler's job. He sent home more than enough to pay the bills and buy the groceries. If Ellen McCall didn't know how to budget, well, he'd give her a crash course before he left Rebel.

He wasn't letting his brother throw away his one opportunity just because the woman needed more cigarettes and another bottle of Jack.

"I can't just look the other way when my brother's in trouble," Tyler told Duffy. "I have to *do* something."

Silence ticked by before the cowboy let loose an exasperated sigh. "Then what the hell are you waiting for?" Duffy asked behind him. "Just get inside the damn house and let's get this over with."

"Thanks, buddy." Tyler grinned. "I owe you."

"Tell me something I don't already know."

"So I know I'm usually the queen of bad ideas and it really isn't my place to point fingers," Ellie said when they pulled into the dirt driveway, "but this is just plain stupid."

"Don't you think I already know that?" Brandy shoved the car into park and stared through the windshield at the beaten-down house with the overgrown yard. "But I can't get any brewer to take me seriously without an actual sample, and I can't take the first sample because that could be just a fluke. I need another sample that's just as good, if not better, than the first." And she needed it by the end of next week. In time for her meeting with Mark Edwards, the CEO of Foggy Bottom Distillers and the man who'd been trying to buy the original Texas Thunder recipe from her grandfather before he'd passed away. She'd called Mark about her new and improved version and he'd quickly cleared an hour from his schedule so that they could meet next Friday morning before he left for a distillers' seminar in Kentucky. Followed by a trip to Germany to study brewing techniques and set up a foreign distributor for his company's product list. He would be gone a minimum of two to three months. Maybe longer.

She couldn't wait months to find out if her recipe would even pay off. She needed money now, or at least the promise of it sometime in the near future, and so she had to meet with Mark before he left and present a viable product that was sure to snag his interest.

In order to do that, she had to have another sample as potent as the first by next Friday.

Otherwise, she was screwed.

"My mash will be ready to run next week and I need someone to run it," Brandy told the woman sitting in the passenger seat of the old Buick.

"So wait until it's ready and just leave it on the

porch." Ellie eyed the bare bulb surrounded by bouncing June bugs. "Kenny Roy will know what to do with it."

"Maybe so, but I have to talk to him. I need to know that whoever is doing the actual distilling doesn't alter or contaminate it in any way. I need quality control." And a primo product.

"You really think Kenny Roy is going to let you talk to his connection? Hell, do you think he even knows who's actually running it? These guys are low-key. For all we know, Kenny drops it off to a guy who knows another guy, who knows another guy, and so on, until they get to the guy who actually runs the still."

"My point exactly. It's passing through too many hands at this point. There needs to be one person overseeing everything at each step."

"And you think Kenny Roy is your person? The guy who wore Crocs to the last VFW dance?"

She shrugged. "Not everyone likes to dance."

"Not everyone spends half his time stoned out of his mind to the point that he *can't* dance. Kenny Roy is an idiot. A sky-high idiot."

"Exactly, which is why I'm going to ask the name of his connection and follow the trail straight to the source."

"That's an even worse idea than talking to Kenny. You don't know these guys." Ellie slid Brandy a sideways glance. "What if they're dangerous?"

A question she'd asked herself a thousand times during the drive over. But she'd never been one to back down when she wanted something, and she wanted this.

She needed it.

And she needed it by next Friday.

Brandy shrugged. "They're businessmen and I'm going to make them a business proposition. They let me watch the entire process and I let them have all the spoils with the exception of one jar." Her gaze met Ellie's. "I need to make sure that I'm really on to something, that the first time wasn't just a fluke, before I take this any farther. If the second batch is just as good as the first, then I'll have something solid to present to the distiller."

Something that was sure to pay off.

She reached for the door handle.

Ellie's hand stopped her. "I don't know about this."

"I'll be careful. I promise. Besides, we probably know the guys involved."

"Even worse. We're not supposed to know who they are."

"It's a small town. I'm sure everyone knows who they are. We're probably the exception." Because Brandy had always been the exception. She'd kept her nose clean back in high school, her focus fixated on the future. On perfecting her brownies and her cookies and her cakes. She'd ignored everything else, from the Friday-night parties to the romantic gossip, to who punched who during the occasional lunchroom brawl. She'd never paid attention to the stuff going on around her, or the people.

Not that it had helped.

She'd still managed to snag herself a reputation. One that had started back in the fifth grade when she'd started to develop well before all of the other girls. By the seventh grade, she'd been a full C cup. And by high school? She'd filled out a D and then some.

She'd been every boy's fantasy, and every girl's enemy. The boys had chased after her and while she'd never let any of them catch her, it hadn't mattered. They'd talked anyway. And spread rumors. People believed what they wanted to believe, and they'd wanted desperately to think that curvy, voluptuous Brandy Tucker was handing it out left and right.

The truth—that she'd been a naive virgin—hadn't mattered in the least.

At first she'd tried to convince them otherwise. She'd dressed conservatively and kept the boys at arm's length. All but one.

One handsome, sexy, charming-as-all-get-out cowboy who'd taken her virginity and made her realize that she was every bit the bad girl that everyone thought.

Not that she'd been ready to fly her crazy flag for the entire world to see.

Not then and not now.

She still walked the walk and talked the talk, denying her lustful nature to the world and playing the good girl.

Most of the time.

She tamped down the sudden memory of a

hot mouth at her throat and strong hands roaming her body and concentrated on climbing out of the old car that had once belonged to her parents.

Brandy had shared the car with her sisters until her grandpa had passed away. Then Callie had started driving his old truck, Jenna had landed an internship with a local vet that came with a company truck, and Brandy had gotten Bertha all to herself.

She shut the door, gathered her courage, and started past the brand-spanking-new black Chevy pickup truck parked off to the side. Kenny Roy might be an idiot but he was obviously doing something right.

Her gaze slid to the cowboy hat parked on the front dash of the truck and an image hit her. A tall, dark cowboy leaning over her, his hat obliterating the handsome contours of his face, his aqua-blue eyes gleaming in the darkness.

A gaze so pale and translucent that it belonged in a brochure for the Bahamas or some other tropical paradise.

She shook away the memory and kept walking, putting one foot in front of the other so fast it was a wonder she didn't trip. But she wasn't about to let her nerves fail her. She knew Kenny Roy. Knew what he was into.

But she'd never seen it firsthand. Never shown up at his house on a Saturday night to score a joint or beg a jar of shine, even though the world might think otherwise.

She'd spent her weekends at home with her sisters. Doing homework. Watching TV. Baking.

Always baking.

And if she wanted to keep baking, she needed to do this. Now.

She drew a deep breath and mounted the steps.

The porch light gleamed, pushing back the dusky shadows just enough to illuminate the rickety hinges and frayed screen door. A beaten-up metal milk can sat nearby filled to the brim with pungent cigarette butts.

At least they looked like cigarette butts at first glance, but based on Kenny's line of work she wasn't placing any bets. An empty Frio Beer case sat nearby, next to several empty cans that had dropped and rolled here and there.

Her foot hit one of the cans. Aluminum jumped and clattered, and a wave of nerves went through her. She steeled herself, balled her fist, and drew her hand back to knock.

The minute her knuckles made contact with wood, the door swung inward and just like that, she found herself staring at a pair of incredible aqua-blue eyes edged in thick, dark lashes.

Eyes that had haunted her more than one night since Tyler McCall had taken her virginity and a dozen of her prizewinning rocky road brownies and rolled out of town without so much as a text good-bye.

CHAPTER 3

Tyler had always considered himself one tough mother.

Focused. Relentless. Game face firmly in place.

Nothing rattled him. Not now when he drew the worst of the worst thousand-pound monster for his next ride. Or way back when his most admired teacher had told him that he was just poor white trash who would never amount to anything.

Tyler didn't stumble when life tossed something unexpected his way. He held his ground and kept his cool. He sure as hell didn't stand there speechless, his heart pounding, the air lodged in his throat, and all because . . . damn, but it was her.

Her.

He stared into eyes as rich and fertile as freshly mowed grass and saw the flash of shock that mirrored his own. Her full mouth parted on a startled gasp and he noted the slight tremble of her bottom lip. "Tyler?" she managed after a few frantic seconds. "Tyler McCall?"

"Brandy." He didn't need to say her last name.

There was only one Brandy in Rebel. Only one Brandy that stood out in his memory and crept into his thoughts when he least suspected it. When he held on for dear life and busted out of the chute or the moment he slammed into the ground after a grueling ride.

He wasn't sure why he saw her face. If anything, she was the last woman he should have thought of, particularly since she never spared him a second thought. Hell, she'd barely noticed him at all back in high school. She'd been too good for the likes of him and she'd made certain that he knew it.

She'd ignored every smile. Every tip of his hat. Every lustful glance.

Until that night, that is.

She'd been more than responsive to him for those few hours, but then she'd morphed back into the same uppity-up. He'd known then that no matter how good the sex—then and now—it didn't make up for the fact that she was a Tucker and he was a Sawyer, and no way was she going to buck tradition and get mixed up with the likes of him.

Not in public.

But behind closed doors?

He was more than good enough for that.

A fact that stuck in his craw even though the last thing he'd ever wanted was a relationship outside the bedroom. He liked his freedom even more than he liked sex and so he'd always kept things easy and uncomplicated.

That hadn't kept the women from trying, however. He'd had more than one chase after him over the years.

But not Brandy.

Never Brandy.

That's why he saw her at the craziest moments. She stood out because she was the only one who managed to keep things in perspective whenever they were together, to give him a dose of his own medicine, to keep it strictly sex.

And while he sure as hell didn't want her falling head over heels, the fact that she never had sort of bothered him. Enough to implant her firmly in his brain.

Crazy, but there it was.

"Is it Cooper?" Duff's voice drew Tyler's attention and he became acutely aware of the strange tingle in his gut and the all-important fact that he had a hard-on for a woman who probably wouldn't piss on him if he were to catch fire right in front of her. Not in front of God and the good citizens of Rebel, that is.

In private? Well, that was a different matter altogether.

He stiffened, shifting his stance and letting the *it's all good* grin he'd become famous for slide firmly into place.

Because it *was* all good.

It didn't matter what Brandy Tucker thought of him. What anyone thought. All that mattered was that Tyler McCall was on his way to the top and nobody was going to pull him back down.

"I didn't know you were in town?" Her soft voice slid into his ears and sent a whisper along the length of his spine.

"It was a spur-of-the-moment thing." He shrugged. "I just got back today." He arched an eyebrow at her. "Don't tell me you're here to score a little smoke off Kenny Roy?"

Her shock eased into a distinctive frown, as if she'd just remembered why she'd never really liked him all that much in the first place. "Of course not. I don't smoke."

He gave her a once-over that went from her head to toes and back up again. Nice and slow. The way he did with every woman. "You want to put twenty on the domino tournament over at the VFW Hall?"

Her expression hardened. "I don't gamble, either."

"So what do you want with Kenny Roy?"

"That's my business, not yours." She glanced past him. "So? Are you going to let me see him?"

"He's not here."

Disappointment furrowed her brow and he had the insane urge to reach out and ease the worry lines with the pad of his finger. She seemed to think. "Any idea when he'll be back?"

He shrugged. "I wish to hell I knew."

"Since when did you start hanging out with Kenny Roy?"

"Since I heard that he's been hanging with my brother." He ran a hand through his hair. "What about you?"

"I've just got a few questions for him. Nothing big." She glanced behind her toward her car as if trying to decide something. "I'll just come back later."

"I don't think that's a good idea. You'd do best to steer clear of Kenny Roy."

"Since when do you tell me what to do?" She planted her hands on her hips. "I don't need your permission. I'm a grown woman, in case you haven't noticed."

Oh, he'd noticed, all right.

Even if he hadn't seen her in over two years.

She was all woman. Lush. Sultry. Beautiful when she was stretched out on a set of flower-print sheets, her skin covered in a slick sheen of sweat, her body open and waiting.

Two years, he reminded himself.

While they might have hooked up from time to time whenever he made it back to town, he hadn't been home since Cooper had gotten his driver's license and started to fend for himself. Plenty of time for things to have changed. A woman like Brandy wasn't meant to keep her sexuality bottled up. And while she'd always done her best to do just that, he couldn't imagine her not going back for more with somebody.

His gut tightened and he eyed her. "Does your boyfriend know you're out slumming without him?"

"Does your girlfriend know you're out harassing women without her?" She stared him down as bold as ever.

As sexy as ever.

The seconds ticked off until a grin finally got the best of him. She'd never had a problem standing up to him. No matter how much of a bastard he was being.

He shook his head. "I don't have a girlfriend."

She nodded. "Well, I don't have a boyfriend."

The words stirred a rush of relief and he felt his body relax considerably.

A crazy reaction for a man who prided himself on keeping things loose and easy with all women.

Even this one.

Especially this one.

"I figured you might have settled down by now," he murmured.

"You figured wrong. I'm still flying solo. Not even a dog. Unless you count the strays that Jenna keeps bringing home. She landed an internship with the Rebel veterinary clinic."

"She always did like animals."

"Um, yeah. So I guess I'd better get going. I'm giving Ellie a ride home." She motioned behind her toward the old car parked in the gravel drive and the shadow of a woman sitting in the passenger seat. "She's my baking assistant. At my bakery." She pushed a strand of blond hair behind one delicate ear as she turned back toward him. "I, um, have a bakery now. I opened up about six months ago."

"I heard. Congratulations. You finally got what you always wanted."

"I did." She stared him square in the eye and he saw the shimmer in her pupils. "I got exactly what I wanted."

Silence stretched between them for several long moments, as if she couldn't decide what to say next. The moment awkward. The way it always was when they weren't humping each other's brains out.

"Well, I guess I'll come back later," she finally murmured.

"Again, I don't think that's such a good idea."

Her gaze narrowed ever so slightly. "Again, I don't think it's any of your business." She turned then and started back down the porch steps. "If you see Kenny Roy, tell him I'm looking for him."

"Not gonna happen, sweetheart." Her shapely butt swayed with each step. His gut tightened, and the words were out before he could think better of them. "But maybe I'll stop by the bakery before I leave. I've got a sudden hankering for a good brownie," he added, not that he was remembering the decadent bite of chocolate she'd given him as a parting gift after their last encounter.

No, he was thinking about the sweet, mesmerizing taste of her. The way she'd squirmed against his mouth. And clawed at his shoulders. And begged for more.

For him.

"You'd better make it early then," she tossed

over her shoulder. "I'm usually sold out by noon."

"I'll bet you are," he murmured, his gaze hooked on the voluptuous side-to-side of her denim-clad ass. "I'll just bet."

CHAPTER 4

"Who knew Kenny Roy had such cute friends?"

"If by *cute* you mean a sneaky man-whore who sails back into town without so much as a phone call, then um, yeah, I guess Tyler McCall fits the bill."

The minute the words were out, Brandy wanted to snatch them back. So what if he hadn't called to tell her he was back in town? It wasn't like he ever called. He showed up. She showed up. And the fun began.

They were strictly sex buddies. No strings attached. No explanations needed.

Just two people enjoying the company of each other behind closed doors.

She just hadn't counted on the crazy emptiness she'd felt when he'd left this last time, and stayed gone so long that she'd almost stopped counting the months.

Almost.

"I meant cute"—Ellie's voice pushed into her thoughts—"as in *cute*. You know, nice hair, good body, handsome face." Ellie slid her a sideways glance. "Vent much?"

"Sorry. I'm just a little disappointed. Kenny Roy's not here."

"Sort of like the universe's way of saving you from yourself and sending a distinctly clear message that I'm right and you shouldn't be pushing for a face-to-face with a bunch of felons. Just drop off the mash when it's ready and let's be done with it."

"I can't." Brandy turned the key and the engine grumbled to life. "I have to follow the process."

"Then tell me about this Tyler McCall." Ellie turned her attention back to the front porch. "Has he always been so hunky?"

Unfortunately.

"So sexy?"

Yep.

"So downright scrumptious?

A frown tugged at her mouth. "Can we talk about something else?"

"I take that as a big, fat yes. So what's the story with you and this hunky cowboy? Was he your steady? Did he stand you up? Did you stand him up? Did you make like monkeys and do it fifty ways till Friday?"

"No, no, and no."

"That's only three nos, which means you purposely ignored the last question, which means you screwed his brains out and then something happened."

"Nothing happened. He left town, that's all."

"And left you behind?"

"It wasn't like that. We were just friends. Occasional friends."

"You mean fuck buddies."

"Can we talk about something else?"

"I thought you'd never ask." Her eyes gleamed. "Tell me about his friend." She motioned to the guy who pushed through the front door and came up next to Tyler. "What do you know about him?"

Brandy peered through the darkness at the other man, who stood a few inches shorter than Tyler. He was slightly leaner than the muscular bull rider, but every bit as good looking with whiskey-blond hair that framed his face and reached just below his jaw.

Even so, her gaze kept going back to Tyler, to the intense way he stared after her, that sexy slant of a grin to his lips that still made her stomach flutter even though she hadn't seen him in two years.

Because she hadn't seen him in two years.

"So?" Ellie's voice pushed into her thoughts. "Who's the sidekick?"

"I don't know." She shoved the car into reverse and backed out of the driveway. "He's not from around here as far as I know."

"Which isn't saying much since you spend your Saturday nights up to your elbows in flour. He could be burning up the dance floor every night at Diamonds and Dust and you would never know. You need to get out more."

"What I need is to find Kenny Roy." One last glance at the two men on the porch and she swung the nose of the car out into the street and stepped on the gas. Gravel spewed and the massive hunk of metal bolted forward.

"We could swing by the VFW Hall. It's Friday night. He could be making a delivery to the domino club. They like to add a little kick to their punch while they play."

"And talk to him in front of the biggest gossips in town?" Brandy shook her head. "I'll stop back by later. Maybe he'll be home."

Hopefully.

Her heart kicked up a beat and her hands trembled.

At the prospect of finding Kenny Roy.

She certainly wasn't getting anxious because Tyler McCall was back in town.

Her gaze went to the rearview mirror and the headlights that sliced through the darkness and settled behind her.

Ellie glanced behind and a smile tugged at her lips. "So what's the scoop on you and Mr. FB?" she asked as she settled back into her seat. "How did you meet?"

"And here I thought the biggest gossips were over at the VFW Hall."

Ellie shrugged. "So I like to get the scoop."

"And spread it around."

"That, too, but I'm due. I've been the object of my fair share of gossip and now it's my turn." She glanced at Brandy. "Tit for tat, you know."

Boy, did she ever. That's why she and Ellie had become friends as well as co-workers. While Ellie wasn't from Rebel, she hailed from a nearby small town and with her good looks and casual attitude when it came to men, she'd learned early on what it was like to have folks talk about her. Yep, Ellie was a kindred soul. The only difference is Ellie had earned her reputation. She wore tank tops and short-shorts and flirted shamelessly.

Brandy, on the other hand, had always done just the opposite. She'd kept her ample curves covered up and played the good girl.

In public, a voice reminded her, stirring a wave of memories that sucked her under and reminded her that behind closed doors, she was every bit the bad girl the town painted her to be.

"So?" Ellie nudged. "Give me the details."

"Tyler and I went to high school together." Brandy tore her gaze from the pair of lights and focused on the blacktop in front of her.

"And?"

"And nothing." She shrugged, ignoring the memories that pushed and pulled at her as she followed the road that led back to town. "We went to school together. We graduated. I stayed here to bake and he left to ride bulls."

"Did you actually date?"

"No. We just fooled around."

"I wouldn't mind fooling around with his buddy. Talk about a hottie."

She slid a sideways glance at her assistant. "Don't you have a boyfriend?" She was reminding Ellie of Bart Wilburn, the hunky ranch hand who'd been picking her up after work for the past few months.

"Sure do."

"And he doesn't mind if you see other people?"

"As long as I don't get caught seeing other people. See, while we like each other, we don't *like* each other. I know it and he knows it, but instead of ending things, we stay together because it's better than being alone. Meanwhile, we're both still looking for something better. At the same time, we don't want to make the other look bad so we keep it discreet."

"That's the most dysfunctional thing I've ever heard."

"So sayeth the woman who's married to her oven. Then again, if I had a hunky FB like the one back there, I might be able to work out my frustrations and keep my focus on work, too. Speaking of which, I've noticed that you're a little tense. I think it's a good thing this guy is back in town."

"I'm not hooking up with Tyler McCall right now."

"Why not? That's what he's for, right? At least take one night off and do the deed. You never know when he'll be back. You know what they say—use it or lose it."

"That's ridiculous." Brandy crossed over the railroad tracks on the outskirts of town and glanced back at her mirror. As expected, the headlights slowed at the small dirt road just on the other side of the tracks. The shiny black truck swung a right and disappeared through the thick trees that shrouded the entrance to Rebel's one and only trailer park and Brandy ignored the strange sense of loss that niggled at her.

"It's the God's honest." Ellie held her hand to her heart. "I heard just yesterday from Amanda Huckaby who heard from Kaitlyn McGuire who said that her cousin spent every second of her twenties building up her hair salon. She worked nonstop. Then all of a sudden, she hit thirty and bam, she wanted to shift into the next gear and have a family. But she couldn't and do you know why?"

"No." Brandy turned right at the next inter-section and followed the street into the heart of Rebel. "But I'm sure you're going to tell me."

"Because her lady parts had been on pause for so long that they forgot what to do." The woman gave a shudder. "Her vagina practically shriveled up and died from neglect. At least that's what her gyno said."

"No doctor said that."

"Not outright. He used some fancy medical terms, but the bottom line is she can't have any kids because her coochie is useless. And all because she put business before pleasure."

"That's crazy."

"Is it? If you think about it, it makes perfect sense. Say you went ten years without using your legs, you wouldn't be able to just jump up and start running. Not without some serious repercussions. We're talking leg cramps. Weakness. Pain. Why, you'd be lucky to stand up at all let alone walk around or run."

"It hasn't been ten years." Brandy pulled up behind the small Ford Focus parked in front of the bakery and killed the engine. "Just two."

"Are you freakin' serious? No wonder you've been so irritable lately." Ellie gathered up her purse and climbed out of the car. "Don't tell me you're going back inside," she added when Brandy climbed out of the car and started for the front door.

"I'm already here. I might as well get everything prepped for tomorrow morning. Besides, I want to check on the mash and make sure it's still bubbling." She slid her key into the lock. "And I'm not irritable because it's been two years. Sweet Somethings has some serious competition for the breakfast crowd. I have a right to be on edge."

"If you say so," Ellie said as she pulled open the door to her Focus. "Use it or lose it, sister." She slid Brandy a glance before disappearing behind the wheel. "That's all I'm saying."

CHAPTER 5

"Did you find him?" asked the petite brunette who sat on the front steps of the faded white trailer. The metal structure sat at the very end of a row of equally run-down dwellings that made up the small community known as the Happy Times Trailer Park.

A place where, contrary to its name, Tyler had had many *not*-so-happy times. The memories stirred but he fought them back down, determined to keep his head on straight and his focus solely on finding Cooper and talking some sense into him.

His gaze went to the girl who'd been waiting for him when he pulled up. Erin Shelton had short black hair that reached for the sky thanks to some heavy-duty hair products. A series of four piercings traced the edge of her right ear. Dark eyeliner rimmed almond-shaped eyes, making them seem wide and, oddly enough, innocent, despite her too-small T-shirt and tight black mini skirt.

Erin was the classic example that looks could be deceiving. She might look like an extra from a *Sons of Anarchy* rerun, but she was smart. Responsible. Driven. She'd been best friends with Cooper since the second grade, when she'd moved in next door with her mother, and his brother's compass on more than one occasion.

Erin wanted out of the trailer park and so she'd studied hard, made straight A's, and earned herself a scholarship, and she'd kept Cooper on track, as well.

Until a month ago when she'd gone off to work as a camp counselor with troubled teens and Tyler's younger brother had taken up with Kenny Roy.

Erin pushed up on a pair of faded combat boots, her expression anxious. Worried.

"You did find him, right?" She glanced past Tyler at the man sitting in the passenger seat. He'd wanted to stop off at the trailer one more time before dropping Duff off at a nearby motel, to check if maybe, hopefully, Cooper had smartened up and reappeared on his own.

"Not yet." Tyler shoved his keys into his pocket and ran a frustrated hand through his hair. "There was no one at Kenny Roy's. I stopped off at the Bucking Horse and the Shade Tree Saloon before that. No one's seen them." At least not today. One of the waitresses at the Bucking Horse had mentioned that Cooper had come in last night, but Tyler wasn't going to tell Erin that. Not when the waitress also said that Cooper had left her a whopping tip and an invitation to get together after work. Erin had a massive crush on his younger brother and while he knew his brother didn't feel the same, he also knew Cooper would never willingly hurt her.

At least not the Cooper that Tyler remembered. But from what he was hearing around town about his brother's recent behavior, he was starting to think that maybe the old Coop had taken a hike. Just like their deadbeat dad.

"We have to be in College Station in two weeks for freshman move-in. We were supposed to ride up together." Cooper and Erin had studied hard, nailing the top two spots in their graduating class and snagging scholarships to one of the best schools in the state.

"He'll turn up before then," Tyler reassured her.

"I thought so myself, but it's been nearly three weeks since I last saw him. He's never been gone that long without at least a text. He even missed pizza night last week. He's never missed pizza night." Her eyes shone in the dim porch light. "I always let him have all the pepperoni."

"I'm sure he just got caught up in whatever he's doing. He'll be home soon. Speaking of which, why don't you head over to your place? I'll catch up with you tomorrow after I check out a few more leads." Namely one that had dropped into his lap thanks to the waitress. She'd mentioned Gator Hallsey, a badass bootlegger from a nearby county who'd been spending more and more time in Rebel. After pocketing the fat tip and turning his brother down on his offer, the waitress had seen Cooper leave with Gator.

Unease niggled at Tyler, making his muscles tight and his gut clench. If his brother was keeping company with Gator Hallsey, then the boy was sure as hell in over his head.

"Stop worrying," Tyler said more for himself than Erin. "I'll find him."

She nodded and headed for the large pink trailer two spots down that she shared with her mother and the woman's current flavor of the month. Not the most responsible setup in Tyler's opinion, but who was he to cast stones? His own mother wasn't likely to win Mom of the Year anytime soon. "Call me if you hear from him," he called after her.

"I will."

"I'll be out in a second," he called to Duff, who still sat in the passenger seat of his pickup.

He thought about inviting the man in for a nanosecond before dismissing the crazy notion.

Duff's parents were a modern-day version of Ward and June Cleaver. His dad was an accountant for a large cattle ranch while his mother owned a small café. The two had been married over thirty years and they were still going strong. Duff had grown up in the same house with the same two parents, three square meals, and a dog named Champ.

Okay, so the dog's name had been Bruiser, but it was the principle. Duff had a normal home life back in Odessa.

While Tyler had this.

He stared at the dented metal door, the peeling aluminum exterior, the small wooden porch that slumped on one side.

Tyler had done his best to fix the porch, but then his mother had come home drunk and rammed her ancient Caddy into the edge and the post had buckled again. Six months of weather and the exposed wood had splintered and started to waste away.

Tyler ignored the sick feeling in his gut and mounted the steps. When he reached for the door handle, the past rushed at him and he stalled the way he always had growing up. Hesitant to go in. Wary of what he might find on the other side. Or what he might not find. Namely an empty space, the fridge cleared out, the furniture gone—all telltale signs that his mother had taken off just like his dad.

Because as different as Ellen Sawyer McCall claimed to be from the worthless man she'd married, Tyler feared deep down inside she was cut from the same cloth. Birds of a feather and all that.

The knob turned, the door creaked and swung inward. True to form, she was still there, sprawled on the sofa like always, a bottle of Jack on the table next to a half-empty cup of the expensive gourmet roast coffee she always bought.

Even if there wasn't enough leftover cash to put food on the table or pay the electric.

"Ma?"

She didn't stir. Instead, the heavy snores of a woman who'd had way too much to drink filled the room.

Tyler closed the door behind him and moved over to the small couch. Sliding his arms under the woman, he lifted her. The scent of whiskey and cheap menthol cigarettes filled his head and made his nostrils burn.

"Hey." His mother's eyelids fluttered open. "What are you doing here?" She'd begged him to come home numerous times on the phone, and yet it was as if he'd just walked in off the street.

"I'm here to help with Cooper."

"Takes after my side, ya know. So smart, that boy. And handsome. And such a gentleman." While Tyler was the exact opposite, which Ellen never failed to rub in his face. "He's a Sawyer through and through, that boy."

"You need to hit the sheets."

"But I'm not ready yet." She twisted, reaching for the cup on the coffee table, but Tyler had already moved her out of reach. "One more drink. A nightcap."

"You've already had one too many." He expected her to argue. She always argued, giving him the lecture that she was the mother and she could do what she wanted. But then her eyes closed and he knew she had, indeed, had one too many, and the snores started again.

He fed her into bed the way he had so many times in the past, tucking the covers around her and making sure she had a trash can nearby just in case she was past the point of passing out and the spiked gourmet roast decided to come back up the way it had gone in.

"Did you find it?" her slurred voice asked him a split second before he closed the bedroom door.

"Not yet, but he'll turn up."

"'Cause I can't sleep without it," she murmured and he knew then that she wasn't talking about Cooper. "I can't sleep without my face mask. These damn shades aren't worth a penny. They're cheap. I told your daddy to buy the nice ones like I had back at home, but he said these would do just as well. Why, the man wouldn't know quality if it jumped up and bit him . . ." She rambled on a few more seconds about his dad's failure to keep her in the lifestyle she'd been accustomed to. She'd been a Sawyer. Accustomed to the finer things in life. And she'd sacrificed it all for a man. For love. And she'd never regretted it, not one single day. Or so she repeatedly told anyone who would listen.

But when the Jack started talking, the optimism that Waylon McCall would come running back and do right by his family faded, and the uncertainty leaked out. The bitterness.

". . . ruined everything, he did. We had a good life."

What they'd had was a trailer they could barely afford and two boys that they could barely feed.

Not that his mother had concerned herself with either. She'd been too busy ignoring their problems during the day, and hiding from them in her damn spiked coffee every night.

"I'll find the mask. Just close your eyes and get some sleep right now. Everything will be okay." He tucked the edges of the blanket around her and killed the small light that burned on the warped nightstand.

Closing the door behind him, he walked back into the living room. Picking up his mom's discarded cell, he typed in her password—Sawyer— and scrolled through her calls, searching for any communication from Coop. There was nothing since last week when he'd left a voice mail telling her that he was fine and he would be home soon.

But *soon* had come and gone. He'd missed freshman orientation already. If he didn't get his shit together, he'd be out for good. Stuck.

Tyler hit the CALL BACK button and listened as his brother's familiar voice came over the line.

"You've reached Coop. I can't take your call right now. Leave a message and I'll call you back." *Beeep*.

"This is your brother. Again. Call me. I mean it, Cooper. Time's wasting." He stabbed the OFF button and tossed the cell to the couch. His gaze snagged on a ragged throw pillow, the edges frayed, the expensive brocade fabric marred by several cigarette burns.

He could still remember the day his mother had bought it. She'd come home from Fancy Designs, an elite shop owned by her second cousin

Liza Sawyer, with a crisp black shopping bag stuffed full of gold tissue, the store's trademark logo embossed on the side. He'd been a gangly thirteen, his feet too big for the worn cowboy boots he'd picked out of the donation bin at the local church, the toes scuffed and the soles worn down to practically nothing. Cooper's boots had been in the same condition, squeezing his eight-year-old feet to the point that he was nursing blisters. The fridge had been empty and the cabinets bare. But none of that had mattered when his mother had plopped down their last forty dollars for the genuine cowhide pillow.

"Liza has one just like this at her place," his mother had declared. "She says it's the latest."

He hadn't been too sure what that meant at the time. He just knew that he'd hated the crisp, ripe smell of cured hide and fancy fabric.

The thing was but a shell of itself now, pungent with the stench of cigarette smoke and spiked coffee. Just like his mother.

Like the entire trailer.

The walls seemed to close in on him in that moment. The air stalled in his lungs. He reached for the bottle of Jack and took a long swig. It did little to ease the anxiety knotting his muscles. There was only one remedy for that.

He set the bottle down and reached for the doorknob. The fresh night air hit him, pulling him out of the stench and the past, and into the present. The door slammed behind him. He breathed deep and hit the steps before crossing the distance to his truck. Climbing inside, he keyed the engine. A Luke Bryan song blasted on the radio, and the air conditioner stirred the new-car scent.

"Any word?" Duff glanced up from his own phone and the text he was reading.

"Nothing." Tyler took one last look at the sad-looking trailer and shoved the truck he'd won six months back at a rodeo in Arizona into reverse.

A few seconds later, he hit the road that led into town. He dropped Duff off at the Rebel Quality Inn then headed for the rodeo arena and the small apartment that sat just above the foreman's office.

The place was reserved for long nights when the events ran late and the arena boss, Jack Gallagher, needed a place to crash that was closer than his spread, which sat a good fifty miles past the county line. Since Jack and Tyler went way back, the man was more than happy to let him bunk there whenever he came to town. A habit that had started out of necessity because Tyler had been tight on funds the first few years and desperate to steer clear of the trailer and all the bad memories it held.

One that continued because the apartment had come to feel more like home than any other place in Tyler's life.

Like hope.

It wasn't big or fancy, but it had a double bed, a set of clean white cotton sheets, a private bathroom with a shower, a small kitchenette, and a bay window view of the arena where Tyler had first started to make something of himself.

Even more, there wasn't a damn throw pillow in sight.

CHAPTER 6

"Where are you?" Jenna Tucker demanded when Brandy set aside the loaf of dough she'd been kneading and picked up her ringing cell. "*Shark Tank* is about to start. I made the queso and you're supposed to bring home an extra bag of Doritos. We're almost out."

"I'm sorry, Jenna. I completely forgot. I'm still at the bakery."

"Surprise, surprise. You're a workaholic, you know that, right?"

"Look who's talking. I haven't seen you in three days."

"I've been inoculating cattle out at the Browns', but that doesn't mean I was doing it twenty-four/seven. I did stop to eat. And sleep. And talk to this really cute cowboy named Tim. He's from El Paso and he's got blond hair and green eyes and the cutest dimples you've ever seen. And don't even get me started on his butt."

"What about Jason?" Brandy mentioned Jenna's current squeeze.

"Jason and I are on the outs."

"Does he know that?"

"Not yet, but he will just as soon as he picks me up tonight. He invited me back to his place later for a quote—special romantic dinner—end quote, and you know what that means." She said the words with the same enthusiasm she reserved for telling pet owners that they were about to lose their loved one. "He'll pull out the ring and I'll tell him it just wasn't meant to be."

"That's what you're going to say?" Brandy added the loaf she'd just finished to the dozen others spaced out on the large metal tray.

"Of course."

"You're sure?" She headed for the sink and shoved her hands beneath a warm stream of water. A quick squirt of antibacterial soap and she washed the flour away before cutting off the faucet and reaching for a hand towel. "You're not going to tell him that you're allergic to platinum and that's why you won't wear his ring, are you?"

"I wasn't planning on it, but now that you mention it, that *is* a pretty clever excuse."

"It's terrible." She set the towel aside. "And it's sure to get you into trouble and stuck with a stalker just like the time you told the last guy that you needed space. He thought you were claustrophobic and now we're still fielding phone calls from that hypnotist who swears he can help you with your *issues*."

"I don't have issues. I just hate killing someone's dream. You know me. I'm an optimist."

"You're a wuss." Brandy grabbed the tray and slid it into the warm oven to let the dough rise overnight.

"I'm an optimistic wuss. It isn't my fault if these guys are so in love that they don't want to let go. It's not like I encourage them. I do exactly the opposite."

"You think you do, but you don't say it outright, and most men, in case you haven't figured it out, can't exactly take a hint. No games. Just break it off. Straightforward. To the point. Drop the ax."

"Consider it done."

"I mean it, Jenna. If you're through with this guy, nut up and let him go. Fast and clean."

"Will do. You sure you can't take a few hours off to make *Shark Tank*? You need a little fun in your life."

Brandy knew that. She felt it in the steady trembling of her body and the ache in her nipples. And all because Tyler was back in town and she couldn't stop thinking about that all-important fact, no matter how many loaves of bread she rolled and kneaded until her elbows ached.

Not that she was admitting as much to Jenna. Or anyone for that matter.

That was the thing about her "arrangement" with Tyler. They weren't an item. They didn't gab on the phone. Or go out on dates. Or swap stories over ice cream cones at the Dairy Freeze. They hooked up. No talking about it. Not to each other. Not to other people. No talking, period.

Which meant she shouldn't be the least bit irritated that he hadn't alerted her to the fact that he was back in town. He didn't usually give her a heads-up. Rather, he rolled back into Rebel, they spotted each other, and bam she showed up or he showed up, and they hooked up.

It was no frills. Easy.

"Tonight's episode is going to be super good," Jenna went on, pulling her from her thoughts. "They've got these guys who make flour out of actual crickets. It's supposed to be really healthy and I imagine there's a market for it, but just the thought of biting into a strawberry-flavored cricket cupcake gives me the heebie-jeebies. What do you think?"

"I think you're going to have to record it and give me a rain check. I'm working on this new recipe and I might be out a little later than usual."

"Late as in an hour or two? Because Jason's working until nine, so we're doing an after-hours supper. I could hit the PAUSE button and wait for you."

Brandy glanced at the full oven ready and waiting for tomorrow morning. "I'm afraid I might be a while."

"Want me to swing by before Jason gets here and bring you some food?"

"No," she blurted so fast that she startled herself. "I mean, I already ate a few leftover muffins to tide me over until I get home. Don't worry about me. I'll be fine. So what's up with Callie? Did she call you about the dress?"

"Yes, and I'm scheduled for a fitting next week. Have you seen it?"

"No. She says it's a surprise that we're going to love."

"It's a bridesmaid's dress. I seriously doubt there will be anything even close to love involved. You remember that last dress I wore in Katie Peterson's wedding? Neon yellow, puffy sleeves, parasol to match. I swear I looked like a giant banana. Stop it, Jez." Jenna said to the yapping dog in the background. "That's *my* Dorito."

"I picked up doggy treats yesterday. They're in the pantry."

"She hates those, but give her a ranch-flavored Dorito and she's all over it."

"She's spoiled."

"She's picky."

"She's you."

"Only when it comes to men. Don't work too hard, sis," Jenna told her. "Gotta go. The show's starting." The line went dead and Brandy hit the OFF button.

She reached for a towel and some cleaner and spent the next few minutes wiping down the cabinets as Luke Bryan drifted from the small iPod dock that sat in the corner, crooning about lost love and stripping it down and getting back to the way it used to be.

And as much as she tried not to, she found herself thinking about Tyler. Wanting him.

Wanting *it*, she reminded herself. She was only human, after all. A normal, red-blooded female with wants and needs.

She turned, her body shifted, and her nipples rubbed against the lace of her bra. An ache shot through her and she caught her breath.

Okay, so maybe she was a little more worked up than the average female. She thought of all the rumors that had circulated about her courtesy of all the boys she'd turned down during high school. Boys too embarrassed to admit the truth for fear that they were the only ones not getting any action. And so they'd lied, and her reputation had grown.

But then Tyler McCall had peeled off her clothes and made her realize she wasn't that far off from the sex-crazed girl the boys had always painted her as. So desperate, in fact, that her hands trembled and her knees shook as she moved about the kitchen. It would be so easy to let her need get the best of her. Just like her mother, who'd fallen hard and fast for Brandy's father and, in the process, forfeited her own dreams.

She gathered the strength her mother had never had and steeled herself against the unsettling thought. She wasn't going to drop everything just because Tyler was back in town.

Sure, she was wound up and due for a little stress relief.

But first she had to finish up here.

Nothing was more important than her bakery, and so she forced herself to slow down, take a deep breath, and focus on cleaning with the same painstaking care that she always did before finally putting the last of her supplies away. She double-checked that she had enough petty cash for the morning stream, restocked extra bakery boxes and bags near the register, and wrote the upcoming specials on the decorative chalkboard that sat propped atop the glass display case.

She made one last pass through the kitchen before stepping inside the walk-in pantry situated near the oven. A careful inspection of the five-gallon bucket and the mash that bubbled and popped, fermenting in the warmth of the small area, and she closed the door.

Killing the iPod, she hit the lights and headed for the front door. Locking up behind her, she walked toward her car parked near the curb and slid behind the wheel. Firing up the engine, she glanced at the dark street in her rearview mirror and shifted into drive. Tires ate up pavement as she pulled out onto the road and headed down Main Street. Her heart beat double time as she neared the first stop sign and gave herself a mental shake.

She forced her grip to relax on the steering wheel. It was just another night. Just another drive through town to the outskirts and a sharp right at the Farm Road that led to the Tucker spread.

Only when she reached the turn and hung a left in the opposite direction did she finally give in to the anticipation that whirled fast and potent in the pit of her stomach.

There was a time and place for everything.

And it was time for Tyler McCall.

CHAPTER 7

There'd been no doubt in Tyler's mind that Brandy would show up now that she knew he was back. Under the cover of darkness, away from prying eyes and wagging tongues.

He just hadn't counted on the sucker punch to his gut when he opened the door to find her standing there in her bakery T-shirt and jeans, her ponytail hanging limp after a long day's work, her cheek still smudged with flour.

Seriously. Hard. Fast. Right below the belt.

Ooomph.

The air stalled in his lungs. His heart slammed to a stop. His throat tightened. And just like that, his dick snapped to full attention.

Talk about bat-shit crazy.

It wasn't as if she'd dressed to the nines in a leather bustier or a red bikini or something equally trashy and sexy as hell.

It was a soft cotton T-shirt, for Christ's sake. A simple pair of jeans. Sneakers. Hell, she hadn't even bothered to take down her hair or wipe her cheek.

Then again, it *had* been two years.

Two years was long enough to make a man find even the simplest things sexy. Like the silky strands of hair that hung loose and framed her delicate jaw and flushed cheeks. The faintest smudge of mascara just below her eyes that gave them that sultry bedtime look.

He swallowed against the sudden tightening of his throat and cursed himself for not turning the air conditioner a few degrees cooler. Damn, but it was hot.

Tyler stepped back and let her precede him inside. She didn't say anything. She didn't have to.

She was here, the warm scent of sweet blueberries and powdered sugar filling his nostrils as she eased past him. A bolt of need shot through his body and his muscles rolled and bunched. He barely resisted the urge to haul her into his arms, back her up against the massive window overlooking the rodeo arena, and take her hard and fast with the last few straggling cowboys watching from below.

He fought the crazy urge because he wasn't in any hurry to fuel the rumor mill that already circulated in Rebel, Texas. Not because he cared a lick about what people thought, but because she did. She always had.

And like it or not, he cared about her.

Not her, specifically, he reminded himself. He cared about their unspoken arrangement. Down-and-dirty sex. No strings attached. No awkward morning after. No expectations. Nothing but the two of them in the moment. Here. Now.

Which meant there would be no fast and furious with the world watching.

But without the world watching?

It could be fast. Furious. Slow. Easy. Any way he wanted it because Brandy Tucker liked it all. She was the most sensual woman he'd ever met and damn if he didn't lose his breath when he drew the shades, shutting out the wranglers closing down the pens below, and turned back in time to see her pull the hot-pink T-shirt up and over her head.

The pale-yellow glow from a nearby table lamp pushed back the shadows and bathed her in a warm light that made her skin seem almost translucent. She didn't spare a glance at her surroundings as she tossed the shirt to a nearby chair.

Not that first time when he'd taken her virginity on top of the king-sized bed not two feet away from him, and not now that he'd had her practically every which way in this very room.

But as many times as they'd met right here, as many positions as they'd tried, as much pleasure as they'd found, he still felt a renewed sense of anticipation. More so because he knew what was about to happen and just how fucking fantastic it could be.

His blood rushed even faster as he watched her peel off her jeans until she wore nothing but a pair of lacy red panties and a matching bra.

"I hope this is a good time," she finally murmured when he didn't step forward, toss her down, and get the party started. The hesitant light in her gaze faded into a wave of bright-green heat as she took the initiative and stepped closer. "I mean, if it's not I can come back later." Another bold step and her nipples kissed his chest. Desire fired in her eyes. "If that's what you want."

"The only thing I want right now is to be inside of you." He pulled her close, his tongue thrusting into the heated depths of her mouth, devouring her as if he might never get another taste.

And maybe he wouldn't.

He knew the sex would eventually stop. It was inevitable. She would find someone and settle down or he would shoot to the top of the leader board and make enough money to buy a sweet little place far, far away from the Not-So-Happy-Times Trailer Park. Or both. Either way, she would stop coming to him and he would stop coming home and it would end. But not just yet.

His hands went to her tight, round ass, and he pulled her even closer. He rubbed his throbbing erection against the cradle of her pelvis. His fingers slid beneath the lace of her panties and felt her bare flesh beneath. Her skin was hotter than he remembered. Soft. Electrifying.

Holy shit.

Urging her backward, he eased her down onto the bed. He captured her mouth in a deep, intense kiss that lasted several heartbeats before he pulled away and stepped back. He thought about slowing down, about taking his time and committing every moment with her to memory, just in case this was, indeed, the last time, but the hard-on throbbing beneath his jeans got the better of him.

He worked the buttons free on his shirt and let the material slide from his shoulders. He unfastened the button on his jeans and pushed the zipper down. The pressure eased and the edges gaped and he could actually breathe for a few seconds.

Until she pushed to a sitting position and leaned forward.

Her fingers touched the dark purple head of his erection where it pushed up above the waistband of his briefs. He ground his teeth against a burst of white-hot pleasure and braced himself against the need beating at his brain. Her touch was just so damn soft and he was so hard and the contrast was tying him into knots.

He needed to touch her. To taste her.

He stared down at her. At the dark-red nipple that pushed through the lace-patterned cup of her bra. He pushed her back, leaned down and flicked his tongue over the rock-hard tip. She gasped, the sound catching in her throat and sending a sizzle of electricity up his spine. It was the sound that haunted his dreams at night. His fantasies.

His memories.

He drew the nub deeper into his mouth, sucking her hard through the flimsy covering.

Her fingers threaded through his hair and held him close. He relished the feel of her flesh for several heart-pounding moments before he pulled away. He gripped the cups of her bra and pulled them down and under the fullness of her breasts. The bra plumped her and her ripe nipples lifted in a silent invitation that he was hard-pressed—literally—to accept.

Still, he wanted to look, to watch the tips pebble and harden beneath his gaze. To see her need in the tight, fierce response of her lush body.

But she wasn't about to let him put on the brakes.

When he didn't lower his head and suckle her again, she reached for him.

"Please. I need it now." There was no shame to the words, no embarrassment to the admission because the Brandy sitting before him wasn't the same girl who kept it all covered up in front of the rest of the world.

She was different.

Wild. Sexy. Bold.

Here. With him.

Crazy.

He didn't know what she did and who the hell she did it with when he wasn't around. But he wasn't fool enough to think he was the only one.

The notion sent a burst of possessiveness through Tyler, feeding the need to stand out in her mind, to brand her his. And that meant not only pressing on the brakes, but holding them down long enough to make sure she felt everything he did to her.

He hooked his fingers at the thin straps of her panties and followed the tantalizing path down her long legs. She had the softest skin. So pale and perfect beneath the rough feel of his fingertips. When he had her naked with the exception of the bra pulled beneath her luscious breasts, he leaned up and let his gaze sweep the length of her.

She was even more sexy than he remembered. Sexier than the first time. The last time. And anything in between.

Sexier than anything he'd ever imagined, and he'd done plenty sitting behind her in English class. She'd been two years behind him in school, but they'd both ended up in the same sophomore English because he'd missed so much school trying to work two jobs and go to class that he'd failed the stupid course twice. He'd passed with flying colors that year because he'd been in his seat every single day. No way was he missing the opportunity to stare at the sweet curve of her neck beneath her blond ponytail. How many times had he wanted to reach out, to trail his fingers down that subtle sweep of skin?

He should have. Hell, half the boys at Rebel had done just that, or so they'd said.

But he'd gotten a different vibe from Brandy herself. Despite her voluptuous body and sultry air, there'd been something innocent in the gleam of her green eyes. She'd never teased or flirted or come on to him. She'd been almost shy.

Then again, she'd been a Tucker. Too good for the likes of a low-life Sawyer, and so he'd taken her reluctance for snottiness.

Until that night after the last football game of the season. She'd been stranded at the game without a ride, her hands stuffed in the pockets of her tight blue sweater as she'd stood outside in the cold, her cheeks pink and her eyes bright. She'd been waiting for her sister, who'd been stuck working late, and he'd been dragging ass out of the locker room after a crushing loss.

They'd had three injuries during that play-off game, enough to kill their chances for a district championship. Not that Tyler had given a shit about any of that. He just liked to hit, to spend his pent-up aggression and take it out on someone with no chance of retaliation. Football had been his saving grace back when he'd been a kid and the world had been against him. His one shot to fight back against that big bitch of life for dealing him such a rotten hand.

His chance to be in control, to call the shots, to turn the tide in his favor.

There'd been no turning the tide that night. He'd gotten two penalties and a bruised shoulder and then his coach had yanked him out of the game.

He'd stayed late to ice his injury and the entire stadium had all but cleared out by the time he'd walked through the locker room door.

Brandy had been the only one still hanging out other than a few of the custodians.

She'd stared at him as if she meant to run the other way, but then she'd walked right up to him and kissed him full on the mouth.

That had been all the encouragement he'd needed. He'd loaded her into his beat-up Chevy, driven her to the rodeo arena and they'd shared the first of many booty calls to come.

He'd been her first, much to his surprise, but he wasn't fool enough to think that he'd be her last.

His muscles tightened at the thought and he trailed a finger down the barely there strip of pubic hair and watched her tremble. He knew what she liked by now and he didn't waste any time giving it to her.

He traced the slit that separated her lush pink lips and she caught her bottom lip as a groan trembled from her mouth. Her legs fell open and the soft pink flesh parted just for him.

Dipping his fingertip into her steamy heat, he watched her eyes go half lidded. A soft stroke and her head fell back. Her mouth opened and a gasp worked its way up her throat. She caught her bottom lip, her teeth digging in as he went deeper, pushing, exploring. He worked her, sliding his finger in and out until her essence coated his flesh. A drop trickled over his knuckle and down his palm, and electricity sizzled up his spine.

Hunger raged inside him and he dipped his

head, flicked his tongue over the swollen tissue, and lapped up her sweet essence. Sure enough, she tasted of blueberries and sugar and something more intoxicating than the most wicked shot of moonshine.

At the first contact of his mouth, she arched up off the bed and her hands grasped his head. Soft, strangled gasps trembled from her lips. He swirled his tongue around her clitoris and felt the tip ripen for him. She whimpered as he sucked the sensitive nub into his mouth and nibbled until she tensed beneath him.

Her fingers clutched at his hair, tugging desperately in a grip that was just short of painful. The sensation fed his ravenous desire and made his breath quicken. He laved her once, twice, and her breath caught on a ragged gasp.

"Please. I need it now. Right. *Now*."

But it had been two long years since he'd been with her and he wasn't about to have it over with just like that. Gathering his control, he pulled away. Not now. Not yet. That's what he told himself.

But then his gaze collided with hers and he saw the fierce glitter in her eyes—a mix of desire and desperation that he felt as fiercely as she did.

She didn't want to wait. She *couldn't* wait.

And suddenly neither could he.

He snatched up his jeans and retrieved a condom from his pocket. After sliding on the latex, he settled between her legs. Bracing himself, he shoved his penis deep into her wet heat and caught himself, his arms braced on either side of her head.

Christ, she felt so good. So fucking *good*.

Her body welcomed him, fitting so tight and snug around him. His heart pounded double time as he relished the sensation a full moment before gripping her lush hips and driving into her again.

She closed her eyes and arched against him, meeting each thrust until his body shook and his cock throbbed. Pleasure drenched his brain and he knew he was close.

But he wasn't going anywhere without her.

He reached down between them and parted her flesh just above the point where he filled her. He caught her swollen clitoris between his thumb and forefinger and squeezed lightly, pushing her higher, pulling him up to the point where he hovered just this side of ecstasy.

"*Yes*," she moaned, her body convulsing around him as the orgasm hit her hard and fast.

He buried himself deep one last time. His body tensed and his muscles tightened and . . . *there*. His cock exploded and he clenched his teeth against the force of it. A shudder ripped through him, vibrating along every nerve ending as he spilled himself. He collapsed atop her, holding her close as her inner muscles milked him and worked another groan from his tight throat.

The seconds ticked by as he fought to draw an actual breath. When he managed, he loosened his hold and rolled onto his back. He reached for her, but she'd already moved toward the opposite side of the bed. Turning on his side, he leaned up on his elbow and watched as she pushed to her feet and started to retrieve her discarded T-shirt.

"I really need to get going," she murmured—the same thing she always said before she pulled on her clothes and hightailed it out of his bed. "I've got a lot to do tomorrow."

"You and me both," he murmured, watching as she pulled the denim up and over her sweet round ass. Regret ebbed through him and he barely resisted the urge to reach out and haul her back into bed for Round Two. He wanted to touch her again, kiss her again, shove his cock so deep inside that he forget where he ended and she began.

Two years, he reminded himself.

Plenty of time to send any normal, red-blooded man over the edge into the land of the sexually deprived.

While he'd had plenty of opportunity to hook up on the road and sate his appetite, for some reason he just hadn't had the time. He'd been too busy busting his ass and keeping his nose to the grindstone. And then, during those few free moments, he'd just been too damn tired. A man had to sleep, after all.

Now he was horny as hell and wanting more from a woman who clearly didn't want more from him.

He sat up, tossing his legs over the side of the

bed just as she shoved her feet into her sneakers and grabbed her keys and purse.

He caught her wrist just as she was about to turn, hauled her down, and gave her a deep, hungry kiss.

And then Tyler did what he always did.

He let go and watched her walk away.

CHAPTER 8

It was six a.m. on the dot when Brandy arrived at Sweet Somethings, after five of the best hours of sleep she'd had in a really long time. She felt rested, recharged.

Mostly.

She had spent the entire drive home from the rodeo arena battling the damn lust that chanted *more, more, more*.

But she'd needed to go home, get some sleep, keep her head on straight and so she had.

Mostly.

She had spent an extra forty-five minutes tossing and turning and thinking that it had been two years. Two long years and so she was definitely due for more than just a one-night stand as was the norm whenever he rolled into town for a day or two here and there.

One fall from grace.

That's all she gave herself. One chance to cut loose and unleash the bad girl deep inside before she bottled it all up and went back to pretending.

But this was different.

This wasn't six months. Or eight. Or maybe even a year since she'd last cut loose. This was two years. Long enough to have earned herself a second encounter. Maybe even three.

Provided she had the time what with everything going on at the bakery.

Her body ached at the thought and she stiffened. Time and place, she reminded herself, and today was neither. It was Saturday. Her busiest day of the week. Add the fact that she still needed to get in touch with Kenny Roy, and she was all but swamped. Too much so to even contemplate cutting out early and paying another visit to Tyler McCall.

Even if she had desperately missed the purposeful glide of his hand down her back these last two years and the press of his fingertips on the underside of her breast and the feel of his lips at the hollow of her throat—

"Looks like somebody was busy last night." Ellie's voice pushed past the images rolling through Brandy's brain and yanked her back to reality and the fact that she was no longer alone in the bakery.

Ellie sat her purse on a nearby shelf and reached for an apron, a gleam in her eyes.

"What's that supposed to mean?" The words were out before Brandy could stop them.

"That somebody was busy."

As in *getting* busy, Brandy's conscience chided. "You made all this bread," Ellie went on, glancing at the tray of fresh-baked loaves. "You must have spent half the night here after we got back from Kenny Roy's."

"I, um, wanted to be prepared." She reached for a tin of cupcakes she'd just scooped and slid them into the oven before setting the timer and turning back to move the bread to the cooling racks. "It's Saturday. Busiest day of the week."

Which meant she would have zero time to think about Tyler or the fact that one night hadn't been nearly enough. She wanted him again. And again.

Not him, mind you. *It.*

She liked sex. She missed it.

Because she was every bit the bad girl that everyone thought.

She forced the thought aside. So she liked sex? Contrary to popular opinion, she wasn't ruled by it.

Not now. Not ever.

"Are you okay?" Ellie's voice drew her attention and she glanced up to find the woman eyeing her. "You look a little flushed. You're not coming down with something, are you?"

"Of course not. I'm fine. It's just a little hot in here." She busied herself pulling down the nearby thermostat. "There. That's better."

"Because if you're not feeling well, I can handle things here."

Brandy gave her a pointed stare. "It's Saturday. That means the Senior Ladies Auxiliary will be stopping by to pick up desserts for their weekly book club and the chamber of commerce will want enough apple turnovers to hand out at the local farmers market, not to mention we've got to furnish the desserts for the PTA luncheon and finish the Wilsons' fiftieth-anniversary cake."

One cake, she reminded herself. As opposed to the two or three or four special-order cakes she needed in order to secure a spot with Hill Country Happily Ever Afters. A dream that would never happen if she didn't get another moonshine sample in time for her meeting with Foggy Bottom Distillers.

"I know we're busy today, but I can still cover if you need to take a break."

"I don't need a break. All I need is more days like today."

Busy. Chaotic. Consuming. Enough so that she managed to push Tyler's image to the back burner and focus on work for the rest of the day.

"So I was thinking," Ellie said later that afternoon, "that maybe I could get off an hour early tonight. If it's okay."

Brandy arched an eyebrow. "Hot date with the boyfriend?"

"Just a girls' night. You can come if you want to. I mean, it's just Lila and me." She motioned to the woman busy decorating the last of the cupcakes that were headed for the First Presbyterian Church and tomorrow morning's Sunday school. "Her hands are always so cramped after doing cupcakes for the hellions, so I thought we'd hit the Watering Trough and unwind."

"I've got way too much left to do here since we started staying open on Sundays," Brandy replied, "but thanks anyway. You two go on."

Ellie shrugged. "You know where we're at if you change your mind and want to toss down a couple of shots."

But it was going to take a lot more than alcohol to relax Brandy. She needed something much more potent.

Some*one* much more potent.

Time and place, she reminded herself. And while a Saturday night was usually the perfect time, it wasn't on this particular Saturday night. Not when she had a bucket of bubbling mash and no one to hand it off to just as soon as it was done.

A few days at the most, she judged after a quick check to make sure the mash was sound and secure and still working its magic.

For now.

But she had a limited amount of time to corner Kenny Roy and get the scoop on his connection, and so she wasn't about to head out to the rodeo arena for another booty call with Tyler McCall.

No matter how much she suddenly wanted to.

CHAPTER 9

"Don't tell me you're still at work," Callie said when Brandy picked up the phone later that night.

"Okay, I won't tell you."

"Darn it, Brandy. You've got to lighten up just a little."

"So sayeth the woman who's held down two jobs since the age of sixteen and is still, the last time I looked, juggling both."

"I'm just helping out Les at the real estate office until he finds a replacement. Then I'll only have the column at the newspaper to worry about." Callie had found not only the man of her dreams, but the job as well. She'd spent years wanting to be a journalist and just recently she'd landed her very own feature column with the local newspaper. *What's Happening in Rebel* detailed the latest and greatest goings on in their small town and was both insightful and funny thanks to Callie's wit.

Brandy's sister really had hit the jackpot.

Brandy's throat tightened. She swallowed and tried to focus on her older sister's voice.

". . . have to slow down and take a breath," Callie was saying.

"I'll do that when I'm turning a substantial profit and business is booming."

If that moment ever came.

She tamped down the doubt and gave herself a mental shake. Sure, she had debt. But she had a plan to get out of that debt, which was why she was parked in front of Kenny Roy's house yet again, waiting for the man to come home so that she could find out the name of his connection.

She stared at the lifeless house, the crickets buzzing around her as she sat in the front seat of Bertha, a bag of fries on the seat next to her and a chocolate shake in the drink holder. So much for an exciting Saturday night.

Not that she hadn't thought about swinging by Tyler's before heading out to Kenny Roy's. She had. So much so that she'd nearly burned an entire batch of cupcakes, which was why she'd decided to ignore her screaming hormones and take care of business first.

"Did you even eat dinner—" Callie started.

"Did you find a photographer for the wedding?" Brandy blurted, effectively switching the subject from her workaholic life to the big event.

"There's a guy here at the paper who's really good. Mike Wheeler. He's from a little town east of here, but he's been at the paper for three years now. Weddings aren't exactly his thing, but I think he'd be perfect. His pictures capture so much character. I think if I can come up with a good bribe, he might do it for me. Which brings me to the real reason for my call."

"You mean you didn't call just to harass me about working too much?"

"Not completely. I mean, that's part of it. You need to take more time off. Have some downtime. Maybe go out to dinner at a nice restaurant. Maybe share that dinner with a certain photographer who went into your bakery the other day and is now convinced you're the most beautiful woman he's ever seen."

"Wait a second. I'm your bribe for the photographer?"

"If you agree to dinner. If not, then I'm stuck looking for someone to capture *the* most important day of my life."

"You're not going to guilt me into this. I don't do blind dates."

"You don't do any dates, and I'm not trying to guilt you into anything. I'm seriously worried about you and your lack of downtime."

Brandy thought of the past night with Tyler and fought down a wave of guilt. "No, you're not."

"Okay, so I understand your dedication, but that doesn't mean I don't want you to have a little fun every now and then. Mike's really cute," she added. "And you'd be doing me a huge favor."

"I'll think about it."

"Well, don't think too long. I need to lock down the date on his schedule."

"I'll get back to you next week."

"How about tomorrow?" When Brandy sighed, Callie added, "It's just that the wedding happens to coincide with the annual Cotton Eyed Joe dance festival at the VFW Hall. Mike will have to find someone to cover for him at the festival if he commits to the wedding, but he won't commit until I can promise him a date and—"

"Okay."

"Okay you'll get back to me tomorrow or okay you'll do it?"

"I'll get back to you tomorrow."

"Oh. Okay. Well, I guess if you really need time to think about whether or not you want to help make the wedding as wonderful as it could possibly be and ease my stress level considerably, then I'm sure you have your reasons—"

"I'll do it. I'll go on the date. Just not right now because I'm really busy."

"Yeah, sure. I would never dump a date on you just like that. You need notice. So how about next week?"

"Make it next month and you've got a deal."

"Great. Thank you. You won't regret it. I know it sounds like I'm just doing this for the wedding, but I really think you two will hit it off. I'll set it up and text the details. Gotta run. Brett's waiting for me. We're having dinner with his pappy. Now make sure you don't work too late."

"Yes, Mom."

"And eat something that isn't loaded with sugar."

"Bye, Mom." She hit the OFF button and set the phone on the seat next to her.

A blind date.

What was Callie thinking?

That maybe there's more to life than work. A first for her because her entire life had been about work. But not by choice. That was the difference between them. Callie had spent years working because she'd had to step up and take charge of the family when their parents had died. She'd *had* to step up and be the mom.

But in all honesty, she was as far from Mary Elizabeth Tucker as a woman could get. Their mother had been a stay-at-home mom, content to move in with her father-in-law so that her family could scrape by on the meager income that her husband managed to bring home. She'd never had aspirations beyond her three daughters, beyond putting food on the table and shoes on everyone's feet.

Or so she'd claimed.

But on those rare occasions when she'd herded Brandy into the kitchen to make brownies or cookies to earn a little side cash, she'd been a different person.

Brandy could still remember her mother talking about her childhood as she rolled out a piecrust or whipped up a chocolate ganache. About how she'd wanted so desperately to be the next Betty Crocker. Childish dreams, she'd said, but Brandy hadn't missed the light in the woman's eyes. The longing.

As if Mary Elizabeth wasn't quite as happy as she professed to be. As if she'd missed out.

Made the wrong decision.

While Brandy knew her mother would never have traded her husband and three daughters for a career, she'd known that the woman had still wondered what life might have been like if she'd followed through with her passion. If she hadn't met and married so young and started having babies right out of the gate.

If she hadn't traded her love of baking for that of a good man.

Brandy wouldn't make the same mistake. She intended to find out just how far she could go before she settled down. If she settled down. She didn't want to have unanswered questions years from now. Or regret.

She wanted to make herself happy now before she felt obliged to make someone else happy.

An image stirred and she saw Tyler McCall wearing nothing but hard, ripped muscles and a sizable erection. She remembered the heat in his eyes and the wicked slant to his mouth and the pleasure gleaming in his eyes.

She shifted on the seat and reached for the chocolate shake in the cup holder. She usually steered clear of sweets when she was off duty. She did enough tasting during the day to keep an extra five pounds on each hip. She wasn't about to indulge after hours and make that ten.

But for some reason, she hadn't been able to

help herself tonight. Her stomach grumbled and a craving ate away inside of her.

Because of him.

Because last night hadn't been nearly enough after two long years on the wagon. It wasn't as if she could go around boffing every guy in town. And risk one of them getting hooked on her? Or worse, her getting hooked on him? Someone she would have to see day in, day out. That would just complicate things and distract her from what was really important.·

No, that's why she kept things going with Tyler. She didn't have to worry about him hanging around, distracting her, tempting her. He was here today, gone tomorrow, and that made him the perfect sex buddy.

Sex, and nothing but sex.

She stuffed her straw into her thick drink. A few sips and she gave up the effort and pulled off the lid. Dipping the straw into the dense chocolate, she scooped a mouthful and closed her eyes as the cold, creamy concoction hit her tongue.

Rich. Sweet. Ahhh . . .

A groan slid past her lips and she went back for another scoop.

"Got a bite for me?" The deep, masculine voice sent a bolt of shock through her. Her head snapped up and just like that, she found herself staring into Mr. Sex Buddy's familiar aqua-blue eyes.

CHAPTER 10

"I, um . . ." Brandy scrambled for her voice. Her hand trembled and the shake sloshed. A glob of chocolate dove over the side and slid down the cup, covering her fingers in sticky goodness. "You scared the daylights out of me." She reached for a napkin and tried to calm the sudden jolt of her heart.

What the hell was wrong with her? She'd slept with the man, for Pete's sake, yet here she was acting like a nervous schoolgirl because he was talking to her.

But then that was the point entirely.

They didn't talk. They didn't socialize. There was no going to the movies or kicking up dust at the local saloon. No running into each other and gabbing like old friends. No picnics or lunches at the Dairy Freeze.

They hooked up and while they might exchange a few choice words in the heat of the moment, it was all about the sex.

This . . . This was different.

This was out in the open for the world to see.

He frowned. "I thought I told you to stay away from here."

"And I thought I told you it was none of your business." She sat the shake in the cup holder and wiped at her messy hands. "I need to see Kenny and I'm not leaving until I do."

"Kenny's a bad guy."

"If he's such a bad guy, then what do you want with him?"

The frown deepened. "Maybe I just came back because I remembered how stubborn you were and I wanted to make sure you didn't get into trouble."

"That would imply that you care, and we both know there's no truth to that." She gave him a pointed stare. "I can look after myself."

He stared at her long and hard as if there was something he wanted to say, but then he shrugged. "My brother's been hanging out with him lately and I'm here to put a stop to it."

"Because Kenny's such a bad guy."

"Exactly." He reached for the door handle.

Before she could hit the LOCK button, the door swung wide and his deep voice slid into her ears. "Scoot."

"What are you doing?" she blurted as he started to climb into the driver's seat.

"We might as well wait together." His muscular thigh hit hers and she found herself sliding to the side a split second before his entire body folded in next to hers.

Vinyl groaned and creaked as he settled behind

the steering wheel. The door slammed shut and suddenly old Bertha seemed much smaller than she'd realized. A hand span of worn seat separated them. The potent scent of sexy male drifted across the space to her and wound tight, pushing and pulling at her already tentative control. The urge to wiggle to her left and snuggle up next to him nearly overwhelmed her.

She pushed aside the crazy notion and finished wiping her sticky hands. "I don't think this is such a good idea."

He shot her a sideways glance. One dark brow arched. "Don't trust yourself?"

Bingo.

"Don't flatter yourself." She cleared her throat. "I need to get some work done, that's all." She indicated the clipboard and supply list. "I've got to order staples tomorrow and I need to figure out exactly how much I need."

"So work." He shrugged. "I don't mind." He was all hard muscle and purposeful intent as he settled back in the seat, one elbow resting on the open window.

Her gaze hooked on his large hand sitting atop the seat between them, his fingers long and strong. The musky scent of leather and horse filled the interior, teasing her senses and making her heart flutter. The air inside the vehicle crackled with electricity.

The chemistry between them fired to life as always, a live wire running from point A to point B, the connection shivering with intensity. She became keenly aware of the chocolate residue coating her fingers and the top of her hand. A thought pushed its way into her head and she saw Tyler's strong hand covering hers, lifting it to his lips, his tongue lapping at the sweetness clinging to her skin . . .

Not that he was doing any such thing. Not out in the open for everyone to see.

A wave of heat washed over her and she barely resisted the urge to tug at the neckline of her T-shirt. The heat rolling off his body made the already humid night air unbearable and she found herself reaching for the door handle.

"Where are you going?"

"I really need to wash my hands," she blurted. "I'll just turn on the hose right there"—she indicated the faucet near the corner of the house—"and cool off." The minute the words were out, her gaze collided with his. A knowing smile crooked his lips and she stiffened. "Clean up," she rushed on. "I need to *clean* off."

The door opened and slammed and she walked swiftly to the faucet, doing her best to ignore the strange prickle of awareness that told her he was watching her.

Her hand closed around the knob and she turned. Water spurted from the end of the hose and she busied herself washing off her fingers.

She wasn't doing anything with him right here, right now. She had more important things on her plate.

Namely, talk to Kenny and get herself home to

bed in time to be at the bakery at four a.m. sharp to prep the way she did every day.

Last night had been enough.

She gathered her strength and her composure, turned off the water, and started back toward the car. Thirty seconds later, she climbed into the passenger seat and reached for her clipboard.

"You're all wet, sugar," he murmured, drawing her attention.

Her gaze collided with his and she felt the familiar ache between her legs. "You have no idea."

He grinned then and she had the crazy thought that he knew exactly what she was talking about. But then he reached out and touched her damp sleeve. "Maybe you ought to go home and change."

"It's just water. It'll dry." She forced her attention to the clipboard. Flipping on the dash light, she focused on counting last week's sales and predicting the coming week, along with specialty items.

"Do you mind?" He motioned to the radio, and she shrugged.

A click of the knob and Jason Aldean's "Burnin' It Down" drifted over the radio.

The music combined with the steady sound of his breathing actually relaxed her and she managed to get a good ten minutes' worth of work done before her gaze snagged on his profile and she found herself remembering a similar moment when she'd climbed into his pickup truck that very first time.

She didn't remember the drive to the rodeo arena or the walk through the stock pens to get to the foreman's office. She just remembered this—his firm chin, the sensual set to his mouth, the slope of his chiseled nose, the shadow of a beard covering his strong jaw.

Everything seemed more defined now, as if the years had added an edge to his features that made him seem older, and much more dangerous.

"I can't believe Cooper would trade a full ride to A and M for this." He motioned to the overgrown yard and the sagging front porch. "It's not like Kenny is making money hand over fist, otherwise he wouldn't be holed up in such a dump."

"You really think Cooper is involved with Kenny Roy?"

"That's what he said. Left our mother a message saying he was doing some work with Kenny Roy and would be gone for a little while. That was three weeks ago. He's been in touch once or twice since, but he just leaves the same message that he'll be back soon. But soon should have come a helluva long time ago."

"Did you call the police?"

He shook his head. "He's not technically a missing person. He's okay or he wouldn't be able to leave messages, but there's no word about where he is or what he's involved with. He mentioned that Kenny Roy had hooked him up with some kind of job, so I figured I would start here."

He eyed her. "What about you? Why do you need to see Kenny Roy? You trying to sell him some cookies?"

"Very funny." She shook her head and fixed her gaze back on the clipboard. "I'm not a Girl Scout, but I am here on business. A new business." She didn't mean to say any more, but he'd been so forthcoming about his brother that the words slid out before she could stop them. "I think I've come up with a new moonshine recipe. One even better than Texas Thunder."

"Seriously?"

She nodded. "I mixed up a batch of mash and Ellie, the girl I was here with earlier, gave it to her boyfriend who gave it to Kenny Roy who found someone who could run it for me. It turned out *really* good, which is why I need to talk to Kenny about running another batch. I've got my mash fermenting right now. It's not ready yet, but when it is I need someone to run it and get me a sample for this meeting I have with a distiller out of Austin."

"Kenny Roy is an idiot. I can't imagine you would trust him with a batch of muffins, much less a bucket of mash."

"I know he is, but he has connections. It's the connection I'm trying to reach. I need to see the mash run myself. To make sure there's no alteration or contamination going on."

"No moonshiner is going to be too keen on an audience."

"Maybe not, but it's the only way I can be sure. The recipe has to be solid, the finished product pure and perfect and in my hands before next Friday, otherwise I'll have to wait months for another meeting. That's time I don't have."

"I'm assuming your grandpa didn't pass down his know-how, otherwise you'd be running it yourself."

"All he passed on was a world of debt, which we've managed to climb out of. At least Callie's free and clear."

"But not you?"

"I had to help Callie." She shrugged. "She spent too many years carrying the burden all by herself. I got a secure loan on my equipment, which I could easily pay back at the time. But then a doughnut shopped opened up around the corner and they're killing my morning rush. That, and I need to expand. I'll never get anywhere if I can't do enough special orders."

"So you perfect the recipe and sell it, and you're set."

"That, and I bake my fingers to the bone. Then I'm set."

He grinned. "Some things never change."

The comment should have made her feel good, but for some reason regret whispered through her.

"What about you?" She eyed him. "I hear you're doing pretty good on the circuit."

"Good enough." His gaze met hers. "So far.

I've got to be in Cheyenne as soon as I settle things here. If I hold my own there, then I'll be on my way."

"So when are you leaving?"

"I'm supposed to be in Cheyenne in a few days to start training for the rodeo in three weeks. I've got a buddy up there who's got a top-notch facility. Cooper has to be at A and M at about the same time. I'll find him and get him to College Station, and then I'll head for Wyoming."

"What if you don't find him in time?"

"Oh, I will." Determination carved his broad jaw. "I'll sit here all night if I have to."

Right here. Right next to her.

So close all she had to do was reach out.

Uh, oh.

"There's really no need for both of us to be here," she blurted. "We could take shifts. I mean, really. Neither of us knows when Kenny Roy will be back. What if he's taking a vacation? I mean, I hope he's not, but my mash still has several more days to ferment, so it's not like I have to talk to him right now. Just sometime before it's ready to go."

"Kenny Roy runs a weekly football pot. He'll be back before Friday, so I doubt he's on vacation."

"Still, he might not be here tonight, so we should prepare ourselves for the possibility that it might take a day or two."

He stared at her a long moment as if trying to

decide something. "I don't think shifts are a good idea."

"Because you don't trust me."

"Because I don't trust Kenny Roy. He's a bad guy, Brandy."

"I'm not exactly all that good, myself," she murmured.

"Oh, I know just how bad you can be." His aqua-blue eyes fired in the center and heat fluttered from the soles of her feet, working its way up and igniting every major erogenous zone along the way. "But this is different. Kenny Roy is a two-bit criminal and the company he keeps isn't much better. You don't need to get mixed up with him."

"I don't need a babysitter."

"Is that so?" He eyed her. "Then tell me, sugar. What do you need?"

"I don't think this is the right place," she started, but then he leaned forward and pressed his lips to hers, and the protest was lost in a sudden rush of heat.

CHAPTER 11

He didn't mean to kiss her.

He'd always let her make the first move and come to him. But there was just something about being so close and not touching her that was eating him up from the inside out.

That, and she just had the most tempting mouth. Full on the bottom with a slight pout that made him think of all the nasty things he wanted to do to her.

Things they'd already done, he reminded himself. Which meant his curiosity shouldn't be getting the better of him. He knew, but damned if that didn't make him want to kiss her that much more.

He slid his arms around her waist and pulled her close. His mouth ate at hers, tasting and exploring and—

The flash of headlights cut through the haze of lust and snapped him back to reality. To the black Ford Explorer that swerved into the driveway and the fact that they were sitting there for all the world to see.

Gravel crunched and brakes screeched. A door slammed, boots crunched gravel. Kenny Roy waltzed up just as they both scrambled from the car.

"Well, well, if this ain't a Ripley's Believe It or Not moment." Kenny stopped a few feet away and took a drag on the cigarette in his hand. "Never thought I'd see the day when a Tucker and a Sawyer got up close and personal right in front of my place. Or anybody's place for that matter. There's a feud goin' on, in case you didn't know."

"We weren't—" Brandy started, but Tyler cut her off.

"We need to talk."

"I'm afraid I'm clear out of smoke." He winked and took another drag of his cigarette. "The good kind, that is. But I do have a little hooch left over to really get the party started."

"I'm not here to buy."

The man shrugged. "I'm not running a new football pot until next week. If you come back Monday, I can get you in on next week's game. It's a pre-season biggee. Texas Tech versus LSU. My money's on Tech. They've got one helluva quarterback this year."

"We're not here to bet."

"So what are you doing here? Don't tell me, the cops chased you away from Rebel Creek and this is the best you could do for a make-out spot."

"I'm looking for my brother," Tyler told him.

Kenny Roy's eyes widened for a split second before he shook his head. "Can't say as I've seen him."

"I don't believe you. An entire barful of customers saw you two together last week," Tyler reminded him.

"That's true enough, but I ain't seen him *this* week."

Tyler stepped forward until barely a hand span separated them. "You're full of shit."

"It's true," Kenny Roy said, clearing his throat as if searching for his voice. "I ain't seen him since last weekend."

"Why not? Where did he go?"

"I think you ought to ask him." He shrugged again. "I ain't gettin' in the middle of somebody else's family business."

"You're already in the middle because you gave him a job that paid more than the crappy Dairy Freeze. He's been selling for you, hasn't he?"

"Maybe. But that was weeks ago. He's moved on since then."

"On to what?"

"Something that pays a damn sight better." When Tyler's gaze narrowed enough to be dangerous, Kenny Roy rushed on, "It's no big deal. He's just doing a little bootlegging with Gator Hallsey. Not cooking or anything like that. Gator don't cook. He's strictly into transport, and he's damn good at it. The best on account of he used to do all that dirt track driving. He knows every back road within a five-hundred-mile perimeter. Saw your brother driving that old Mustang of his and thought he might be halfway decent at transport. They left day before yesterday with a truck full of hooch for a high-end buyer up around Dallas. The guy's got money coming out his ass."

"So why doesn't he just hit up a liquor store?" Brandy voiced the one question that most people came up with when they thought of modern-day moonshining. It was a crime not worth the risk and easily preventable.

At the same time, old habits died hard in a small town.

"Because that would be too easy," Kenny Roy chimed in. "This guy's got *money*, and when you got money it's always fun to see just what you can do with it."

"How much you can get away with," Tyler added.

"Exactly. It's always fun outsmarting the cops. That, and it *is* some pretty damn good hooch thanks to your girlfriend, here. Speaking of which." His gaze slid past Tyler. "You gonna help us out with another batch there, sugar?"

"That depends." She stepped forward, her shoulder brushing Tyler's as she came up next to him.

"On what?"

"On whether or not I get to see the process through from beginning to end."

Kenny Roy smiled. "You're kidding, right?"

"Not at all. My mash. My hooch. I should be there."

He shook his head. "Not no, but hell no. My boy don't run anything with an audience."

She shrugged. "Then you and your boy can mix up your own mash."

Silence settled for a long moment before he arched an eyebrow. "You really got another batch ready to go?"

"It's fermenting right now. You can either let me watch the process and give me the first good jar while you keep all the rest for yourself, or you can lose out on the opportunity to make some easy money. There's no shine out there as good as mine."

Tyler had to give her props. She stood her ground as she faced off with Kenny Roy. While the guy was little more than a small-time criminal, he still came off as intimidating with his beady black eyes and stout body. But Brandy wasn't the least bit put off. Determination gleamed in her eyes and he knew then she wasn't giving up on her recipe any more than he was giving up on his brother.

"I guess I could talk to him." She nodded and Kenny Roy hooked his fingers in his belt loops. "Is that it? 'Cause I'd really like to get inside. I just won the big enchilada."

"You play the Lotto?" Brandy asked.

"I ain't talking Lotto. I won a free dinner at Maria's House of Enchiladas. She's got chili cheese tonight and I aim to get there before the doors close." He moved to walk past them, but Tyler caught him by the collar.

"Not so fast. When is Hallsey getting back to town?"

Kenny Roy didn't look as if he wanted to give an answer, but Tyler wasn't leaving without one. He tightened his grip and the material pulled tight around the man's neck. "You can tell me now, or you can get used to seeing my truck parked in your driveway because I'm not leaving." He glanced past Kenny's Ford to another car idling at the end of the drive. The old burgundy Cutlass had just pulled up, the driver little more than a shadow. "I bet that would put a cramp in your business." He let loose a whistle and motioned to the car. "He's closed. Get out of here."

"Hey—" Kenny Roy started, but the grip on his collar went tighter and the words snagged in his throat.

The Cutlass stalled for a second before shifting into gear and hauling ass down the road.

"Either tell me something or I can promise that won't be the first customer you lose," Tyler vowed.

"Next week," Kenny Roy rasped. "They ought to be back by Monday." When Tyler narrowed his gaze, Kenny Roy added, "Tuesday at the latest. At least that's what Gator said before he left."

"It doesn't take three days to drive to and from Dallas."

"It does if you're stopping off to make some

drops along the way. Most of Gator's customers aren't too keen on taking deliveries during the day, which means he has to hit 'em up at night. He's got several, so it'll be a few days. Three. Maybe four days." He shrugged. "How the hell do I know? I just know he's gone until I hear that he's back."

"And as soon as you do, you'll call me, right?" Tyler's fingers tightened. The material grew taut. Kenny Roy's gaze went wide. "Otherwise, I'll be telling the sheriff about those plants you've got growing in the bathroom."

"How do you know—"

"I just know," Tyler cut in. "Call me, understand?" Kenny Roy nodded and Tyler motioned to the Explorer, "Now back that thing up so we can get the hell out of here." He thrust the man forward and Kenny Roy stumbled a few feet before catching himself.

He stood, tugging at his collar before pulling a cigarette from his pocket and flicking the flame on his lighter. The tip flared and smoke curled.

"A Tucker and a Sawyer," Kenny Roy said after a long drag. He stepped toward his vehicle, the smoke following him. "Who woulda thought?"

CHAPTER 12

She wasn't going to follow him.

That's what Brandy told herself after they'd left Kenny Roy's house. They ambled over the railroad tracks before hitting Main Street. A few more blocks and she watched Tyler's truck turn off the main road and head for the outskirts of town.

It was still early. Just shy of ten o'clock on a Saturday night. There was no guarantee he was even going back to the rodeo arena. He could be hitting up a nearby bar and picking up some local girl for all Brandy knew.

Her lips vibrated from the feel of his kiss.

Just a kiss, which meant it shouldn't bother her. Not when they'd done so much more so many times before.

But this one kiss had felt different.

More potent. Intense. Meaningful, even.

And the last thing she wanted—needed—was *meaningful* when it came to Tyler McCall.

She was all about hot, fiery, intense, do-me-*now* passion. Nothing more. No sitting next to him with the crickets buzzing in the background. No music playing softly while they talked about . . . everything. Anything.

Talking, of all things.

She turned in the opposite direction and headed to the main turnoff leading to the Tucker spread. Pavement gave way to gravel and dirt as the car bumped along the last half mile leading to the house. Brandy rounded a cluster of trees, the foliage growing more sparse until she spotted the peeling two-story house that she'd lived in for most of her life.

Ever since her dad had moved the family from Austin to help take care of his ailing father. At least that had been the story her parents had told their three daughters. Grandpa needed them, and it had been true. But they'd also needed Grandpa since her dad had lost yet another job and had been hard-pressed to keep a roof over their heads.

They'd had little more than a few suitcases and the clothes on their backs when they'd walked into James Harlin Tucker's home, but that fact had never bothered her parents. They'd had each other and as long as they'd been together, they'd been happy.

For the most part.

But Brandy hadn't missed the look of longing in her mother's eyes whenever she'd whipped up a few pies to bring in some extra money at Thanksgiving, or baked a dozen loaves of cranberry walnut bread to sell at the Christmas Bazaar.

Her baking hadn't just been a means to an end. It had been something she'd loved. Something she'd been proud of. Something she might have had an opportunity to actually pursue if she hadn't married so young and given up everything for her husband and children.

Brandy's hands tightened on the steering wheel as she pulled to a stop in front of the house. The place was dark except for the bare yellow bulb that flickered on the front porch, the driveway empty.

But then Brandy hadn't expected anything different. It was Saturday night, which meant Callie was with Brett, and Jenna . . . well, she was, hopefully, setting the record straight with Jase.

And Brandy was, as usual, alone.

She licked her suddenly dry lips and tried to ignore the hum that vibrated along her nerve endings as she remembered the press of Tyler's mouth. She stiffened and pulled a box of leftover bread rolls from the backseat, along with a box of thumbprint cookies, before making her way to the steps. She was one shy of the front porch when she heard the echo of an engine. She set the bakery boxes on the porch and turned just as twin beams sliced through the darkness and bathed her in stark white light.

Her own gaze narrowed, her vision going blurry as she fought to see past the sudden plunge of headlights. Her heartbeat kicked up a notch and excitement gunned through her as gravel crunched and brakes growled. The lights died and anticipation wound tight in her belly.

She blinked once, twice until her eyes adjusted and she could make out the silhouette of a man climbing down from the driver's side of a beige SUV.

Beige, not black. A beaten-up Suburban rather than a brand-spanking new, sleek diesel pickup.

The realization sliced through her and her anticipation took a nosedive while her unease snapped to attention.

"Hey there, Brandy." Sheriff Hunter DeMassi's voice carried through the darkness a few moments before he stepped into the dim halo of porch light that pushed out into the yard. "Hope I'm not catching you at a bad time."

"Not at all. I'm just getting home from work." She waited while he stepped up onto the porch, the light turning him from a shadow to an actual man. "What can I do for you?"

Another search. That's what she expected. The sheriff had been out numerous times over the past few months to walk the path to the site of her granddad's old still. The place where he'd finally blown himself to smithereens after decades of making his own shine.

But then everybody makes mistakes, and while James Harlin had been every bit as good as his daddy and his granddaddy before him, he hadn't been the legend himself—*the* Elijah G. Sawyer— and so the odds had finally caught up to him.

That, and his failing eyesight and withering liver had contributed to the tragedy. Both had made him slower and more susceptible to errors, and so he'd finally made one.

His last one.

She eyed the sheriff. He was just a few years older than she was. Tyler's age, to be more exact. Like Tyler, he was well over six feet, too. But that's where the similarities ended. His dark hair was cut much shorter than Tyler's, his face clean-shaven. He had golden eyes that caught the porch light and gleamed with an intensity that told her he hadn't shown up just to see how she was doing. There was something else driving him. Something far more serious.

"You can have another look out back if you want," Brandy offered.

"No need." He shook his head. "I'm here because there have been new facts that have come to light. See, we made a few arrests last month. Caught some moonshiners that were poaching on Sawyer land."

She nodded. "I heard about that. You guys arrested Big Jimmy, didn't you?"

"Him and a few others working with him." The sheriff nodded. "Since moonshining is a federal offense, Austin sent a crew out to go over the still site, and they found a few interesting pieces of evidence."

"Such as?"

He didn't say anything for a long moment, as

if picking and choosing just how much to tell her. "Your grandfather's DNA was found at the site," he finally murmured.

"My grandfather had his own still. Why would he be nosing around at Big Jimmy's place?"

"You tell me. There's no denying the evidence. Some way, somehow, he was with Big Jimmy at his still at some point prior to his death. And we're not talking years. The weather would have washed away any old evidence. This was fresh. He paid a visit to that still not a week or two before he died."

"That's crazy. My grandpa hated Big Jimmy." James Harlin had hated most everyone who'd threatened his livelihood. Not that Big Jimmy had cooked up hooch that good. But he had gone so far as to try to push his stuff on James Harlin's customers, and so her granddad had seen the man as a threat. At least he'd cussed up a blue streak whenever anyone had made mention of him.

"Maybe Granddad went there to threaten him. You know how territorial he was."

"That's what the Feds are thinking. The thing is, this place was deep in the woods. Far enough out that James Harlin would have had a devil of a time getting out there. It seems he could have run across Big Jimmy at any number of places without having to go to so much trouble. The diner. The VFW Hall. Cavanaugh's General Store. There are a dozen places that don't involve crawl-ing onto a four-wheeler and roughing it three miles over raw terrain. Did he have access to an off-road vehicle?"

"Are you kidding? If his truck couldn't get the job done, then he didn't bother." She glanced toward the old barn that sat several yards from the house. "There's the old tractor, but it died years ago."

"Which means it's doubtful he headed out there on his own."

She eyed him. "What are you trying to say?"

"That something's off." He seemed to think. "Something doesn't add up."

"Which makes you wonder about everything that does add up," she added for him. He didn't respond, but she didn't miss the gleam in his eyes that said she'd hit the nail on the head. "You're thinking there was more to the explosion, aren't you?"

"No, no," he said much too quickly to ease her mind. He pulled off his hat and ran a hand through his dark hair. "I went over the scene myself and didn't find anything that would indicate the explosion was anything other than a terrible accident. It's just . . .." He shook his head again. "I'm sure I'm just making a mountain out of an anthill." He sat the hat back on his head. "But I'd still like to be sure. Maybe look around a little more just to ease my own mind."

"Be my guest," she said, motioning to the back. "But the dozers were already out plowing down everything so I can't say that you'll find much of anything besides crushed timber."

"I'm not interested in poking around out back." He shook his head. "I'd like to look around inside, if that's okay. Your grandfather's room, in particular."

Because no one had even thought to go through his personal belongings. There'd been no reason to when all signs had pointed to a tragic accident and nothing more.

Until now.

The realization sent a whisper of unease through her. "Callie packed most everything away, but it's all boxed up in his bedroom." While her older sister had worked up the courage to face her demons where their grandfather was concerned, Callie hadn't actually parted with any of his stuff. Rather, she'd left it for Brandy and Jenny to do away with as they saw fit. Since Jenna's idea of dealing with things was to look the other way, the boxes had been left to Brandy, who'd yet to decide between the local Goodwill or the church donation box. "You're welcome to have a look through them if you think there might be something helpful in there."

"I'd appreciate that." He waited while she unlocked the door and stepped inside.

She scooped up the white ball of fluff that met her and cuddled the yapping animal close while she motioned the sheriff in. "Hush, Jez," she told the dog. "It's just the sheriff." But Jez didn't care. She was a ballsy teacup–mutt mix that Jenna had brought home from the veterinary clinic, along with half a dozen other strays—two rabbits, two more monstrous dogs that lived on the back porch, and a small cat now camped out in the barn. While little more than a handful, Jez considered herself the ruler of the Tucker household and she meant to establish dominance.

Until the sheriff reached out a hand and tickled her behind the ears. The barking turned to panting and soon she was lapping at his fingers and wagging her tail excitedly.

"I think she likes you," she told the sheriff as she led him down the hallway. Their footsteps echoed off the old hardwood floor the way they had done her entire life whenever she'd ventured to James Harlin's room.

Not that she'd made the trek very often.

He'd been a mean old coot and so Brandy had avoided him for the most part, just as he'd avoided her. Callie had been the pain in the ass, facing off with him, calling him out whenever she had the chance, and Jenna had been the chip-off-the-old-block, giving him a good chuckle with her wild and crazy ways. Meanwhile, Brandy had been invisible to him. The nonexistent middle child. Until he'd come looking for cookies to chase down his liquor, that is. But even then, he'd rarely made eye contact with her. As if looking at her bothered him even more than the damnable hemorrhoids he complained about so religiously.

She'd hoped to coax a smile from him with her famous gingerbread.

But James Harlin hadn't been capable of smiling. He'd gone to his grave with the same frown he'd worn throughout his life, leaving Brandy to wonder if he'd ever really liked anything.

Her cookies. Her.

That's why she'd yet to part with the boxes. Because she was still trying to make up her mind about him, just as she was trying to decide what to do with his stuff.

She pushed aside the thought and focused on the panting dog. "She definitely likes you," she told the sheriff.

"What can I say? It's the animal magnetism."

He grinned and she remembered their high school days when he'd asked her out a time or two and she'd turned him down. He'd been one of the few who hadn't written anything about her on the bathroom wall, and so she'd always liked him.

"This is it," she said, showing him into the small room that her grandfather had occupied near the back of the house. She pushed open the door and flipped on the light. "Take your time."

"Thanks," he said. "I shouldn't be too long."

She nodded. "I'll be in the kitchen if you need me." She stalled for a split-second, drinking in the familiar smells of mothballs and moonshine that still permeated the small space. An empty Mason jar sat on the nightstand next to an old *Reader's Digest* and a half-empty pack of Juicy Fruit gum. The man had liked his gum as much as his shine and so it had been all too typical to find him smacking away in between sips during his TV time.

Her gaze hooked on the worn quilt that covered the full-size bed and she remembered James covered up to his neck on a particularly cold night, a jar of hooch next to him, a frown on his face.

Until she'd handed him one of her homemade cookies. The expression had slipped then for just a heartbeat. Not a full-blown smile, mind you. Just the hint of something besides his usual disdain.

Then he'd shifted his attention back to *Wheel of Fortune* and she'd been left to wonder if it had just been her imagination.

Or if maybe, just maybe, she wasn't invisible to him after all.

She shook away the past and turned to leave the sheriff to his work. Brandy spent the next half hour storing the extras she'd brought home from the bakery and cleaning up the mess Jenna had left in the kitchen. Her younger sister had never been strong on housework, not with Callie to pick up the slack. Since Callie had all but moved in with her fiancé and left Brandy and Jenna to fend for themselves, Brandy had taken over most of the domestic duties.

She cleaned the kitchen and was just picking up in the living room, Jez yapping at her heels, when the sheriff appeared in the doorway.

She arched an eyebrow. "Find anything helpful?"

"Not really. There sure are a lot of empty Bengay tubes."

"I said Callie packed up." She grinned. "I didn't say she threw anything away." Her sister had had a hard enough time putting away the old man's belongings. She hadn't been able to bring herself to toss out anything. Brandy had promised to do that for her sister when she found the time. Which, thanks to the bakery's demanding hours, hadn't happened yet. "If you need anything else, let me know."

He nodded. "Thanks for letting me look around. The Feds are probably right. James Harlin could be a determined SOB when he wanted to be. I'm sure he probably found a way out there to give those boys a piece of his mind for poaching on his business."

Only he didn't sound so sure.

A fact that followed Brandy around for the next hour as she showered and changed and tried to get some much-needed sleep.

Tried being the operative word.

Instead, she tossed and turned and thought about her granddad and the night of the explosion. There'd been nothing off about that night.

He'd gone out to work like always and she'd crawled into bed early in order to be at the bakery at the crack of dawn. She'd been sleeping like a rock, too, until the sound had rattled the walls. The next thing she knew, she was standing with her sisters, watching the flames lick at the pitch-black night while sirens wailed in the back-ground.

A terrible end to a terrible man.

Right?

The question haunted her until she gave up trying to sleep and finally climbed out of bed. She curled up on the old vinyl couch in the living room and fired up the ancient console TV, a throwback to Christmas ages ago when she'd been just seven and her dad had brought home the cherrywood console as a surprise for her mother.

Brandy could still see the smile on her mother's face, the kiss she'd planted on her husband's lips. She'd been so thankful. So happy.

Most of the time, Brandy reminded herself.

But there had been those weak moments. The unhappiness. The longing. The regret.

Because she'd married too young and given up a promising career.

Not this girl.

Not now. Not ever.

Brandy held tight to the notion as she reached for the remote and pulled up a rerun of *Ace of Cakes*. But even that wasn't enough to ease the unsettling feeling in the pit of her stomach. The only thing that did that was the image of Tyler McCall that rushed into her head when a partic-ularly extravagant wedding cake topped with an exact likeness of the bride and groom filled the screen.

The figurine wore a cowboy hat and suddenly she saw Tyler wearing nothing but his hat tipped low and an expression that said he wanted her. Now.

Her lips tingled and her stomach hollowed out, and try as she might, she couldn't seem to shake the crazy reaction. Not after two more episodes and a cold shower.

Because there was only one thing that could get him off her mind.

Anticipation coiled through her and need vibrated along her nerve endings. She glanced at the clock. It was half past midnight. Late for her, but early for most of the other folks in town when it came to a Saturday night. Was Tyler still out? Was he asleep? Awake? Restless?

There was only one way to find out.

CHAPTER 13

Tyler blinked, but Brandy didn't fade and disappear the way she did in his fantasies.

Because this wasn't a fantasy.

She'd come knocking on his door again, searching him out, fanning the flames that already blazed so fiercely between them.

And it didn't matter that he was tired or worried or frustrated to the point that he wanted to put his fist through a wall. Nothing mattered but this.

Her.

She sat astride him, her skin pale and silky in the moonlight that drifted through the parted curtains and bathed the room in a celestial glow. She shimmied her body and hiked her sundress to her waist to free her legs. With the material out of her way, she spread wider and settled more fully over him.

She wasn't wearing any underwear.

He'd known that the moment he'd opened the door and she'd pushed him back inside, to the edge of the bed. She'd lifted the hem and just like that, she'd been on top of him.

Her bare sex rested atop his cock that throbbed beneath his jeans. She gripped his shoulders, stared deep into his eyes, and rubbed herself against his length. Side to side. Back and forth.

She flung her head back and went wild for the next few moments and it was all he could do not to touch her smooth thighs or knead her sweet, round ass or slide his fingers into her wet heat.

But Tyler had been waiting for this moment all damn day and he wasn't about to have it over with as quickly as it had been last night. He balled his hands into fists and let her have her fun.

"This feels so good," she murmured, her voice low and breathless and oh, so stirring. The sound prickled the hair on the back of his neck and sent an echoing vibration along his nerve endings.

"Damn straight," he managed, his own voice thick and raw and . . . Christ, but she felt amazing.

But for all her boldness, there was a hesitancy. As if she wasn't as sure of herself as she should have been with that face and that body.

She wasn't, and the realization eased some of the tension knotting his stomach. He knew then that Brandy hadn't spent the past two years warming the sheets with another man. She'd waited for this. For him.

"I missed you," he murmured, the words little more than a growl of appreciation at what she was doing to him with each slide and shimmy and . . . holy *shit*. He clamped his lips as a hiss worked past them and then the movement stopped.

"Really?" she breathed as her entire body went still. "You really missed me?"

"You bet your sweet ass." His words reassured her and she smiled, a brilliant slash of white in the darkness of the room. "And it is a sweet ass. The sweetest."

"I bet you say that to all the girls," she murmured, her smile fading into something more primitive and possessive and daring.

She wanted him to step up, to tell her that she was wrong. That she was his.

The thought stalled in his brain for a long, fierce moment before she moved again. That's all it took to effectively distract him from reality. Everything scrambled into a furious swirl of pure, raw need and he stopped thinking altogether.

She kept riding him, rubbing herself up and down, creating a delicious friction before she finally leaned back. Soft fingertips reached for the waistband of his jeans. He was already so hard that the zipper caught and refused to budge.

"Easy," he murmured, catching her hand with his.

He lifted his pelvis and guided her hand down, helping her work the zipper the rest of the way. Pushing his jeans down, he caught his underwear along with it and stripped both free until his erection sprang thick and heavy toward her.

Her touch was sure and purposeful as she reached out. One fingertip traced a throbbing vein up his rock-hard length, pausing just shy of the silky-smooth head.

Not because she was hesitant again. Hell, no.

She knew exactly what she was doing. Exactly how to drive him crazy. That's what he loved about her. There was nothing tentative about Brandy Tucker when it came to the sex itself.

Even that first time, she'd been bold, provocative, erotic despite being naive. A woman who had no problem taking pleasure.

Or giving it.

She'd embodied every wild thing ever written about her on the bathroom wall and then some. A bad girl in every sense of the word, and he'd been the lucky man to touch her first.

To touch her, period, a voice whispered. A crazy-ass voice because no way was he fool enough to think that while she might have held off for the past two years, that it meant anything. That she'd waited because he was the only man for her.

The first.

The last.

Right.

But he was the only man at this moment, and so he meant to make it count.

Contrary to the back stall of the boy's first-floor restroom at Rebel High, Brandy had never been all that mesmerized by the male member.

Until Tyler McCall.

Bold and beautiful, his penis jutted tall, throbbing beneath her steady touch. She caught her bottom lip, barely resisting the urge to lean down and lick the engorged purple head. Instead, she circled the underside with a trembling finger and watched him suck in a breath.

The sound fed her confidence and she wrapped her hand around him. Heat scorched her fingertips and he arched into her grasp. Still he didn't touch her with his strong hands.

Instead, he waited.

She didn't waste even a second in taking the lead.

Her gaze trailed up over a ridged abdomen, a broad chest sprinkled with dark, silky hair, a corded neck, to the chiseled perfection of his face partially hidden in the shadow of his cowboy hat. It was her latest fantasy come to life, and heat rushed through her.

She took his hat off, set it aside, and stared deep into his bright-aquamarine eyes. There was no mistaking the raw, aching need that gripped him.

"I wasn't sure if you would show up tonight."

"Me either, but then I started thinking and it seemed like such a shame to waste this." She touched the ridge of his penis, just a gentle sweep of her fingertip but enough to make him shudder.

"I'm glad you came," he murmured.

"But I haven't," she said, stroking him again. "Come, that is. And neither have you. Not yet."

The words seemed to feed something dark and primitive inside him. Before she could draw another breath, his mouth covered hers and his tongue thrust between her parted lips. The kiss seemed to go on forever and when he finally pulled away, Brandy couldn't seem to catch her breath.

She fought for air while he reached down into the pocket of his jeans and retrieved a foil packet. A few seconds later, he slid the condom onto his erection, gripped her waist, and pulled her closer.

He pressed his hard sex between her legs. The plump head pushed into her a delicious inch until she felt her body pulse around the top of his thick shaft. She felt the wetness between her legs, drenching him and making the connection that much hotter.

A shiver ripped through her and she slid her hands around his neck. Her fingers plunged into his hair. Her nipples tightened, pressing against the thin material of her sundress, and her thighs trembled.

He kissed her slowly, deeply, before he finally drew away. His heated gaze held hers as he lifted her hips again, pushing into her a fraction more. But it wasn't enough.

That's the way it always was with him. He gave a little, but she wanted more. She always wanted more. Harder. Faster. *Now.*

Bracing her hands against his chest, she climbed to her feet. She backed up just a few steps and reached for the edge of her dress. Bunching the hem, she pulled it up and over her head. Her nipples hardened against the sudden rush of cold air from the window unit blasting nearby and she trembled.

As soon as the chill hit her, it slipped away as Tyler's gaze swept the length of her. Fire flared in his eyes, warming her skin and sending a flush through her body.

"You are the most beautiful woman I've ever seen, Brandy Tucker." It was a compliment she'd heard many, many times. But there was something different about the way he said it. As if he really and truly meant it.

Duh.

He thinks you're super hot and you think he's sexy as sin. Otherwise you wouldn't be here getting naked together.

Still . . .

She watched as he stood and shed his jeans completely. He settled back down on the edge of the bed and motioned for her.

"Come here, baby," he murmured, his voice raw and husky and oh, so stirring.

Anticipation rippled through her and every nerve in her body tingled. She straddled him again, her knees and calves cushioned by the soft mattress.

She slid the swollen bud of her clitoris against his engorged penis until she reached the head. She rubbed from side to side, feeling him pulse against her most tender spot. She gasped when his teeth caught one nipple and he closed his lips over the sensitive peak. He drew her deep into his mouth and sucked so hard that she felt the tug between her legs.

She moved a fraction higher and pressed the wet opening of her body over the head of his erection. His hold on her nipple broke as a ragged gasp escaped his lips. She pushed down slightly, letting him stretch her, fill her, just enough to make her insides tighten.

And then she stalled, determined to stop at that exact moment and relish the sweet pressure that tightened.

He bucked beneath her and she did it again, pushing down just enough to make her body crave more before pulling back and gasping for air. His hands slid down her back and his large fingers pressed into her bottom as if to pull her back down. But he didn't. He wanted her to take it at her own pace.

Sweet and slow. Or hard and fast.

She kissed him then, sucking at his tongue the way her body grasped at the head of his erection.

Over and over.

His muscles bunched tight beneath her fingertips, his body hard and stiff, until she knew he couldn't take any more.

With a shudder, she slid down over him until she felt the base of his shaft fully against her. The soft silk of his pubic hair teased the sensitive lips of her vagina. He sat there inside of her for a long, heart-stopping moment before the sensation seemed to overwhelm him and he had to move. He gripped her bottom with both hands and his hips lifted.

He slid deeper. The sensation of being stretched and filled by the raw strength of him stalled the air in her lungs.

The pressure between her legs was razor-sharp and oh, so sweet. But not half as sharp and sweet as the sudden tightening in her chest when he looked at her, his gaze so fierce and possessive, as if two years had been way too long and he never meant to let her go again.

As if.

He would let her go. He always did.

That's what a booty call was. Here today. Gone tomorrow. *Temporary.*

She held tight to the notion and shifted her attention to the desire coiling tight in her body. She rocked her hips, riding him with an intensity that made her heart pound and her body throb and her brain short-circuit.

She held tight to her senses for as long as possible, determined to memorize every movement and brand his every expression into her brain. Until sensation gripped her, so wild and tantalizing that her breath stalled and her heart all but stopped beating. She couldn't help herself. While she wanted to watch, the only thing she seemed capable of in that next instant was feeling.

Her eyes closed.

Her head fell back.

Strong arms anchored her tight as he pushed her down hard on his throbbing erection. Tight. Until her body released a warm, sucking rush of moisture.

His deep groan vibrated the air as his strong fingers clasped her bottom. He bucked beneath her and the muscles in his neck went tight. Once. Twice. His erection pushed deep one final time and he exploded.

She collapsed against him, her head in the curve of his shoulder as she tried to catch her breath. His arms tightened around her and he simply held her then, stroking her back and her bottom as her heart slowly returned to normal.

Oddly enough, it was those stroking, soothing moments afterward that stood out in her mind long after she'd pulled on her clothes and walked away.

Because for the first time he hadn't let her go right away. He'd held on for just a little longer this time. Holding. Touching. Caressing.

And as much as she hated to admit it, she'd liked it.

The realization made a twenty-minute drive home last only fifteen. Anxious, she pressed on the gas and hauled butt in the opposite direction. Because the last thing Brandy Tucker wanted was to *like* Tyler McCall.

CHAPTER 14

Tyler checked his phone for the umpteenth time before collapsing back onto the bed to stare at the ceiling, his heart still pounding, his body still throbbing.

He listened for the sound of her car, but the only noise that carried was the hum of the nearby window unit and the murmur of the livestock below. Everything was quiet. Asleep.

Except for him.

He rolled over and hauled his ass out of bed, straight into a cold shower.

Cold, of all the crazy things. He should be more than sated. Enough to roll over and fall right to sleep.

But he kept smelling the sheets, which still held the sweet aroma of blueberry muffins, and he found himself thinking about her. Wanting her. Needing her—

Hold up.

The only thing Tyler *needed* was to get his hands on Cooper. Since that wasn't going to happen anytime in the next few hours, he might as well make the most of his downtime and actually do something productive.

Climbing out the shower, he pulled on a pair of shorts, a T-shirt, and some old sneakers. It wasn't his usual boots and jeans, but it was perfect for an early-morning run. The arena was dark and quiet as he left the small apartment and headed down toward the back corral.

It was still just an hour shy of dawn and so the working cowboys had yet to show up to feed the animals, but the place would be bustling with life all too soon.

Not soon enough.

Tyler eyed the mechanical bull situated in the small enclosure. It wasn't a top-notch machine, but it had been good enough to get him to the point he was at today. And it would get him to Cheyenne in less than three weeks. Likewise, the choice bulls penned nearby would be prep enough to ensure that he was as quick and tough as he needed to be.

If he was stuck here, he might as well make the most of it. He wasn't falling short in Cheyenne. He might never get this opportunity again what with his cousin Brett Sawyer, the reigning PBR champ, retiring. The spot was wide open and Tyler wanted it.

He knew he was the long shot. The dark horse.

But then that was the story of his life.

He'd always been the odd man out. The black sheep. The outsider among the prestigious Sawyer clan thanks to a mother who'd married a worthless sonofabitch. Mr. Least Likely to Succeed, but he'd defied the odds and done just that. Now would be no different.

He left the arena behind and headed for the large fenced-in area out back and the small path that ran its perimeter.

And then he started to run.

Ellie Clark had done the walk of shame before.

Many times before.

And so the strange feeling that she wanted to climb back into bed and say to hell with everything caught her completely off guard.

Particularly when she stared at the cowboy responsible for it.

A *cowboy*, of all people. She'd never been into cowboys even though her hometown had been crawling with them. She'd wanted someone wearing something besides a pair of shit-covered Wranglers and charming smile to sweep her off her feet.

And get her the hell out.

Away from the map dot where she'd been born and bred and the ever small-minded mentality of a hick town.

Which didn't explain in the least why she'd moved to Rebel. Same small-minded mentality. Different hick town.

But at least the faces had been fresh and she'd been able to escape the mundane without moving more than fifty miles away from her sick grandmother. For a little while.

Still, even though she liked Rebel and she loved her job at Sweet Somethings, she was starting to feel a little restless again. Particularly since her nana had passed on last year and eliminated the main reason she'd been sticking somewhat close to home. Nana was gone, the weekly visits to nearby Lawless, Texas, no more. She was free now.

Antsy.

Which explained tonight's bad decision.

Well, that and four Buttery Nipples.

She'd never done well with shots, but since Lila had been icing all day and she'd needed a big dose of pain relief, Ellie had forfeited her usual Bud Lite in favor of something much stronger so that her coworker didn't have to get shitfaced all by her lonesome.

Bad move.

The more she'd drunk, the more restless she'd gotten, and soon she'd been dancing around the small bar, ripe for someone, anyone to sweep her off her feet. She'd been hard-pressed to shake things up. And while a hunky cowboy was usually the norm in this neck of the woods, there was nothing normal about the man stretched out on the bed in front of her.

He had the hard lines of a professional rodeo man. A calf roper to be more specific, or so he'd said. Half of an award-winning duo. She found herself wishing she'd asked which half. That, and his name.

She still couldn't believe how fast things had progressed. One minute they'd been at the bar, the next she'd been following him into his motel room. No name. No details. He could have been a serial killer for all she knew.

Then again, the rodeo circuit hadn't had a known serial killer in its ranks in forever. That, and the rest of the bar seemed familiar with him, even if she hadn't known him from Adam.

Not that it mattered.

He didn't matter and the less she knew about him, the better.

It made leaving easier and forgetting all about the past four hours a plausible plan of action.

She glanced at the deeply tanned body resting atop the crisp white sheets, his legs dusted with the same fine gold hair that swirled across his chest and surrounded a very impressive penis. Even asleep, he looked half-cocked and loaded. The sight stirred an ache low in her belly.

Definitely impressive. Not only visually, but physically, as well. He'd certainly managed to do some impressive things since they'd stumbled into the room. She still couldn't believe she'd come a whopping three times in as many hours. Not her record, mind you, but definitely a record with a living, breathing human being rather than Big Red, her favorite vibrator. Even her current "boyfriend" hadn't managed to stir more than one, and that had been a record in and of itself.

Until now.

She picked her way around the room, pulling on a shirt here, a pair of blue jean shorts there, until she stood fully clothed and ready to get the hell out of Dodge. Now. Before he cracked open an eye.

That would just make things weird.

She grabbed her purse and keys and reached for the door knob, but the deep voice stopped her cold.

"You're up awful early."

"I, um, need to get to work."

"It's Sunday."

"Yeah, well not all of us keep banker's hours," she blurted even though Brandy gave her the mornings off. "I work for a living."

"This early?"

"Church then," she quipped. "Gotta make the early service. Especially after last night."

His warm chuckle vibrated the air around them and sent a whispering heat through her. "We did do a few things that would give new meaning to the word *hedonism*." Bedsprings creaked and just like that, he was standing in front of her, his naked body filling up her line of vision and making her breath catch. "I guess it makes sense you might need to repent." He took her hand and touched the palm to his lips. "You definitely racked up the sins last night."

Heat bolted from her head clear to her toes, and a dozen erotic images bombarded her brain. Memories. Fantasies. Of what he'd done to her

out to fill the case. The girls' choir loves my chocolate ganache and they'll be letting out just after one so I want to have plenty ready and waiting. All that singing makes them hungry."

Brandy spent the next hour mixing and baking and frosting. She slid the last cupcake into place just as the doors swung open and a whopping two customers walked in.

Betty Dupree and her neighbor, Eliza Jamison. Both women were in their eighties and lived over at the senior center. Every Sunday they rode the bus to church just down the street and walked over for muffins and coffee—along with the other two dozen residents—to eat and talk and wait for their ride back to the home.

"Decaf for me, sugar," Betty said when Brandy went to fill her mug. "I'm watching my caffeine."

"Me, too," Eliza chimed in. "On account of it aggravates my heart condition."

"You don't have a heart condition," Betty pointed out.

"Maybe not, but too much caffeine makes me feel like I do. My heart starts racing and I get all hot around the collar."

"That's not caffeine. That's lust. You got a hankering for that new Wayland Carmichael. He's the new beefcake over at the home," Betty told Brandy. "Doesn't live there yet. His daughter just brings him over for dominoes every afternoon. He's fresh meat and Eliza here is sweet on him."

"Am not."

"Are, too."

"Ladies, have a muffin," Brandy said, distracting the women from their bickering. "I just made a fresh batch."

"I hope you didn't make too many," Betty said, taking the plate that Brandy slid across the counter. "On account of the rest of the ladies decided to stop off at the doughnut shop instead of coming here."

"But the bus picks you guys up here," Brandy reminded the woman.

"Not today. Our driver is anxious to try this new French thing the doughnut shop is doing called a beignet. It's all the rage in New Orleans. Since Missy Stevens's grandma relocated here after Katrina, she's been teaching Susie Mae all her Cajun baking secrets. That's where the habanero jelly came from. Anyhow, they was handing out samples this morning during Sunday school, so a whole mess of us decided to go over after church. The driver, too, on account of his grandma is Bernice Vernon, who's the one leading the switch from muffins to doughnuts. I swear the woman ain't got no loyalty." She glanced behind her at the windows and the pair of old men who hobbled past. "See there? Headed after one of them fancy beignets. It's shameful, I tell you. Downright shameful."

"That's what's wrong with men today," Eliza chimed in. "Always wanting something fancy when they could have what's right in front of them."

"Don't mind her," Betty added when her companion turned and headed for a nearby table. "She's just upset because Wayland likes Genevieve Flowers. She's that woman from Austin. Moved here with her grandkids until she got too old to get around by herself and now she's at the senior center. She wears a fresh daisy tucked behind her ear every Sunday to church. Drives the men wild on account of it masks the mothball smell and makes her downright irresistible."

"That would do it," Brandy said, turning to fill a cup of coffee for Betty.

"None for me, sugar," the old woman waved an arthritic hand. "Not on account of I'm sweet on anybody. The stuff just don't sit well on my stomach anymore. Why, I used to have a cast-iron constitution. Could eat those fellas at the VFW under the table when it came to chili night. One time I ate six bowls in a row of Merle Jaggart's Chile From Hell. Washed it down with an entire glass of your daddy's hooch, too. Now I can't even eat a can of Wolf Brand. And don't even get me started on what I can't drink. It's a good thing all that brew died with your grandpa, bless his soul. It did, didn't it?" she asked, one penciled-in eyebrow arching ever so slightly. "You and your sisters aren't taking over the family business, are you?"

"Not at all, Miss Betty. I've got my hands full here."

"Of course you do. And it's a good thing, too. I'd hate to see any one of you girls blow yourself up like that James Harlin. And speaking of blowing"—she touched her stomach—"I think I need to use your little girls' room. That tapioca I ate this morning is grumbling like Old Faithful."

When Brandy motioned toward the small restroom near the door to the storeroom, Betty shook her head. "Saw Melvin Abercrombie waltz straight in there right as we come in. Based on the fact that he went back for double tapioca, I'm sure he's going to be a little while."

"You can use the employee restroom just on the other side of the kitchen."

"This way?" Betty asked as she followed Brandy's directions and rounded the counter. "My, my, it's something back here what with all the cakes and pies. Why, it's like I've died and gone to that great big Dolly Madison in the sky . . ." Her words faded as she disappeared into the back room.

Brandy turned back in time to see yet another handful of seniors stroll past the bakery, headed down the street to Brandy's competition.

While she'd seen the breakfast rush slowly dissipate, watching the same thing happen to her Sunday brunch bunch made her feel even worse.

And that much more determined to get her mash into the hands of Kenny Roy's moonshine connection before her meeting with Foggy Bottom Distillers on Friday.

After Betty returned and Brandy got her set up with a cup of tea, a blueberry muffin, and two Tums, she spent the next few hours dealing with the handful of customers that found their way into the bakery.

It seemed the girls' choir wasn't half as excited about the chocolate cupcakes as they were to try the chocolate-filled doughnuts down the street. Ditto for the men's prayer circle, who traded their usual apple bread to stroll past toward the doughnut shop. Brandy fought down the anxiety and tried to keep her thoughts positive, but by the time she handed over things to Ellie and grabbed her keys and purse, she was sucking down a few Tums herself.

Forget waiting around for Kenny Roy to call her. She needed to make something happen. And she needed to do it now.

"Do you know what time it is?" Kenny Roy demanded when he hauled open the door and found Brandy standing on his doorstep.

"Three o'clock on Sunday afternoon," she told him, her gaze shooting past to the dim interior of the house and the shadow stretched out on his living room couch.

"You have to be shittin' me," he growled, glancing up and shielding his eyes from the sun that blazed overhead. "Where do you get off banging on a man's door at all hours of the morning?"

"Again, it's not morning and I wouldn't have to bang if you had opened the first hundred times that I knocked."

"Damn nut job," he muttered, moving to close the door.

But Brandy was quicker. She shoved her foot in the open doorway and bit back a wince when the wood hit her big toe. "We need to talk."

"I told you I'd get back to you."

"That's not good enough." She pushed her foot even more firmly in place, and Kenny Roy frowned.

"You know I could call the cops."

"Please do. I'm sure they'd be very interested in that garden in your bathtub," she murmured, remembering Tyler's words from the night before. "Listen, all I want is a name. You don't even have to talk to them for me. I'll do that myself. I just need to know who." When he hesitated, she added, "They'll never know I heard it from you."

"Really? And how do you figure that?"

"It's a small town. I come from a long line of moonshiners. I could have gotten their name from my granddad. He knew every moonshiner in the county, and then some. He could have given me the name and I just so happened to track them down myself."

"That's real weak."

"True, but it could work."

He seemed to think. "And if it doesn't?"

"They still won't know it's you. My lips are sealed. I swear."

He wiped a hand over his bleary eyes and she knew he was at least considering it.

"You like muffins?" she added, desperate to tip the scale in her favor.

He seemed to think. "I could eat a muffin every now and then," he finally said.

"What if I can guarantee you free muffins every day for an entire month?"

"Throw in a few of those triple chunk brownies and you've got yourself a deal." She nodded and he added, "The Silver Dollar."

"That's a bar, not a person."

"It's all I got. My connection makes a delivery at the Silver Dollar out on Route Six every Sunday afternoon just before sundown. The bar's closed then, but the back door is open. He stops off and drops off. He's the only guy I know personally in the operation. You talk to him and he can hook you up." He eyed her. "That, or mess you up. Don't say I didn't warn you."

"Don't worry about me." It's not as if she meant to go in with guns blazing. No, she was just going to watch and gather some information. Then she would pick and choose a time to approach and plead her case.

"That was some really good hooch you came up with," he added. "I hope it's worth all the trouble you're about to find yourself in."

"Me, too," Brandy murmured as she descended the porch steps, walked over to old Bertha, and headed back to the bakery.

She spent the next few hours closing down shop for the day, prepping for Monday morning and listening to Ellie talk about how she wasn't in any way attracted to Tyler McCall's hot-looking rodeo buddy.

She'd finally broken down and mentioned that her hookup had been none other than the cowboy they'd seen with Tyler at Kenny Roy's that first night.

"I mean, I knew he was good looking, but he was even hotter when I got an up-close-and-personal look," Ellie said. "I was like, wow you're something, and he was like, wow, so are you, and bam, the next thing I know we were going at it like a couple of rabbits."

"Too much information," Brandy told the woman, placing a tray of bread loaves in the warmer before checking the timer on the oven.

"I know, I know. I don't usually kiss and tell, but this is different. I just can't help myself. Do you know I even mentioned him to Betty when she was poking around back here looking for the bathroom? Spent ten minutes listening to her tell me what a hellcat she used to be back in the day before her stomach started acting up and she got bunions." Ellie shook her head. "What bunions have to do with a sex drive, I'll never know, but Miss Betty seemed convinced there is a direct correlation."

"That's crazy."

"Exactly, which shows you just what a number this guy is doing on me. I was actually taking pointers from Miss Betty. I don't know, I just feel like the more I talk it out, the more I can understand why I can't stop talking about him."

"Maybe you're talking about him because you like him."

"Are you freaking serious?" Ellie gave her a horrified look. "I don't even know him. It was just a one-night stand."

Sometimes that's all it takes.

The thought floated through her mind before she could stop it. A ludicrous notion because it most certainly took more than one night of sex—or even a few dozen—to really know someone.

It took talking, connecting.

Which she'd done last night with Tyler Mc-Call.

"I really need to get out of here," she blurted. To get her mind on something more productive. "Lock up for me?" she asked Ellie.

"You know it. Say, maybe I can see what Lila thinks." She turned toward the back room where the short, squat woman stood icing coffee cakes for the following morning. Lila was a no-frills kind of girl when it came to looks. Her hair lay straight and limp, her face free of makeup. "Not that she has lots of experience, but it doesn't hurt to ask." Ellie headed for the kitchen, and Brandy grabbed her purse.

She pushed Tyler to the farthest corner of her mind and walked out to her car.

The sun was just shy of dropping below the horizon when she pulled up to the Silver Dollar Bar & Grill.

CHAPTER 16

The parking lot was all but empty with the exception of an old red pickup truck parked off to the side and a small Ford Fusion that sat next to it.

She pulled into the spot next to the Fusion and busied herself looking at her phone, as if waiting for someone. Seconds turned to minutes and minutes to half an hour before she heard the rumble of an engine and saw an old rusted-out silver pickup truck pull into the parking lot.

She sank lower in her seat and stared through the slats in the steering wheel as the vehicle pulled around the back and disappeared.

Fifteen minutes passed painfully slow before the truck reappeared. It rumbled past and she strained her eyes to see the driver. It wasn't a face she recognized and she knew it wasn't going to be as easy as discovering that it was, indeed, someone she already knew. She was going to have to go to a lot more trouble if she wanted to find out the man's identity.

The truck pulled out of the drive and headed

down the road. Brandy counted to five and then she started the car and followed. She stayed a decent way back as the truck neared the interstate and prayed that he wouldn't get on and haul ass.

He didn't.

Instead, he pulled into a small convenience store that sat on the left. She felt a surge of victory.

She swerved into a parking spot while the man eased up to a gas pump, killed the engine, and climbed out. Sure enough, she'd never seen him before. He was tall, with dark hair pulled back into a ponytail, a jaw that was three days past a five o'clock shadow, and dark-brown eyes. Tall. Attractive even, if Brandy had been looking to hook up.

She wasn't.

She needed a name. An identity.

She watched him walk inside. The glass door rocked shut behind him. A few minutes later, he strolled back out, a bottled Coke in one hand and his wallet in the other. He climbed into the old rusted-out truck, gunned the engine, and then pulled out. A few seconds later, he hit the entrance to the interstate and disappeared down the highway.

Brandy drew a deep breath, climbed out of Bertha, and walked inside. While she might not know the driver, she most certainly knew the clerk standing behind the counter at the Pac-n-Save.

Ivy Earline Sawyer-Hilstead had bright-red

hair teased into a perfectly coiffed beehive that had gone out of style decades ago, along with her cat's-eye glasses hanging from a gold chain around her neck. But since she was just this side of seventy, no one had enlightened her to that all-important fact. The glasses slid down her nose, revealing bright-blue shadow and heavily rimmed eyes.

"Well, lookee who we have here," Ivy said. "If it ain't Brandy Tucker."

"Hi, Miss Ivy."

"Stopped by your place a few days ago and had one of them brownies. Wasn't nearly as good as the ones I make at home, mind you, but I guess it'll do for most folks around these parts that ain't never had a decent batch."

Ivy wasn't just old, she was mean, too. Add a heavy dose of snobbiness courtesy of her last name and the one-hundred-year-old feud that had been raging between the Tuckers and the Sawyers, and to say Ivy was unpleasant would have been a huge understatement.

Still, the woman was old. That is, just this side of heaven and so Brandy minded her p's and q's even though she wanted to tell Ivy that a box of Betty Crocker Fudge Brownie Supreme couldn't hold a candle to her award-winning chocolate nirvana brownies.

"I'm sure you could teach me a thing or two," she told Ivy. "You've got so many years of baking on me, after all. A lot of years." The emphasis on *lot* wasn't lost on the woman and she stiffened.

"But I didn't come to swap tips," Brandy added. "That gentleman, the one who was just here in that old pickup truck, he lost something on the road back there," she blurted out—the first thing she could think of. "A blanket flew out of the bed and fell on the side of the road. I grabbed it. I was hoping to return it but he pulled out of here before I could stop him."

"A blanket?"

"A horse blanket," Brandy nodded, feeding the lie with an ease that actually surprised her. "You know how expensive those things are. I'd hate for him to get to wherever it is that he's going and realize it just blew away. If you knew his name, I could get it back to him."

"Ain't got time to play the Good Samaritan, little girl. I got work to do." Ivy indicated the half-answered crossword puzzle on the counter next to her. "Find out yourself."

"Okay, if you're not interested in a reward, then I guess I'll just figure it out on my own—"

"Reward? What reward?"

"The one I'm offering for information."

"And why would you offer a reward just to return a smelly old horse blanket?"

"Because I don't want to be saddled with someone else's belongings." When Ivy didn't seem the least bit convinced, Brandy added, "That, and he's awful cute."

"So now we get to the real reason." The old woman swept a glance from Brandy's head to the sizable chest pressing against her bakery T-shirt.

"I should have known what you were up to the moment I saw you."

The dig sliced through Brandy, but she wasn't about to flinch. It didn't matter what Ivy thought. What anyone thought for that matter. She knew the truth. She knew she wasn't the slut that everyone believed her to be.

But if playing the part now would help get her that much closer to Kenny Roy's moonshine connection . . .

"What do you say? You don't want to stand in the way of true lust, do you?"

The woman's gaze narrowed. "What's in it for me?"

"I'd offer brownies, but yours are so much better—"

"I'll take 'em. Not 'cause they're better than mine, mind you. But I'm so tired after being on my feet all day that I don't get much time to whip up any. They're a damn sight better than store-bought, I suppose."

"Great. Stop by tomorrow and I'll have a dozen waiting for you."

"Make it two and you've got yourself a deal." Brandy nodded and Ivy added, "Never seen him before." She turned toward the register. "But he used a credit card. Let me see . . ." She licked her finger and started picking through the small stack of receipts. "Here we go. Name's Ryder Jax."

The name echoed in Brandy's head, pushing and pulling at her memory. He was one of the bootleggers her grandfather had done business with on occasion and part of the infamous trio of moonshine runners who delivered from here to Houston, and every county in between.

While she'd never seen the man firsthand, she'd heard his name mentioned more than once by her gramps. Ryder and his buddies were local legends, and more than a little dangerous. But then, that was the nature of the business. "Thanks, Miss Ivy," Brandy said as she turned to walk out of the store.

"Don't thank me," the woman called after her. "Just make sure my brownies are boxed and ready by two."

She had a name.

While it wasn't much, it was enough to fuel her hope despite the crappy day at the bakery. She made one last stop at Sweet Somethings to box up some muffins before leaving them on Kenny Roy's doorstep and heading home.

Home, she vowed. She'd spent two nights with Tyler already. It was time for a break.

She held tight to her decision as she started down Main Street. Besides, it was way too early. Barely eight o'clock. She couldn't very well show up now.

That's what she told herself. No way did her reluctance have anything to do with the fact that she was starting to like Tyler McCall. Instead, she turned left and hit the road toward home.

CHAPTER 17

"You're not going to believe this," Callie declared when Brandy walked into the small kitchen a short while later to find both of her sisters seated at the old weathered table, an empty bakery box between them. "Tell her what you did."

"I didn't actually do anything," Jenna replied, licking what was left of a chocolate cupcake off her fork. "I'm the innocent, here. The victim."

"You're the wimp," Callie said, reaching for Jenna's left hand. "Look at this."

"Is that what I think it is?" Brandy stared at the princess-cut diamond that could have doubled for a marble. "That's huge."

"I know, right?" Jenna said, a smile touching her lips for a split second. "I've had four engagement rings to date, but this one's the biggest by far. Jase really outdid himself."

"You say that like it's a good thing," Callie said, "which it most certainly is not because you don't want to marry him."

"You didn't tell him, did you?" Brandy eyed her younger sister, who looked uncomfortable.

"Of course I did. I told him it wasn't a good time when he cornered me last night, so he waited until today and met me at the veterinary clinic. I was helping Willa birth her calf when he drops down on his knee and pulls out the ring. Seriously, who does something like that in middle of a birthing?"

"Obviously Jase. Why did you say yes?"

"I didn't actually say yes. I said, 'Wow, what a great ring.' Which he took to mean yes."

Callie shook her head. "You're such a wimp."

"I am not. You didn't see him. He just looked so happy. And he's been so unhappy since he had to put his dog to sleep six months ago and I just couldn't kill his dreams just like that. I couldn't be that mean."

"So you're just going to marry him?" Callie shrugged. "On account of his dog died and you don't want to see him upset?"

"Of course not. That would be crazy. I'm going to break it off. I just thought I'd let him bask in the moment a little longer."

"That's only going to make it harder," Brandy chimed in.

"Not necessarily. See, I figured I'd give him some time to see that we're really not right for each other and then it would make the breakup a little easier. In fact, he might even be the one to break up with me."

Callie grimaced. "I doubt that."

"I don't know," Brandy interjected. "She can be sort of a pain when she wants to be."

"Exactly. I'm picky. I work too much. And I've got a wandering eye. We've been in the honeymoon phase and so he really hasn't seen what a bitch I can be, but now that the proposal is out there, he'll start to see that he's made a mistake. That I'm not really all that."

"So that's your plan?" Callie demanded, her own ring catching a reflection of light as she waved a hand. "Just to wait until he changes his mind?"

"It could work."

"It's stupid. What if he doesn't change his mind?"

"He will. I mean, he has to, right? I'm totally not his soul mate. I like chocolate ice cream and he likes vanilla. I love *Grey's Anatomy* and he gets queasy at the sight of blood. We're totally wrong for each other. It's just that the sex was so good that he's thinking I'm all that—"

"Too much information," Callie cut in. "You need to be straightforward with this guy. Honest."

"That, or you could marry him," Brandy added. "Maybe you couldn't say no because deep down, you actually like him."

"I do like him," Jenna shook her head, "but that doesn't mean I have to sacrifice the rest of my life. It's just *like*. I mean, really, it's hardly enough to even contemplate such a big step. I like Jez and

I'm not marrying her. I like Doritos and I'm not marrying them. I like One Direction and I'm not packing my bags and turning into a groupie. I like lots of things. It's no big deal."

The words echoed in Brandy's head and made her realize exactly how silly she was being. So what if she did like Tyler McCall? *Like* didn't constitute *love* and as long as she wasn't in love with him, she didn't need to be so worried about following in her mother's footsteps.

"I'm just going to give it a couple of days," Jenna added. "Let him see what a real bitch I can be. Then he'll end it."

"And what if he doesn't?" Callie voiced the one question that Brandy was thinking.

"Then I'll break it off myself. I swear," she added when Callie started to say something.

"We're talking about an engagement," their older sister reiterated. "As in the rest of your life. *Forever*. This is serious. This isn't something to play with."

"So sayeth the soon-to-be Mrs. Brett Sawyer. Listen, I know you take this stuff to heart, but it's not that big a deal. Jase doesn't really love me and I don't love him and it's just a matter of time before he realizes it. He's a smart guy."

"Fine then, but no more sex," Callie said. "Sex complicates things."

"Or not." The words were out before Brandy could think better of them. "I mean, if it's a strictly sexual relationship with zero expectations, then it doesn't complicate anything. It does the opposite, right?"

Callie stared at her a long moment. "Right, I guess. In a different situation. But the ring complicates things, so it's better to steer clear of the sex. That'll force him to see what kind of person Jenna is and he'll drop her just like that."

"Thanks a lot," Jenna said.

"Don't get your panties in a wad. I'm just pointing out the obvious. While you're a super-nice person, you're not wife material. You've got a wandering eye and you're a commitment phobe. You refuse to even sign up for a credit card."

"The interest rates are killer."

"Maybe, but that's not the point. You don't like to commit to anything. Not an interest rate any more than a man."

"I might commit one day."

"When hell freezes over, but we're talking about right here, right now. Let him see the real you."

"I'm on it."

"I mean it, Jenna. No agreeing with him just to agree. Voice a real opinion. He'll see how shallow you are and bam, you're out of the engagement."

"Sounds like a plan," Brandy agreed.

"You both suck."

"Hey, we see the real you and love you anyway. That has to count for something."

Jenna made a face before adding, "I'm going to watch last week's episode of *Scandal*. If Jase calls, tell him I'm too busy to talk. Better yet, I'll call and leave a voice mail telling him not to disturb my TV time."

"Add that you want to meet him tomorrow to register for towels. That'll definitely leave a bad taste in his mouth. No man likes to register for towels," Callie told them.

"Brett did it," Brandy pointed out.

"Only because I agreed to sign up for power tools while we were at the department store. Speaking of which, if you really want to get us something off the registry, try the blower. It's a V8 with wind direction. He'll love you forever. Oh, and speaking of love, you're all set," she told Brandy. "The date is next Saturday. Lunch at the diner with Mike. Wear red."

"I've been thinking and I—" Brandy started, but Callie looked so suddenly distraught that she caught herself. "Fine, I'll be there."

"Have I told you that you're the best sister in the world?"

"I thought I was the best sister in the world," Jenna chimed in as she pulled her head out of the avocado-green fridge, half a leftover apple pie in her hand.

"You were before you went and added a plus-one to the reception menu. What do you think Jase likes? Fish or chicken?"

"Neither. He won't be around by then."

"The wedding is only four weeks away and you're not known for your ability to clean the slate." Callie eyed the humidifier parked on the counter. "You went back and forth for four months with the last guy. And honestly, I still think he thinks there's a chance."

"He does not think there's a chance."

"Only because I had Arnie hypnotize him and make the suggestion. Speaking of which, maybe you ought to introduce Arnie and Jase."

"Or you could just be honest," Brandy offered.

Jenna seemed to think. "Arnie does come into the vet clinic on Thursdays to bring in his pit bull. Maybe I could ask Jase to pick me up. They'll have a chance meeting and bam, problem solved."

"She's too much of an optimist," Callie said as Jenna grabbed a fork and headed for the den, pie in hand, Jez yapping after her. "It's going to bite her in the ass one day."

But as Brandy stared after her youngest sister, she started to think that maybe optimism wasn't such a bad thing. While Jenna found herself in a pickle every now and then when it came to men, things always seemed to work out in the end.

Because her sister didn't let worry hold her back. She didn't sit around thinking about the future. She lived for the moment. She followed her instincts, and while they might occasionally lead her into the deep end sometimes, she didn't panic even then. She just kept her hopes up, scarfed down pie, and miraculously enough life worked itself out.

Brandy was definitely worrying too much when

it came to Tyler McCall. They were buddies of the carnal variety. End of story. Nothing more. Not even if she did like him just a little. The key was not to worry over her slip-up the night before, rather to move forward from this moment with her priorities in order. Top of the list? To keep things strictly physical.

To move fast and furious whenever they were together and leave little time for anything else like talking or teasing or falling even more into *like*.

At least that was the plan.

One she didn't get a chance to initiate just yet because Callie pulled out the bridal magazines and Brandy found herself poring over dresses for the next few hours until her sister called it a night and headed home to Brett. And then Jenna snagged her attention with a rerun of *Cupcake Wars*. Before she knew it, midnight had rolled around and she still needed to spend at least half an hour online to see if she could find an address for a certain Ryder Jax.

Thirty minutes that soon turned into two hours until she hit pay dirt with a monthly membership at FindMyPeeps.com that produced a viable home address.

Three to be specific, but then that was the Internet. Luckily all three were within a forty-mile radius and shouldn't be too difficult to check out. Tomorrow. First, she needed some sleep. Four a.m. was only a few hours away. Which meant sex with Tyler McCall would have to wait.

But next time . . . She would most definitely keep her priorities straight and her brain on target.

No more talking.

Or getting to know each other.

Just sex and nothing but sex.

CHAPTER 18

Tyler glanced at the clock for tenth time in as many minutes. Half past one a.m. She wasn't coming. He knew it, yet he stayed put anyway, listening for the grumble of an engine, the click of footsteps. Hoping.

Like hell.

He sat up and reached for his phone. A quick text and he decided to hit a nearby bar and join Duff for a nightcap, but he'd have to hurry if he meant to get there before last call at two a.m.

He sure as hell meant to make it, to stop biding his time, staring at the door, and *do* something. The waiting around for word from his brother was driving him insane, to the point that he'd stopped by at the trailer today and offered to fix the failing porch. Anything to fill the time when he wasn't training.

Or having sex with Brandy.

From the looks of it, he was going to have a damn sight more time on his hands than he'd originally thought.

He'd dropped off a load of wood earlier, left

another voice mail for Cooper, and met with Jack Gallagher about climbing onto a few of his bucking bulls.

Not the best that the Rebel area had to offer, but the cream of the crop belonged to Brett Sawyer and Tyler wasn't up to picking that sore just yet. His cousin hated him and so he knew the answer would be no.

But he would make do.

He always did.

He'd never had the best facilities, never had an easy ride like Brett and a few other golden boys in professional bull riding. Tyler didn't have it easy. Not when he'd been living on cheese sandwiches and training on a rusted-out barrel behind his trailer, though things were a slight bit better now. At least he had cash in his pocket, a roof over his head, a good meal, and enough left over for a bottle of whiskey on those nights when his muscles ached clear to the bone.

Like tonight.

He pulled on a T-shirt, grabbed his keys, and walked out to his truck. A quick glance down the road just to make sure there was no blaze of lights, and he swung up behind the wheel.

Give it up, buddy. She's not coming.

Because he'd screwed up last night. He'd held her just a little too long, made things just a little more complicated. Not on purpose. Hell, he'd been tired and she'd felt good and, seriously, it's not like he was starting to *feel* anything for her.

Tyler made it his business not to feel anything for anyone. He didn't need anything else pulling him back to Rebel, Texas, not when he was this close to breaking the last few ties. He would see his brother off to A&M, fix the damn porch for his mother, and that would be that. His work here finished.

Finally.

Yep, last night had had little to do with feeling and more to do with the fact that he'd had a weak moment. He'd been tired as hell, and well, he'd let his exhaustion cloud his thinking.

A weak moment.

That's all it had been.

One that had spooked the living shit out of her.

A good thing, he told himself. As tired as he was right now, as stressed, he was liable to haul her close, bury his nose in her neck, and fall dead asleep without ever having peeled off even a stitch of her clothes—and that wouldn't work at all. No, it was better that she kept her distance tonight and let him get his head on straight.

Because the last thing he meant to do was feel anything for Brandy Tucker besides lust.

Gunning the engine, he sent the truck screaming down the road toward the first turnoff and the small bar that sat just off to the right.

"So what do you think?" Duff asked him after he'd spent ten minutes giving Tyler the quick rundown on his rocky love life.

Love, because Duff had broken down and mentioned the L word just last night, in the heat of the moment, just when he'd erupted like Old Faithful. A big no-no for any man.

"It's hard to tell. What did she say?"

"She didn't say anything," Duff said, his words slightly slurred thanks to the half-empty bottle of Crown Royal sitting on the table in front of him. "I don't even think she heard it."

Oh, she'd heard it, all right.

Tyler would be willing to lay money on it, particularly since the woman in question was a local. Not that Duff had mentioned her name.

That was the telltale sign that something was different with this woman, because Duff had a habit of kissing and telling, only he wasn't spilling his guts right now, not to the point that he'd violated the local's identity. "Tell me what I should do now."

"Right now? At this moment?" Duff nodded and Tyler said, "I think you should call it a night and head back to the motel." Tyler took a swig of the bottled water in front of him, his drink of choice once he'd caught up to Duff and realized the man was three sheets to the wind. "I'll drive."

"But don't you think I should call her? I mean, I said I would last night before she left. But then I woke up and realized what I'd said and I started to think that maybe I shouldn't have said it. What if it scared her?"

What if it didn't?

That was the question that would have startled

Tyler more than anything else when it came to pouring out his feelings for a woman. The notion that she would return those feelings, that he would find himself anchored to the one town he'd vowed to leave behind.

"What if it did?" Tyler decided to play devil's advocate. "Then it's a good thing you didn't follow through and call her."

"But what if she waited the entire day and then I didn't call. She'll know I didn't mean it."

"Maybe that's a good thing."

"It's terrible. What kind of guy drops the L word and doesn't mean it?"

"I hate to break it to you, Opie, but most guys in the free world."

"I don't do that," Duff said. "I've never done that. Why now?"

"Is she good looking?"

"Damn straight."

"Is she good in bed?"

"The best."

"Then that's why."

"I'm an asshole."

"You're human."

"A crappy human. I told her I would call her. But then I wanted to see her so damn bad that it scared the shit out of me. I couldn't call her. And now she's going to think I didn't want to call her."

"You didn't," Tyler pointed out.

"Yeah, but not because I don't like her. I do. Hell, I like her a lot. I don't love her. I mean, I don't think I do. That's crazy, right? I don't even know her."

"Crazier than crazy."

"Seriously, there's no way I can really *love* her. Not when I don't even know her middle name. I don't know what her favorite food is or what kind of music she likes or her favorite color. I don't know anything except she can damn well scream up a storm when she cuts loose. That ain't enough, right? I mean, I actually mentioned her to my mother this morning before I could stop myself. Told her I might be bringing someone home for dinner. What the hell was I thinking?" He shook his head. "I should call her."

"That would make things worse. Trust me. Just get some sleep. Call her tomorrow if you still want to talk to her."

"I might not, right? I mean, it might be a good thing that I didn't call her on account of I need some distance right now to get my head together. Do you know I almost asked her to come with me to Cheyenne after I dropped the L bomb? Seriously, how crazy is that?"

Almost as crazy as Tyler thinking for even five seconds that it might not be so bad to wake up tomorrow, and the next day and the next, with Brandy Tucker curled up next to him.

"I'm blowing this way out of the water, right?" Duff tossed him a questioning glance, his eyes bleary and red. "No way can I love this girl. I need to slow down, pull back."

Amen.

"That's it." Duff downed the finger of whiskey left in his shot glass and slammed it down on the scarred wood. "Get me out of here. I need to sleep."

"Yeah," said the bartender, who came up and reached for the empty bottle. "Get the both of you outta here. It's closing time."

Tyler nodded, grabbed Duff by the arm, and hauled him to his feet. Hiking an arm around the cowboy's waist, Tyler led Duff outside and hitched him up into the passenger seat of his pickup before slamming the door and rounding the truck.

"Thanks, buddy," Duff said as Tyler climbed behind the wheel. "Here," Duff said, handing over his phone. "You take it. I don't trust myself. I might get horny and call her up." He slumped down into the seat, his head lolling against the headrest. "Who knows what I might say? Hell, the next time I see you, I might be engaged." He shook his head again. "What was I thinking?"

"You weren't, but at least you came to your senses. You're ending it now. No more leading her on."

"Damn straight. No lame excuses. No eating my words. Just a clean break. So what if she thinks I'm an asshole?"

"Better to disappoint her now than do it later when she's even more hooked on you."

"Yeah, more hooked," Duff mumbled, closing his eyes. "That would be bad. Probably."

Tyler gunned the engine and pulled out of the parking lot. Fifteen minutes later, he pulled into the parking lot of Rebel's one and only motel. He hauled the man out and steered him toward his room. A few seconds later, he let Duff collapse on the bed while he turned to pull off the man's boots.

"Thanks, buddy," Duff's voice drew him back around. "You saved me. At the rate I was going, I might be married by now if you hadn't shown up to talk some sense into me."

"That's what friends are for. Now get some sleep." He finished pulling off the boots, plopped Duff's hat on the nearby dresser, and turned toward the door.

"Maybe you ought to leave the phone." Duff's voice stopped his hand on the doorway. "I should at least leave a voice mail and tell her that something came up. I wouldn't want her to think I'm a total jerk."

So much for breaking ties.

But Tyler couldn't say that he blamed his buddy. Great sex made even the strongest man do and say the craziest things.

Tyler knew that firsthand.

But he wasn't making that mistake again.

CHAPTER 19

It was the longest morning of Brandy's life. Not because the bakery was slow, though that in itself was torture to watch. But because she had three possible addresses for Ryder Jax and she couldn't wait to do a little recon and narrow down his whereabouts.

Once she knew the location and she'd checked it out to make sure she wasn't liable to get her head blown off, then she would approach him and talk to him about running her shine.

She thought about ducking away at lunch and leaving Ellie in charge of the minimal stream of customers, but the woman seemed more quiet than usual.

Depressed even.

"Don't tell me things went sour with the new cowboy?"

"No. Yes." Ellie shook her head. "I mean, I guess it's how you look at it. I think he likes me more than I like him and so I had to break it off because, you know, the last thing I want is to get involved with anyone. I like my freedom."

"You're preaching to the choir."

"I mean, he really is cute and there's just something about the way he looks at me that's kind of cool. But not *that* cool. It would never work anyway. He's not even from here. He's just here until he heads up to Cheyenne. Which is why I hooked up with him in the first place, you know? He was new. Exciting. But most of all, no strings."

Yep, she was preaching to the choir, all right.

"If I want some guy blubbering how much he loves me, I could just stick it out with Bart, you know?" She shook her head. "No, thank you."

She said the words, but there was something about the distant look in her eyes that told Brandy she wasn't nearly as sure as she wanted to be.

And so Brandy dug in her heels for the rest of the day and did her best to distract her baking assistant. She went over a new recipe for s'mores cupcakes and showed Ellie how to whip up a rich frosting using fresh whipped cream and mascarpone cheese, and she helped her look for Miss Betty's purse.

It seemed the old woman had left it in the restroom on Sunday.

"Thanks ever so much, dearie," Betty told her when Brandy handed over the giant white patent-leather bag that had been sitting in the corner of the employee bathroom. "Why, I thought I'd lost it for good."

"I'm sorry I didn't find it sooner. I usually notice things like that." But then she hadn't been thinking straight the past few days since Tyler had rolled back into town. It made sense that she would have missed the giant purse when she closed up on Sunday night.

"You've got your hands busy what with all these great muffins." Betty held up the blueberry that Brandy had handed her after finding the missing purse. "Take care now, sugar. And thanks again."

Brandy watched as the woman walked out of the bakery and climbed into a small blue pickup truck driven by a young man in his twenties. Her grandson Mitchell, Brandy knew from seeing him with Betty at the last picnic. While Betty's daughter and son-in-law didn't get over to see her too often from Austin, her grandson lived nearby in the old house where Betty had grown up. He drove her around whenever she missed the bus and visited her every week.

For a quick moment she found herself thinking how nice it would be to have a grandson to look out for her when she got older. But in order to have a grandson, she would have to have a daughter or son. And in order to do that, she'd have to find a husband.

Not that she believed all women had to have a husband to settle down and have a family, but it was her own personal belief. What was right for her.

If she'd wanted to settle down, which she most certainly did not. Even if it would be kind of nice to have a loving grandchild drive her around in her old age.

She gave the idea thought for a few more seconds, until Betty's grandson swerved out into traffic without signaling and a loud honk shattered the air. Mitchell hung his head out the window, shouted a few choice obscenities before giving the ultimate salute, and the image of the kind, loving, helpful offspring was shattered.

Okay, so maybe *not* settling down wasn't such a bad thing.

She held tight to the thought and finished closing down the display cases before heading into the back room and packing up. She had more brownies for Kenny Roy and another two dozen for Ivy. Once she dropped both off, she was hitting the road to check out the addresses.

At least that was the plan.

She gathered up her purse and bakery boxes. Her free hand went to the lights. She'd just plunged the back room into darkness when she heard Tyler McCall's deep voice directly behind her.

"What a shame, darlin'. You know how much I like it with the lights on."

Her breath caught and she felt his body so close behind hers. Close enough that all she had to do was lean back just a little. Turn. Kiss him for all she was worth.

Fast and furious.

Sex, and nothing but sex.

Before she could think too much about what

she was doing—or rather, what she wasn't doing—she flipped the lights back on. The shadows disappeared and she turned.

"What are you doing here?"

"I thought I'd stop by to see if Kenny Roy called you?"

"Did he call you?"

He shook his head. "Cooper's still out of town. At least that's what most everybody is saying. Anybody who's seen him with Gator Hallsey, that is. What about you? Did Kenny Roy call?"

"No." Not that she'd waited for him to call. "I didn't give him a chance. I stopped by his place and he gave me a name."

"Seriously?" He eyed her a long second before adding, "Just like that?"

"Well, I did sort of have to promise him something." A strange look came over his face and she had the crazy thought that he was jealous.

A strange warmth spread through her, and she had the even crazier thought that she liked the fact that he looked ready to murder someone on her behalf. She enjoyed the sight for a few more moments before giving in to her conscience. "Brownies," she blurted. "And some muffins, too."

"Kenny Roy does like to eat," he said after a long moment, and the tension between them eased just a little. "So who's the connection?"

"Ryder Jax." When his gaze narrowed ever so slightly, she added, "Do you know him?"

"I know of him. He's partners with Gator Hallsey." She nodded and he added, "I've been asking around about Gator ever since Kenny mentioned him. He's a bad guy, so I'm guessing Ryder isn't much better." His gaze caught and held hers. "You're not going to track him down on your own, are you?"

"That's exactly what I'm going to do. In fact, I was headed out to do just that. I Googled him last night and came up with three possible addresses. One of them has to be right."

"Let's go then."

"I don't think that's such a good idea."

"Actually, I think it's a great idea. I'm out of leads. Maybe Ryder can shed a little more light on the Cooper–Gator connection."

"So this offer to come with me is strictly self-serving?"

"Why else would I want to go?"

Because he was worried about her running off after a bad guy all by her lonesome. Because he cared.

She ditched the thought and held tight to the all-important fact that while she might be excited to track down Ryder, she wasn't stupid, either. It was better to have reinforcements.

She certainly didn't say yes because, in all honesty, she'd missed him.

The sex, she reminded herself. She'd missed the sex and maybe they could get back to it after they found Ryder's whereabouts.

In the meantime, she wasn't getting all chummy. No talking and cozying up on the way.

"Suit yourself," she murmured, summoning her most disinterested shrug.

"Oh, I will, darlin'. I most definitely will."

CHAPTER 20

He wasn't going to talk to her. That's what Tyler told himself as he climbed into his truck and glanced at the passenger seat where she'd already settled in.

No talking.

No glancing at her, watching her worry her bottom lip.

No wondering what she was thinking when she caught the plump fullness and stared mindlessly through the windshield.

"This recipe really means a lot to you, doesn't it?" The question was out before he could stop himself.

She didn't look as if she wanted to answer any more than he'd wanted to ask, but then she shrugged. "It's everything. The bakery is barely scraping by right now. Another month like this last one, and we'll be losing money. I have to make sure that doesn't happen. That means I need another source of income to expand so that we're not just competing with a doughnut shop.

We need to be a go-to cake venue for everyone in the Hill Country. That won't happen without another oven and another specialty decorator. And neither of those will happen if I don't run this mash and present a product to Foggy Bottom Distillers by Friday."

"That's four days away."

"Which is why I couldn't wait around for Kenny Roy. At least you've got a few extra days to play with. I'm down to the wire. My mash is just about ready to go. Then I'll have less than twenty-four hours to run it before it sours. That means I need to talk to someone *now*."

"I'm sure Ryder Jax can hook you up. The question is—will he?"

"I'll bribe him if I have to." She glanced out the window, her brow furrowing. "Let's hope he likes brownies."

"There isn't a man out there who can resist your brownies, sugar."

She slid a glance toward him, a grin tugging at her lips and easing the worried expression. "Why is it I get the feeling you're not talking about an actual baked good?"

"Oh, it's good, all right."

"You're a horn dog."

"I've been called worse."

"I'll just bet." Quiet settled between them for a few moments, but it was an easy silence. Her worry had faded and she seemed to have relaxed just a little. "You still haven't heard from your brother?" she finally asked as if the easy silence bothered her as much as the uneasy silence had bothered him.

"Not yet. Kenny said he might be back today, but I've got a few people at the local bars—the usual haunts—keeping a lookout for him. So far, nothing. It's looking more like tomorrow. If he even shows up at all."

"You really think he might have taken off for good?"

"Not so much as I'm thinking he might have gotten himself into some deep trouble. More than he can handle. These dudes . . . They're no good."

"Still, folks have seen them together. It seems stupid for anyone to hurt him when they'd more than likely be the most obvious suspect."

"If I didn't know better, I'd say you were trying to make me feel better."

"Maybe I'm just returning the favor. So how's your mom?"

They spent the rest of the drive talking about the falling-down porch he'd reframed just that morning and about the woman who seemed oblivious to anything but her spiked coffee.

"It had to be hard for her, growing up with so much and then having it all taken away when she married your dad."

"True. My grandparents hated my dad." To the point that they'd disowned not only their daughter for marrying poorly, but her offspring, as well. They'd gone to their grave hating their daughter and her two mistakes. "But she made that choice willingly."

Because that's what it was—a choice. His mother hadn't had to fall in love with his dad. She'd made her choice, and then she'd blamed the world for it.

Not Tyler. He took responsibilities for his own actions, and he wasn't making the same mistake. His mother couldn't let go of the past even though the past had let go of her. Not Tyler. He was letting go. Getting away. Forgetting. Once and for all.

But first he had to make sure that Cooper was okay.

That, and finish the damn porch.

"I hear Callie's tying the knot," he added, eager to change the subject.

"Next month," she said. "If she can make her mind up about a bridesmaid's dress. I've got a fitting on Thursday, but so far there are over six possibilities and nothing for sure."

"Maybe she wants you to choose for yourself."

"If she wanted that, she wouldn't have hooked me up with her photographer."

"Come again?"

"Nothing. It's just a lunch date that I got wrangled into because Callie wants perfect pictures and her top candidate wants me." She shook her head. "You'd think after ten years, things would have changed."

"Are you kidding? Nothing changes in a small

town," he murmured, voicing the one fear that lived and breathed deep inside of him, that no matter how well he did, how much money he made, or how much fame he gained, he would still be *that* worthless Tyler McCall.

"I don't know about that. I think people change. It's perception that doesn't change. And that doesn't mean anything anyway. Who cares what someone else thinks?"

"Sounds like you've forgiven all those boys for all that writing on the bathroom wall."

"Forgiven, yes. Forgotten, no. But no matter what they wrote, it didn't make it true. It didn't," she said, more to convince herself than him.

"Here," he said, eager to change the subject. He handed over his cell. "Type the first address into my Google Maps and let's see if we can find this guy."

They didn't find Ryder Jax.

But they did find out where he was living. At least, according to the neighbor who happened to be watering her plants when they pulled up outside the small clapboard house that sat just beyond the interstate, about ten miles north.

"You can try him back, but good luck with that. He keeps terrible hours. Nothing like his mommy or daddy, God rest both their souls. They would be beside themselves if they could see the way he's let that house fall to ruin." She pointed to the dried-up rosebushes that lined the front porch and the overgrown grass. "You'd think he could at least mow. Keep up the property values and all that, but no. Even flipped off Martin Jenkins—he's the president of the neighborhood association—when he stopped by and kindly suggested it. Then he fined Ryder and the war started. The more notices he got, the higher he let the grass get until Martin got tired of looking like an ineffective idiot and cut it himself. At least that's what folks are saying. Martin says he got tough with Ryder and convinced him to mow last month, but there ain't a one of us alive who buys that nonsense. That Ryder is a stubborn one. But then so was his daddy. Mean, too, so it makes sense his boy would be just as bad. Runs in the family, it does . . ." Rose Hamper went on for the next five minutes about meanness and families and her own ungrateful children until Brandy interrupted her.

"Brownie?"

"Why, I don't mind if I do." She took the bakery box and opened the lid. Taking one goodie out, she started to hand it back, but Brandy waved her off.

"You keep those. It's the least I can do for putting you to so much trouble."

"All I did was answer a few questions."

"And graciously agree to call us if Ryder shows up. We really need to talk to him."

"I suppose I could do that," the woman said after swallowing a mouthful. "I surely could.

"That was useless," Tyler said when they climbed back in the truck.

"Are you kidding? That woman will be sitting by her window all night."

"For a brownie?"

Brandy shrugged. "What can I say? They're that good."

"You're that good," he heard himself say. She slid a glance his way and their gazes locked and Tyler knew that there was no way he was taking her back to the bakery.

Instead, he turned and headed for the rodeo arena. It was early, but he didn't care. He needed her.

Now.

And everything else would just have to wait.

CHAPTER 21

"Where the hell are you?" Jenna's frantic voice carried over the line the minute Brandy answered her cell phone the next morning. "You're not hurt, are you? Oh, crap, you're not dead, are you?"

"Yes, and it sure is hot down here."

"Very funny. Seriously, I all but freaked when I came in early from my date and realized you weren't home."

Brandy glanced at the clock. "You know, five a.m. isn't early for most people."

"Stop trying to change the subject."

"Which is?"

"Your bed is untouched, which means you didn't come home and sleep in it last night." Silence stretched between them for a thoughtful moment before Jenna's excited voice carried over the line. "So whose bed did you sleep in?"

"Maybe I slept in the storage room at the bakery. I have to get an early start."

"Did you?"

She wanted to lie, but she'd never lied to either

of her sisters. That was her thing. Jenna was blunt and in-your-face. Callie was responsible and motherly. And Brandy was brutally honest. "I'm at the rodeo arena."

"With who?"

Brandy glanced at the empty bed next to her and a wave of disappointment flared before she managed to tamp it back down. "By myself."

Jenna didn't say anything for a long moment, as if weighing the truth of Brandy's answer. But it was Brandy and so she finally sighed. "This is about the dogs, isn't it? They're keeping you up. I'll find Jez a home. I swear. I've just been busy at the clinic, and then there's Jase, who won't leave me alone even though I really want him to."

"You were out all night with the man. That doesn't exactly put off a get-the-hell-away-from-me vibe."

"I tried to bail out earlier, but he was so nice and sweet. He made dinner."

"So you figured you would sleep with him one more time."

"I was lost in the heat of the moment, but then he woke me up with pancakes and I realized my mistake. I couldn't get out of there fast enough. I pretended to have a reaction to a chocolate-covered strawberry and made him bring me home."

"I'm surprised he didn't take you straight to the hospital."

"He suggested it, but I swore I had my EpiPen

at home and since the house was closer, he went with it."

"He just left you in the midst of a fake reaction?"

"Actually he's parked out front, watching through a pair of binoculars, which is why I'm standing in front of the window, jabbing my leg with a Pixy Stix. That should give the right silhouette against the shade, don't you think?"

"That or you could try one of those beef treats that you give Jez. It's got the right shape."

"You're right. Let me grab one—"

"Jenna, I'm just joking. The Pixy Stix is fine. Just finish up, wave to him from the window, and turn off the light."

"You think that'll get him to leave?"

"No, I think a direct 'I'm not as into you as you are me and I think we should call it quits' would get him to leave, but since I know you aren't going to say that, just stick with the allergic reaction for now."

"I *will* tell him. It's just that he's so excited when we're together and I do like him. Just not *that* much."

They talked for a few more seconds before Brandy managed to hang up. She hit the light on the nightstand and a warm yellow glow pushed back the shadows. Outside, dawn was just creeping past the shades, indicating that morning was soon to follow.

Morning.

The realization rushed through her, reminding

her that she'd not only slept with Tyler, but she'd *slept* with him.

There'd been no creeping out before dawn. No *Thanks, but gotta go.* Or *I really appreciate it, but have a nice life.* No, she'd snuggled right up next to him and closed her eyes and now the sun was about to rise and she was past due at the bakery.

At least one of them had kept things in proper perspective.

Her gaze Ping-Ponged around the room, looking for boots or clothes or *something* before stalling on the open bathroom door. She strained her ears for some sound, but there was no water running. No footsteps. Just the distant sound of the animals below.

She ignored the disappointment that niggled at her, pushed the blankets to the side, and scrambled from the bed. She grabbed her undies, which lay on the floor a few feet away.

She spent the next five minutes plucking her clothes up off the floor and damning herself for forgetting the all-important fact that she'd agreed to sex only. Fast and furious, and then a quick *Bye, bye.* She'd had every intention of being the first one to hit the road after the deed had been done, the first one to pick up and walk out.

Like always.

She certainly hadn't meant to close her eyes. To get too comfortable. To forget for even a split second that Tyler was not the morning-after type and, even more, that neither was she.

Luckily that all-important fact hadn't slipped *his* mind.

She spared a quick glance around the room. A black duffel bag sat in the far corner, but otherwise there was nothing there. No clothes hanging in the closet. No personal items spilled out across the dresser.

Because this place was just temporary for Tyler. He was leaving soon and so there was no need to get comfortable.

And the problem is?

No problem. Sure, she preferred being the one out the door first, but at least he'd had the good sense not to linger and make things that much more awkward.

Anxiety pushed her that much faster, and she pulled on her clothes at the speed of light. She was getting out of here now, and she wasn't going to think that maybe, just maybe, it might have been nice if he'd at least waited for her to wake up. Grabbing her phone, she called the only cab company in Rebel and arranged for a ride to her car.

Slipping out of the small apartment, she rushed down the stairs that ran outside the building. While she could hear the occasional *Hell, yeah!* that echoed from inside the arena and the stomp of hooves, the outside parking lot was all but empty with the exception of the few trucks parked here and there.

The cab pulled up a few minutes later and she climbed inside. She headed back to the bakery for the spare change of clothes she kept in the storage room for emergency spills and the ever-popular red velvet volcano that always erupted when she was forced to use her ancient mixer for backup when her one and only commercial model was occupied.

Not that she'd been that busy since the doughnut shop had opened up. Her sales were down, her orders smaller and less frequent.

For now.

But once she snagged herself more equipment and handed out samples at the upcoming Travis County Bridal Fair being held next month, she was sure to pick up more cake orders.

But neither was going to be possible if she didn't sell her moonshine recipe. And in order to sell it, she needed to run this latest mash and make sure she was on to something.

And that meant she needed to talk to Ryder Jax.

When she reached the bakery, she let herself in the back door, thankful that she was the first one there.

She was always first.

Except this time she was late, too.

Two hours to be exact. Ellie would be walking in the door in less than half an hour and Brandy had yet to do any of her usual prep work.

She changed her clothes and stopped at the fridge to grab a bottled water. Her gaze snagged on an Orange Crush and she could practically taste the sugary sweetness on her tongue. She'd always loved the stuff. To the point that she'd perfected an Orange Crush cupcake topped with whipped orange marshmallow creme.

But while she used the stuff in her baking, she couldn't actually pinpoint when she'd last chugged one down. Since her occupation required a lot of on-the-job tasting, she'd sworn off sugary drinks on her own time and tried to eat a fairly healthy diet when she wasn't in the bakery.

She never just enjoyed herself for the sake of it.

She'd never wanted to. Her work had always been enough to satisfy her sweet tooth. To keep her busy. To fill the emptiness.

Until now.

She popped the top and took a long draw on the icy soda. Unfortunately, it did little to ease the thirst that clawed at her. The need.

Because as great as last night had been, it hadn't been enough. Brandy Tucker wanted more, and damned if that realization didn't bother her even more than the fact that she'd violated her precious schedule and was late getting her coffee cakes in the oven that morning.

Late.

The truth followed her for the next few minutes as she frantically tried to catch up, her own conscience telling her what a fool she'd been. She'd wasted an entire night—

The truth stalled as she walked into the small room that sat behind the oven. Her gaze snagged on the lifeless blanket that sat on the floor. The one she'd wrapped around the five-gallon bucket that held her precious mash to keep it warm and buzzing.

Except the blanket was lifeless now.

She glanced around, anxiety ripping up and down her spine. Her heart stopped. An invisible hand hit her chest like a whopping punch and the oxygen stalled.

Yep, the blanket was lifeless, but even worse, the mash was gone.

CHAPTER 22

Kenny Roy might deny having anything to do with the missing mash—which he'd done repeatedly when she'd questioned him not a half hour ago—but Brandy wasn't buying it. He might not be the one responsible, but he knew something and Brandy meant to find out exactly what it was.

She eyed the rusted-out silver pickup truck parked in front of the crumbling bar that sat just off the interstate. A few motorcycles leaned near the entrance. A couple of pickup trucks sat off to the side. A few more beaten-up cars sat here and there, along with Kenny Roy's black Ford Explorer. Smoke drifted from the open doorway, along with an old George Jones song. The Possum had been one of her grandpa's favorites. Not *the* favorite, mind you, but close, and so she'd heard every song a thousand times over. The familiar lyrics echoed in her head and the beat thrummed down her spine as she climbed out of Bertha and headed for the entrance. The clack of pool balls, followed by the *crackkkk* as a bottle hit the floor, brought her up short and she stalled.

Her nerves trembled for a few seconds before she swallowed against the fear and drop-kicked the notion that she should have told someone where she was going. Tyler maybe.

But he would have wanted to come and she wasn't ready to face him just yet. Last night had thrown her for a loop. Add the missing mash on top of that, and she didn't trust herself to talk to him without totally freaking out.

She was a nervous wreck and her only hope was to recover the mash. Since Kenny Roy was the only one who knew about the mash besides Ellie—who had been totally oblivious when Brandy had questioned her earlier—Brandy was placing her bets that he'd either had something to do with it or mentioned it to his connection, who'd decided to cut her out of the loop completely.

Not happening.

She eyed the bar again. Still, she wasn't about to get herself killed. She debated heading back to her car to send a quick text. But reception way out here was poor at best and she didn't want to waste any time worrying over a signal. Kenny Roy could be in and out in a moment and she would lose her chance to see him in his element.

No, she might not get another opportunity like this.

She drew a deep breath and walked inside the neon-lit interior.

The place was just a shell of an old tin building with a concrete floor littered with cigarette butts and scuff marks. A bar lined the far wall, the backdrop lit with a string of old Christmas lights. Similar lights crisscrossed the ceiling, helping out the bare bulbs that flickered here and there. A jukebox lit up one corner. An old cigarette machine from years gone by sat next to it, the display still advertising smokes for twenty-five cents.

"If you're wanting to light up, you'll have to fork over twenty times that much, sugar."

Brandy turned to see the young woman carrying a small tray, a black apron tied around her waist.

"The machine still works," the woman went on, "but Bubba, there"—she pointed to the hefty man tending bar behind the counter—"has it rigged to take tokens. You can buy a token for five bucks over at the bar."

"I don't smoke."

"Neither do I, sugar. At least not until quitting time. Then it's the only thing that helps calm my nerves after dealing with the jerks in here. Nothing like a good drag every now and then."

"That ain't no way to talk about your favorite customer, Meg." A man glanced up from a nearby table. He wore biker boots, a black leather vest, and a *Duck Dynasty* beard. Gray streaks hinted that he wasn't anywhere close in age to the young woman serving his beer, but that didn't stop him from going for a quick pinch on her butt cheek as she leaned in.

"You're right, Cecil. Calling you a jerk is putting it mildly." She swatted his hand away and slammed the beer down on the table in front of him. "You're more like a dirty old man."

Suds flew and he chuckled. "A dirty old man who knows how to tip."

"That's the only reason you're not wearing that bottle as a hat, sugar." Meg winked and turned back to Brandy. "What can I get you, girlfriend?"

"Diet Coke," Brandy said, sliding onto a nearby bar stool and glancing around, her gaze scanning the interior for Kenny.

She spotted him in a matter of seconds standing near the pool table. Her gaze went to the now familiar man who leaned over the table to line up his next shot. He wore a pair of worn jeans and a black button-down shirt, his sleeves rolled up to his forearms. His hair was long, framing his face and falling a few inches below his chin. Stubble shadowed his jaw, lending him an air of danger that said Ryder Jax was a force to be reckoned with.

The man playing opposite him was no different. He was a few inches taller, his shoulders a bit thicker. He had dark hair as well, only his was longer, brushing the tops of his shoulders. He wore a button-down white shirt, the tails hanging free. His jeans were worn in all the right places, his boots scuffed as if he'd put in the same hard day's work as every other man in the bar.

But he was different. There was something commanding about him. Tough.

The ball flew into a nearby pocket and the man turned to face the two-bit dealer. Kenny pulled out a wad of cash, followed by a hasty spiel that looked more like pleading. As if he'd come up short somehow and he feared telling the man.

Mr. Tall, Dark, and Dangerous didn't react. No displeasure. No anger. No nothing. He just stared at Kenny for a long moment before taking the cash and sliding it into his pocket. He turned away then, leaving the man still talking, and went back to his pool game with Ryder.

Kenny's mouth snapped shut as he watched the next shot. He started to talk again, but Ryder waved a stick at him and that was that. Kenny headed for the door.

Brandy turned back to her drink before Kenny caught sight of her and counted to fifty to give him time to leave before she turned around again, her attention going to the pool game in the corner and the man lining up his eight-ball to Ryder's dismay.

Downing a long sip of the icy drink, she slid off the bar stool and crossed the room.

"Nice shot," she said as the ball slammed into the pocket and Ryder let loose a string of curses.

"Thanks." The man spared her a quick, unreadable glance before turning back to his opponent. "Pay up, Ryder."

"No fair, Gator. You hustled me."

As in *the* Gator Hallsey.

Ryder frowned as Gator held out his hand. "I swear I don't know why I let you hustle me," Ryder grumbled as his hand dove into his jeans pocket and pulled out a few hundred-dollar bills.

Shock bolted through Brandy. He handed the money over as if they'd been playing with ones.

"There's no hustle involved," Gator said, taking the cash. "I'm just better than you. At pool, and everything else," he murmured as he turned back to Brandy. "*Everything*."

His meaning rang loud and clear and she stiffened. "That's nice, but I'm not interested."

"Hear tell you're always interested, Miss Tucker. Every night, in fact."

"Don't believe everything you hear."

"So." He reached for a chalk cube and dusted the end of his stick. "If you're not here looking to get lucky, then what are you here for?"

"I know you're mixed up with Kenny Roy. Ryder, here, is his moonshine connection. And since you guys are affiliated, I'm guessing you're part of that connection."

"I can't say I know what you're talking about. How about you, Ryder? You know anything about any moonshine going on around here?"

"Not me."

"Cut the crap. I know it's you two and you know I know, so let's stop pretending. Kenny Roy gave you some mash a few weeks back and

you either ran it yourselves or gave it to someone to run. I just want to know who." She swallowed. "I need to talk to them."

"First off, I don't run shine," Gator said, putting his back to her. "I don't know what you're
talking about."

"You know exactly what I'm talking about.
You're just lying because you're afraid I might be
a snitch and you aren't too keen on spending the
next ten years behind bars."

He stiffened and turned to face her. "If that
was true then that would make me one mean
mother," he murmured, leaning so close she could
feel the rush of air against her lips.

Lips that were fuller than she'd first thought.
Kissable, even, if she'd been the least bit interested.

She wasn't, she realized as she stared him
down. She didn't catch her breath. Or fight down
a rush of heat. Or feel her knees tremble. Nothing. Because as good looking as he was, he wasn't
Tyler McCall.

The sudden truth shook her even more than
the fact that she'd just called out the most dangerous man in the county.

"I'm not looking for trouble," she added. "I
just want what's mine. I made another batch of
mash and now it's missing. Since Kenny Roy is
one of the few people who knew about it, I'm
banking that he took it and handed it over to
you."

"I don't know what you're talking about."

"Fine, deny it. It doesn't matter." She thought about arguing quality control, but at this point, she was too desperate. Beggars couldn't be choosers and she was this close to dropping to her knees because the last thing she had time to do was come up with another batch of mash. "I don't care who took it at this point. All that matters is that I get a jar of the finished product."

He seemed as if he wanted to tell her where to go and how fast to get there, but then he shrugged. "I can get you a jar of shine, sweetheart, but I can't promise it's your product. I didn't touch your mash and I don't have a clue who did."

"And I should believe you because of your stellar reputation?"

A slow grin split his face. "If reputations were in play, then you'd be doing a striptease on this pool table right now instead of arguing with me." He shrugged. "Believe me or don't believe me. I really don't give a rat's ass." He peeled off a few twenties from the wad Kenny Roy had given him and laid them on the table before signaling the waitress. "Let's cut out," he told Ryder. "We've got work to do."

"Wait a second. Where's Cooper McCall?" she called out, her voice bringing him up short.

His brow furrowed. "What do you want with Cooper?"

"His brother's looking for him. Kenny Roy

said you two were delivering together, so if you're back, then where's Coop?"

Gator's gaze narrowed ever so slightly. "He headed for Austin on business. I was going myself, but I got held up here."

With her mash.

That was the only reason he was standing here right now. He'd come back for her mash and stuck around because he was going to hand it over to someone to run as his own. It was just one of the dozen theories pushing and pulling at her brain.

"Cooper's a big boy," Gator added. "If he wants to talk to his brother, I'm guessing he will. If not, then it's his business."

"Who are you working with?" she called after him when he started to walk away. "Who ran my mash the first time?"

"Trust me, you'd rather not know." With that, he left her staring after him.

She debated following, but Gator Hallsey was the best driver to ever haul shine. As good as his daddy and granddaddy before him had been back in the day.

She might try, but she would never manage to keep up.

Even more, she couldn't shake the crazy hunch that he was telling the truth.

Yeah, right. He was a criminal and she was no closer to getting a jar of the finished product before her meeting on Friday.

She was so screwed.

Professionally and personally.

The truth dogged her as she walked out of the run-down bar and climbed back into her car. Because there was no more denying that despite her best efforts, she'd done the unthinkable— she'd fallen head over heels for Tyler McCall.

CHAPTER 23

"He's in Austin," Brandy told Tyler when he picked up his phone later that evening. She'd thought about stopping by to tell him in person, but after her recent realization, she'd decided that distance was better.

Safe.

"Who?"

"Cooper."

"How do you know?"

"I saw Gator Hallsey. He's back, so I asked where your brother was."

"And you think he told you the truth?"

"I don't see a reason for him to lie. Not about that anyway."

"What do you mean?"

She wasn't going to tell him. That's what she told herself, but the hopelessness inside of her welled up and suddenly, the words tumbled out. "My mash is missing. Someone took it and I'm laying my money on Kenny Roy, or Ryder Jax or Gator Hallsey, or all three. At the very least, they know who has it and what's going on."

"Where are you at?"

"The bakery?"

"I'll be there in a few minutes."

"I don't think that's a good idea—" she started, but it was too late. The dial tone echoed in her ear and Brandy had all of fifteen minutes to gather her courage and prepare herself for a visit from the last man she wanted to see at the moment.

Why did everything have to be so complicated all of a sudden?

"There's no sign of breaking and entering here," Tyler said as he examined the small back door that led into an alley behind the building and then walked back to the small closet behind the oven. "This pantry door wasn't locked?"

"Why would I lock it? It's not like someone's going to break in to steal flour or sugar, and that's all that I keep back there."

"Ellie knew it was here?"

"Ellie's so preoccupied right now, I seriously doubt she knows her last name anymore. She's really into your buddy, Duff."

"I think the feeling is mutual."

"Uh, oh."

"What's that supposed to mean?"

"That Ellie doesn't like being hooked on anyone. She likes playing the field."

"Duff's pretty much the same."

"Which is why Ellie's determined to break things off and stay away from him."

"Sounds like a good plan."

It was, which was exactly why Brandy was following Ellie's lead. Except Ellie didn't have Duff barging over to check her back door and fog her common sense.

"The back door had to be unlocked at some point," Tyler said. "Unless you think someone came in through the front door. Was it unlocked last night?"

"Of course not. I never leave it unlocked."

She thought about how she'd rushed in at the last minute that morning because she'd let Tyler McCall distract her last night. And every night before then.

"Maybe I left it unlocked. I mean, I had to have, right? Otherwise there would be some evidence of an actual break-in."

"Unless it's a really experienced thief."

"In Rebel? We haven't had any sort of break-in around here since the Rebel Softball Team went on a scavenger hunt and dared each other to steal two rolls of toilet paper from the Mercantile. Even then, they didn't actually break in. One just distracted the clerk while another girl snuck the toilet paper past him under her shirt. It's not like there's a big crime wave around here."

"And you sure as hell can't call the sheriff."

"No."

He nailed her with a gaze. "You can't go chasing after Gator Hallsey and his crew. I don't care if they did have something to do with taking the mash."

"They did," she said, more to convince herself than him. Because ever since she'd left the bar, she hadn't been able to shake the voice telling her that while Gator wasn't the most upstanding guy, he'd been telling the truth.

Which meant something else was going on.

"Leave it alone and make another batch," Tyler told her.

She shook her head. "I don't have time. Speaking of which, I need to get home. Thanks for stopping by, but I promised Jenna we would hang out tonight."

"What about later?"

She ignored the rush of excitement. "I'm committed for the long haul. Maybe we can get together tomorrow." Even as she said the words, she knew she wasn't going to call him. Or drive over.

Distance.

"Listen—"

"I really have to go."

He looked as if he wanted to say something, but then his phone blinked and he shook his head. "Fine, but you're sure you're going home? No more poking around?"

"Scout's honor." She crossed her heart and watched as he turned and walked away.

"He called," his mother told him when he walked into the trailer a few minutes later. "Told me he was fine and he'd try to stop by sometime soon. I told him I needed him here now, but that boy

doesn't listen. Why, you just wait until your
father gets home . . ." Tyler's mother went off on
a rant about how things were going to change
and shape up before she ended the tirade with a
long swig of her coffee.

"Where's he at?"

"He didn't say."

"Did you ask him?"

"'Course, I did," the woman said, her words
slightly slurred. Then again, it was after sundown.
Well past happy hour. And to say Ellen McCall
was happy by now was an understatement.
"Say, when are you going to pick up that mess
out front?"

"I should be done by tomorrow," he told her,
particularly since he wasn't doing much else tonight.

He thought of Brandy and her reluctance earlier, and his gut tightened. She was scared.

He didn't blame her. Last night hadn't gone
exactly as he'd planned. Things had started off
good enough. Fast. As planned. But then she'd
sighed and he'd found himself slowing down,
and then they'd both been so tired that falling
asleep had seemed like the right thing.

Until the neighbor had called to tell him his
mother was singing at the top of her lungs and
she was going to call the police if Tyler didn't put
a stop to it. He'd gone by the house, poured his
mother into bed, and then headed back to the
rodeo arena only to find that Brandy had left.

So? Good riddance. That's what Tyler told

himself, but damned if he hadn't actually liked falling asleep with her. Enough that he'd had one hell of a practice session that morning. He'd been focused. On point.

"You keep riding like that," Jack had told him, "and you'll give those cowboys a run for their money in Cheyenne."

Yep, he'd done good, and all because he'd gotten some much-needed sleep. Some peace. The most he'd felt in a long time.

Unfortunately, Brandy hadn't had a similar day. Her mash was missing, she was rattled, and now she was scared.

Of him.

Of them.

The urge to hop into his truck and haul ass over to her place hit him hard and fast, but Tyler wasn't about to go there. Sure, he'd had a good day. But maybe it hadn't been because of Brandy. Because he'd had some decent sleep.

Maybe he was just pushing himself.

His mind made up, he spent the next few hours clearing away the leftover wood and nailing up a few of the last pieces, until the porch stood strong and tall. He jumped to test the weight and satisfaction rolled through him.

Short-lived when he headed back to the empty apartment and the soft sheets that still smelled like Brandy Tucker.

CHAPTER 24

"Maybe I'm not interested in talking to you." Brandy tried to sound nonchalant as she fed a lemon tart into a pink bakery box early Wednesday morning, but it was next to impossible when she caught a whiff of his scent.

The enticing aroma of leather and male and that unnameable something that made her think of soft cotton sheets and the moonlight peeking past the blinds of the small apartment . . . Forget it. Forget him.

Forget.

She tried for a steadying breath. "Look, I thought we got this straight last night—I don't think it's a good idea for us to continue to get together." She added the last word on a whisper, eyeing the four women sitting at a nearby table, nursing coffee and slices of her cranberry walnut bread, their gazes hooked on Tyler. "I think we should call it quits."

"Really?"

"Really."

"You know what I think? I think," he said,

stepping toward her, "you're pushing me away on purpose because you're scared."

"There goes that word again." She gathered her courage and focused every last ounce on holding her ground. Last night she'd given herself every reason why she needed to cut all ties, namely the sex was starting to interfere with her daily life.

Her business.

She was thinking about him too much when she should be focusing on work. That, and she was falling for him.

Really and truly falling to the point that she saw his face when she closed her eyes instead of visions of specialty cakes and pies.

"Walking away doesn't mean I'm scared," she heard herself say. "It means I've got other things on my plate. Things that are a lot more important than sex."

"All the more reason to see this through now." He stared at her, his eyes bright and mesmerizing. His lips hinted at the faintest of grins and his gaze dropped, peeling away her clothes and caressing every bare inch. "I'll be gone soon enough. We might as well make the most of the time we have left. Then you can get to all of those other things on your plate without any distractions."

Her skin tingled and her heart stalled.

Bad heart.

She tried for a disinterested shrug. "I'm not

distracted now. I know you hate to hear this, but I'm just not that interested anymore."

"You don't have to be afraid."

"For the last time, I'm not afraid of you."

"Not me, sugar." He leaned over the counter, his hand brushing hers as he reached for the bakery box. "Us." The word trembled in the air between them, his fingers soft and warm against hers.

She swallowed and managed to pull away and shift her attention to the cash register. "There is no *us*."

"We're good together."

"We *were* good together. I was horny. You were horny. I'm no longer horny. So that's the end of it. Look, if you're looking for more, that's great. I'm sure you can find any number of girls ready and willing to spend time with you—"

"I'm not talking about spending time. I'm talking about burning up some energy. Some lust. I'm not looking for a relationship." He ran a hand over his face, and she noted the weariness around his eyes. Something tugged at her heart. "I'm looking for my brother and I'm having shitty luck finding him. The wait," he ran a hand through his hair, "the wait is killing me. I need a distraction, Brandy. I need you."

"So I'm a distraction to you? That's it?" The notion sent a rush of regret through her, followed by a wave of relief. Because that's all she wanted to be when it came to Tyler McCall.

At least that's what she was desperately telling herself.

"You help me work out my frustration, which helps me focus. And sleep. I know it sounds crazy, but you don't know how worked up I've been. I haven't slept a solid three hours in weeks." He ran a hand over his face and she noted the weary light in his eyes. "I'm stuck here for the next few days and while I am, I need to train or I can kiss my next rodeo good-bye." He shook his head. "I have to hold it together. That means I need a distraction from worrying about Cooper every damn night." His gaze locked with hers. "You were sleeping pretty soundly, too, when I ducked out."

"About that," she started. "You could have left a note or something."

"Worried about me?"

"Afraid that I was going to have to find a replacement after I've put so much time and effort into training you for the job."

He grinned, the expression slow and wicked, and her heart gave a double thump. "Good to hear that I'm not so easily replaced."

"I didn't say that. I just said I don't want to have to train." Another grin and her chest tightened. "Listen, why are we doing this? If you just need to hook up, so be it." She motioned to the table of women. "Take your pick."

"Sure thing." He took her arm and joined her behind the counter.

"What are you doing—" she started, the

words drowning in the lump in her throat as he hauled her up against him.

"I pick you."

She stared up at him, wishing he wasn't so tall, so handsome, so . . . close. "I'm not ripe for picking."

His eyes darkened and she realized she'd said the wrong thing . . . or the right thing depending on the part of her doing the thinking. From the heat pooling between her legs, she'd bet money it wasn't her head.

"I'd say you're plenty ripe, sugar." His thumb grazed the side of her breast, and her nipple throbbed to awareness. "Ripe *and* juicy, and damn near ready to burst."

"That's not what I meant." She fought for an extra breath to send a much-needed jolt of oxygen to her brain. "From what I've seen, there are plenty of women in this town who wouldn't mind being your distraction."

"That's where you're wrong. The women in this town don't give a lick about distracting me. They'd rather wife me up, and I'm not here for that. This is a small town, sugar. The local girls aren't thinking about having a good time. They're more worried about what time you're going to call them tomorrow. And whether or not you're going to ask them to the church picnic. And when you're going to order the ring and pick out the crystal." He shook his head. "To hell with that. I'm more a red Solo cup kind of guy. Always have been. Always will be."

"I'm sure there's a nice girl—"

"I don't want a nice girl. I want you, Brandy. And you want me. For now. That's why this works. We both know what's going to happen and what isn't."

And that was the problem in a nutshell. She knew. She just wasn't so sure she liked that truth so much anymore.

The notion struck and she stiffened. The last thing she wanted was a relationship, even if she was falling for him a little. All the more reason to say good-bye, which she would most definitely do.

But it didn't have to be now.

"I'm not the least bit interested in an actual relationship and neither are you," he went on. "It's a match made in heaven. Like peanut butter and chocolate. Strawberries and whipped cream." He quoted her favorite cake flavors from the menu hanging overhead. "Coconut and vanilla."

"Cookies and cream," she murmured—the next selection—her gaze meeting his. "You're serious about this, aren't you?"

He didn't answer. Instead, he dipped his head and kissed her smack-dab in the middle of her lunch rush, with her bakery brimming with customers. Not quite as many as usual. Not with the doughnut shop cranking out new flavors every five seconds. But still . . . there were people.

His hand cupped her cheek, shattering her thoughts. His other palm splayed along her rib cage just inches shy of her right breast, his fingers searing through the fabric of her blouse. His mouth nibbled at hers. His tongue slid wet and wicked along her bottom lip before dipping inside to stroke and tease and take her breath away.

Now, this . . . this was the reason she should turn and walk away right now. Because despite the audience, she was this close to sliding her arms around his neck and begging for more than a kiss.

Because she was every bit the bad girl the entire town thought her to be.

The thought rooted as his fingers crept an inch higher, closer to her aching nipple, which bolted to attention, eager for a touch, a stroke, something—anything.

His fingers stopped inches shy, but his mouth kept moving, his tongue stroking, lips eating, hungry . . . so hungry. His intent was pure sin, and Brandy couldn't help herself; a moan vibrated up her throat.

He caught the sound, deepening the kiss for a delicious moment that made her stomach jump and her thighs quiver, and left no doubt as to the power of the chemistry between them.

"I really do have a lot of work to do," she said, trying one last time to preserve her sanity when he finally pulled away, leaving her dazed and trembling.

He leaned in, his breath warm against her ear. "So do I, but none of it's getting done until we take care of business." His words made her shake and quiver all the more.

Shaking? Quivering? Over some cowboy?

This cowboy, a voice whispered, that same voice that had warned her off him the minute she'd seen him standing in the doorway. The voice that had urged her to cut and run when he'd approached her counter.

At the same time, it wasn't like Tyler had set up shop in Rebel permanently. It was a few days more, maybe a week at most—just until he located his brother and talked some sense into him. Then he was back on the road, out of her life, her thoughts.

"I guess it would be foolish to put a stop to something that seems to be working for the both of us."

"We spend the nights together. We have sex. We sleep. That's it."

"And then you go your way and I go mine?"

"That's the plan."

"Hasn't it always been?" Her gaze locked with his and her heartbeat kicked up a notch as he nodded and she added, "Okay. But on one condition. You help me find my mash."

"I think that ship might have sailed."

"Maybe, but I've still got two days. It's not over until it's over."

CHAPTER 25

"What can I do for you?" Brandy asked Betty later that afternoon, after a lunch hour spent casing Gator Hallsey's most recent hangout. The man hadn't come in again and the bartender had no information, and so Brandy was no better off. The only thing keeping her spirits ups was her plan to keep seeing Tyler.

Crazy, but there it was.

"Muffin?" she added, motioning to the freshly baked goodies on the top shelf.

"That would be delightful, sugar." The old woman rummaged in her purse for her wallet. "And give me some of that Earl Grey tea you mixed up the other day. It did wonders for my stomach. 'Course, a shot of something a little stronger would be better, but then I'm not as young as I used to be, am I?" Betty smiled, her face breaking into a mass of wrinkles. "That's what you ought to start working on instead of another cake. You ought to whip up some shine that don't tear up my stomach. Told my grandson that just the other day, bragged about how good your granddaddy's stuff used to be and how you were a chip off the old block."

"Moonshine isn't my specialty." Not anymore. Not now that her shine was missing and the chances of her finding it in time to run it and come up with a viable product before her meeting on Friday with Mark, were slim to none.

Maybe Tyler was right.

The notion was too depressing and so she tried for a smile. "Honey butter to go with the muffin?"

"Told Mitchell I ought to try my hand at making my own moonshine," Betty went on. "But he waved me off like he always does. Don't get old, sugar. Nobody takes you seriously anymore."

"You thinking about brewing up some shine?"

"Why not? It ain't like I ain't tasted my fair share. I bet I could come up with something. Then again, I'm too old to go to the pokey. Hear tell, Sheriff DeMassi's closing in on all the moonshiners in this area. Did you hear about that big arrest out at the Sawyer place? The one where they took down Big Jimmy? Heard about it from my Mitchell, who said he saw with his own two eyes when they hauled the guy in. It was ugly. Pure ugly. And just for a little cooking."

"That's because it's illegal."

"Horse shit. It's the government, I tell you. Always trying to tell us what to do. Why, I'm of a mind to run some shine just to show them there are still some red-blooded Americans left who ain't afraid to exercise their God-given rights."

"I don't think running shine is mentioned in the Constitution."

"Me, either." The deep voice sounded and Brandy's head snapped up to see Sheriff DeMassi standing at the counter.

"Sheriff," Betty said, her spine instantly straighter. "I was just talking here about God and country."

"I heard, but I doubt the big guy would condone breaking the law. Contrary to what a lot of folks think, running shine *is* illegal and any parties caught participating will be tried according to the law."

"Law schmaw," Betty snapped. "Why, it's a shame what this world's come to where an old woman can't say what she wants without an officer of the law stalking her."

"I'm not stalking you."

"You were just at the Quick Stop and so was I."

"That's because I was picking up a newspaper and you were buying panty hose."

"Ah, hah. You *were* stalking me. Otherwise you would never know that I was buying panty hose."

"You were standing in front of me in line, Miss Betty. You argued with the clerk about a different brand. I couldn't help but notice."

"Right." She slid a glance to Brandy. "I'd watch my step around him if I were you. He's liable to haul you in."

"I only do that with criminals, ma'am."

"My point exactly." She gave Brandy another glance before grabbing her muffin and heading for a nearby table.

"So what can I do you for, Sheriff? I've got fresh apple bread."

"I'm afraid I'm not here on break."

Anxiety rushed through her and she thought of the missing mash. Had the sheriff gotten wind of it and confiscated it? And now he was here to arrest her?

"Big Jimmy is being transferred to Huntsville Prison on eight counts of making illegal alcohol and tax evasion."

"That's good."

"Is it? Because I just keeping thinking he knows something and now that they're transferring him out, I'm not going to get another chance to find out what that is."

"Maybe it's just what the Feds say. Grandpa paid Jimmy a visit. Threatened him. It could be that simple."

He nodded, but the affirmation didn't touch the taut line of his mouth. "Even so, can I stop by your place again and take a look in your granddad's room? There's something still bothering me from the other night."

"I didn't think you found anything."

"I didn't. That's the problem. I keep feeling as if there's something there." He scratched his temple. "Something I'm missing."

"I usually stay late to prep for the next day, but I was actually going to cut out early tonight."

Thanks to Tyler. They were going to ask around some more about Gator and then head back to his place.

But first she needed to swing by home.

"I should be home around seven."

He nodded. "I'll see you then."

Tyler slid off the mechanical bull and wiped his hands on his jeans. His phone beeped from his pocket and he slid it free to see the latest stats from the rodeo going on in Blackwater, South Dakota. It was a small-time venue with little in the way of prize money, but it did feed the national standings. Not enough to knock Tyler out of his spot, but enough to shake things up and make him think twice about crawling back on the mechanical bull.

He needed a real bull. A mean sonofabitch.

He needed Junkyard Dog.

He eyed the sleek black animal in the nearby pen, the familiar Sawyer emblem blazing on the sign mounted just outside the railing. While Brett had issued a press release stating that he was going to retire to work his family's cattle ranch, he'd decided to put some of his effort into bulls.

Grade A, prizewinning bulls like the one only a few feet away.

Junkyard Dog was just one of a handful penned at the rodeo arena in anticipation of the weekly Saturday-night event that the venue hosted. A small-time show that didn't feed into national standings, but certainly afforded some really good practice.

If Brett had been inclined to share with Tyler.

The thought struck as he watched his second cousin in the nearby arena, talking to one of the cowboys who'd just hit the dust after an unsettling ride. Tyler couldn't help but wonder what words of wisdom the reigning champ was passing on. If any. Maybe they were smack-talking the way he and Brett used to do.

Too much smack for Tyler to turn around and ask for help now.

That's your pride talking, a voice whispered.

But Tyler had gone without so much for most of his life that pride had been all he'd had. And while things had changed, old habits died hard.

He checked the rest of his texts, his heart pounding ever so slightly when he saw Brandy's name and the message that she would be a little late tonight.

Cold feet?

That was his first thought, but then she hadn't called things off between them, so it could very well mean just what she said—she had to take care of something at home. The notion filled him with hope, a rare commodity for him these days, and eased the tension in his shoulders just enough so he could take a deep, easy breath.

He checked Coop's number yet again and listened to the familiar voice mail. He didn't even bother to leave a message this time. Maybe Cooper was still out of town. And maybe he was just hiding. Either way, Tyler intended to find out. They might be hunting for Brandy's mash tonight, but he fully intended to find out as much as he could about his brother's new line of work at the same time.

Cooper hauling moonshine.

It didn't make a bit of sense since his brother had barely gotten his driver's license the last time Tyler had been home. He'd been so timid, so determined to walk the straight and narrow—unlike their father—that he'd been fearful of even getting a parking ticket.

And now he was running with the fastest in the county.

It didn't add up.

No, it just started the throbbing in his temples that said he had a major migraine coming on.

So much for hope.

He slid the phone into his pocket and walked around to another nearby pen and a bull by the name of Grenade. He wasn't fast, but he was brutal and so Tyler spent the next few seconds prepping his hands before climbing over the edge of the stall. His ass hit the bull and the animal jumped and jerked. He dug in, wrapping his fingers under the rope and tilting his head forward for a long moment.

He gave the signal and just like that, the bull shot forward, bucking and bolting this way and that while Tyler held tight. The seconds ticked by . . . three . . . four . . . five—

Whumph!

He hit the ground. The air bolted from his lungs and pain jolted him.

But he moved anyway, springing to his feet and moving out of the way as the cowboys fought the bull back into its pen.

He stopped and drew a deep, shaky breath, his backside screaming, his shoulder throbbing. Okay, so he'd gotten faster in addition to being mean.

"Good ride," a cowboy called out.

Half-ass came the text message a split second later when Tyler's phone beeped and he hauled the iPhone out to stare at the screen.

He glanced at the familiar number before his head snapped up to catch the stare of the man who stood clear across the rodeo arena. Brett Sawyer shook his head before turning back to his own phone.

When you ride, you have to do it like you mean it. Pull your head out of your ass came the next message.

Tyler's fingers flew over the keys. *If you know so much, get over here and show me how it's done.*

I might came the blinking reply. *I just might. But first you need to get your head in the game. Whatever's bugging you, deal with it and then get back to work.*

Tyler stared at the screen long and hard, the unanswered questions about his brother beating at his senses. That, and he was still thinking about Brandy, about the fact that she'd come so close to putting the brakes on and that while she'd agreed to more sex, she'd been almost reluctant. As if she wasn't half as anxious to spend time with him as he was to spend time with her.

That, or she just didn't want to admit it.

Deal with it, came the next text.

Tyler stuffed his phone into his pocket, dusted off his jeans, and headed for the small apartment on the second floor. A quick shower and he intended to do just that.

CHAPTER 26

"Here you go," Brandy said, showing the sheriff into her grandfather's room. "It's all just the way it was the last time you were here." She still hadn't made the decision between Goodwill and the church. "Take your time."

He nodded. "Thanks." And then he walked into the room and started moving around boxes, peering inside.

Jez yapped at Brandy's feet and she spent the next fifteen minutes feeding the small dog as well as the handful of strays around the house. She'd just finished scooping some rabbit food when she heard the deep male voice behind her.

"I hate to bother you, but is Jenna home?"

Brandy turned to see blond-haired, blue-eyed Jase standing in the kitchen doorway, a Tupperware container in his hands, a worried look on his face. "I don't mean to barge in, but I just had to see for myself that she's feeling better. We were supposed to go to the annual dry-cleaner awards banquet tonight. I'm getting the award for best creases in the county."

"That's great."

"It was, until Jenna got sick. Now it just doesn't seem like such a big deal. I know she can't get out of bed yet and I don't want to disturb her, but I thought I could drop off this soup. I made it myself."

"You made soup? For Jenna?" Who'd left that morning for a two-day equine clinic in nearby Blue County. Not that she'd told Jase as much. Not after faking an allergic reaction. "I, that is, how sweet. I'm sure she'll love it."

A smile touched his lips. "It's the least I can do considering it's my fault she's out of commission. I knew I should have gone with chocolate chips and whipped cream to garnish the pancakes instead of the chocolate-dipped strawberries. But the guy on the YouTube video—Romeo Ron is his name—said that women love fruit and, well, talk about a disaster." He glanced behind him down the hallway. "I'll just take this up to her—"

"No," Brandy cut in. "That is, she's finally sound asleep and I'd hate to wake her. She really needs her rest." So much for brutal honesty. "Just leave it with me and I'll see that she gets it."

He didn't look as if he wanted to, but then he seemed to think. "I guess that would be okay. Just make sure you tell her how sorry I am. And that I love her. And that this is just a bump in the road leading to a long and bright future—"

"Go," Brandy heard herself say. "Get your award. You deserve it."

"It just won't feel right without Jenna."

"About that . . ." *Just tell him.*

That's what she thought about doing, but Jenna had to do her own dirty work. That, and Brandy didn't have the heart to disappoint the young man.

For the first time, she could understand how Jenna constantly found herself in such dilemmas when it came to men. Jase looked so smitten, and there was something sweet and wonderful about that.

Brandy found herself wondering what it would be like to have a man so hopelessly in love with her.

To have Tyler so hopelessly in love with her that he would give up everything just to bring her chicken soup.

Not that she had anything to worry about. He'd said himself that he was just here a little while longer. There would be no hanging around. No moving back home. No chicken soup. No being in love. No giving up anything.

Thankfully.

If he had felt that way, then she would find it hard to deny her own feelings and bam, she would find herself marching the same path as her mother.

No, she wasn't going there.

Still, it didn't hurt to at least think about it.

She took the soup from Jase, shooed him out the door, and headed down the hall to check on the sheriff. She found him neck-deep in a box of old shoes. He held up a battered black tennis shoe.

"Was this James Harlin's?"

"I'm assuming so since it's in his box. Why?"

"Because we found one just like it at Big Jimmy's place."

"Which proves James Harlin went out there to threaten Big Jimmy."

"Not necessarily. It proves he was there, but it doesn't prove why. What if he went out there for another reason?"

"Which is?"

"That's what I'm not sure about, but I've got a few ideas. Mind if I take the shoe?"

"Be my guest." She pushed aside the endless questions swirling through her brain and showed the sheriff to the door. A few seconds later, she headed back to her room to change clothes.

She'd just unhooked her bra when her hand grazed her nipple and a strange tingle of awareness shot through her.

Because she couldn't stop thinking about tonight.

About him.

About how much she wanted him.

Too much, a voice whispered, and while she wanted to think that was a good thing, suddenly the fact bothered her. To the point that she ditched the rest of her clothes, stretched out on the bed, and did her damndest to curb that want herself.

She was almost there.

Brandy clutched the edge of the sheet, her knuckles white, as she stared at her bedroom ceiling. Dusk crept past the edge of the curtains and filled the room with shadows. Her nerves buzzed. Her legs trembled. Her heart beat a frantic rhythm.

Almost, but for some reason she couldn't quite get there.

She let the images from those few nights with Tyler replay in her head. The impression his fingertips had made against her heated skin. The rasp of his jaw against the tenderness of her breasts. The warm press of his lips against the side of her neck. The soft feel of his arms wrapped around her. The press of his fingers . . .

The thing was, she didn't feel Tyler. She was all by her lonesome. Lonely.

The notion struck, but she pushed it aside. She wasn't lonely. She was horny.

That was it. One quick orgasm and she would stop thinking about him so much, wanting him.

And so she did what any healthy, red-blooded female would do. She trailed her fingers down to Funland for a quick visit.

Oddly enough, it didn't feel quite as good. Her hands weren't callused, her skin raspy, or her touch quite as purposeful as that of the man who lived and breathed in her thoughts.

She frowned and stepped up the action, moving lower to the tender flesh between her legs. She closed her eyes and tried to picture her favorite singer, Luke Bryan, particularly in his "Country Girl" video. The man certainly could shake his ass.

Instead, it was Tyler who was shaking it in a pair of skintight jeans, a wicked smile on his face, a gleam in his eyes. Tyler looming over her, driving into her . . .

She came quickly, clamping down on her bottom lip to contain the scream and the screech and . . . Ahhh.

Delicious sensation gripped her for a few blessed moments and she slumped back, welcoming the satisfaction sure to follow. The rush of warmth she'd felt their last time together. The punch of *oomph* that had drained the tension from her body and left her limp and lifeless and completely sated.

If only.

Instead, she still felt edgy. Nervous. Needy.

She ignored the strange emptiness and focused on the positive: the clenching and unclenching between her legs, the trembling of her body, the numbness in her toes, and the all-important fact that while she might still want him, it wasn't the all-consuming, rip-off-your-clothes-right-here-and-now want she'd felt five minutes ago.

This she could handle.

That's what she told herself, but she still felt a rush of excitement when she opened her door half an hour later to find him standing on her doorstep.

"What are you doing here?" she asked him. "I thought we were meeting at the bakery."

"I thought I'd save you a drive back and just pick you up here." He noted the flush to her face. "What's going on? Are you sick?"

If only. "I'm fine," she said, turning to draw a deep breath and pull herself together while she snatched up her purse.

"What's this?" he added, when she handed him the chicken soup and motioned him out the door.

"Dinner."

The grin on his face was enough to make her wish she'd made the soup herself. "Thanks."

"It's nothing. Jase made it for Jenna. She's not here but he doesn't know that. No sense in letting it go to waste."

"True enough." But the explanation didn't kill the smile on his face, or the sudden longing that stirred deep inside of her. "Where to?"

"To find Gator Hallsey and get my mash back."

CHAPTER 27

Gator Hallsey seemed to have disappeared right along with Brandy's mash.

That's the conclusion she came to after four hours spent bar-hopping, talking to waitresses, and chasing down all leads. No one had seen him. And if they had, they weren't inclined to talk. Even to Tyler, who wore the most menacing look Brandy had ever seen.

They were no closer to answers when they finally pulled into the rodeo arena later that night than when they'd started out.

But Brandy was this close to going up in flames.

She wasn't sure if it was the constant bounce of the pickup or the knowledge that Tyler was so close, or the anticipation of having him even closer, but she wanted him in the worst way by the time they walked into the small apartment.

So much so that she hadn't even cared that they'd waltzed by two cowboys who'd lingered down near the pens. Men she'd recognized from her high school days. Timmy Carson and Eli

Walley. They'd both tipped their hats and given her that knowing smile that had sent her home in tears more times than she could count.

Embarrassed.

Ashamed.

Not this time.

The door closed behind them and she reached for her sundress. Pulling down the straps, she shed the clothing at the speed of light as he flipped on the lights and walked over to draw the shades that edged the massive window. He paused just shy, his gaze drinking her in, and her stomach hollowed out.

Been there. Done that. *Get a grip.*

But that was next to impossible with Tyler McCall's powerful body filling up the room and his hot-as-a-Texas-summer gaze scorching her from her head to her toes and back up again.

He made her feel so excited and anxious and needy.

Correction—she didn't *need* Tyler McCall, or any man for that matter.

She simply wanted him physically. Right now. This moment.

Temporary.

She forced her thoughts away from heat swamping her and shifted her attention to the six-plus feet of warm male who hadn't so much as budged an inch near the window.

At least his feet hadn't budged.

Her gaze lingered on the very prominent bulge

beneath his jeans. Her throat went dry and she licked her lips before she could think better of it.

"Come over here and do that, sugar."

She hesitated and he reached for the shades. They slid over the window and she waited for the rush of comfort that it usually brought.

Not this time.

"Well?" he drawled, his voice distracting her from the unsettling thought.

"Well, what?"

"Well? Why don't you stop giving your bottom lip all that attention and come over here and give me some?"

"Why don't you come over here?"

He didn't say a word. Just stared at her with those liquid aqua blue eyes and that ever-widening grin, as if she'd said just the right thing and impressed the hell out of him in the process.

"What are you thinking?" she demanded before she could stop herself.

"That you're about the most stubborn woman I've ever had the misfortune to meet."

"I'm not stubborn enough. Stubborn gets things done. Usually."

"I know you wanted to find the mash, but you'll just have to think of something else. Meet with the distillery man on Friday and give him the recipe."

"I can't do that without a sample."

"Yes, you can. If he's that interested, he'll work something out."

"Maybe, when he gets back from his trip in

three months. I can't wait that long. The business won't wait."

"You'll figure something out," he told her, and while she'd said the same thing to herself more times than she could count that day, for some reason it rang true when he uttered the words.

"Now stop worrying and come over here." He stood barely a hand span from her. Filling up her line of vision. Drinking in all her oxygen. Zapping her common sense and making her forget all about Friday's disastrous meeting.

She licked her lips as her gaze riveted on his mouth. He really had a great mouth, with firm, sensual lips that made her skin itch and her insides tighten in anticipation. "It's really hot in here." She blew out a breath and fought for another. "Hotter than usual."

"It's me. Or you." He reached out and caught a drop of perspiration as it slid down the valley between her breasts. His touch lingered and her heart thudded a frantic rhythm against his fingertip. "Probably both." His mouth touched hers.

Her lips parted at the first moment of contact, so eager and desperate, for several heartbeats Tyler actually forgot that he meant to take his time tonight, to enjoy every moment.

There was nothing slow about the way he stroked his tongue along the length of hers and plunged deep into her mouth. Nothing teasing about the purposeful way he ate at her lips, as if she were his only sustenance and he'd gone far too long without.

He barely resisted the sudden urge to bend her over in that next instant and sink as deep as possible into her soft, warm body. He wanted to forget where he ended and she began. Hell, he wanted to forget everything—the upcoming ride and the pressure to find his brother and get Cooper the hell out of Rebel the way he'd gotten himself out—everything save the woman in his arms and the need heating his blood.

Slow and easy.

He gathered his control and fought for a leisurely pace because after a disastrous evening, this was all they had. Each other. And he meant to make the most of it.

The kiss softened as he suckled her bottom lip and wrung a frustrated moan from her.

He slid his hands up her arms, over her shoulders, learning her shape, the dips and curves near her collarbone, the soft, satiny slopes of her breasts.

He lifted her onto the nearby dresser. Parting her long legs, he stepped between her thighs. Her heat cradled the rock-hard erection pulsing beneath his jeans. He thumbed her nipples and caught her cry of pleasure with his mouth, the sound exciting him almost as much as the knowledge that he was going to haul her close and fall asleep next to her when it was all said and done. For a little while, he reminded himself.

That's all this was. The two of them. Together. For now.

He gave up her lips after a deep, delicious kiss

to nibble down her chin, the underside of her jaw. He licked a fiery path to the beat of her pulse, and teased and nibbled at the hollow of her throat until she gasped. Then he moved on, inhaling her sweet, fragrant smell, savoring the flavor of her skin. An echoing flame leapt through him, burning hotter, brighter . . .

He leaned back long enough to drink in the picture she made.

She had her head thrown back, her eyes closed, her breasts arched in silent invitation.

Dipping his head, he took a slow, leisurely lap at her nipple. The tip quivered, expanded, reached out, and begged for more. He licked her again, a quick swipe followed by a slow, thorough lap that tightened the flesh even more. Finally, he drew the pouty flesh into his mouth and sucked long and hard. A moan vibrated up her throat and she gasped, grasping at his shoulders.

The grasping he could handle. But then she wrapped her legs around his waist. Rubbed herself up against his aching length. Scattered his common sense. He felt her heat through the tight denim and it shot his intentions to hell and back.

Her desperate fingers worked the button of his jeans, then the zipper. It stuck for a heart-pounding moment, the teeth stretched too tight over his straining length. A swift yank, a frenzied *zippp* and . . . *there*. He could breathe again.

He caught her head in his hands, his fingers splaying in her hair, anchoring her for the long, deep probe of his tongue.

"Tyler!" The slam of a door punctuated the shout. The noise shattered the passionate fog Tyler found himself lost in. He stiffened, breaking the kiss to gasp for air as footsteps sounded on the stairs outside.

Brandy's forehead furrowed and her eyelids fluttered open. "What's wrong?"

Before Tyler could answer, a man's voice sounded on the other side of the door. "It's Eli Walley," the man called out. "I feed the animals," the man prodded, reminding Tyler of the cowboy who toted hay bales and filled up troughs. "Listen, man, you left your cell down by the bull pen. It's been beeping like a mother. Tyler? You in there?" But he already knew because he'd seen them walk the stairs not fifteen minutes ago.

He knew they were in there, and he knew just what they were doing.

The realization seemed to hit them both. Brandy stiffened and started to move, but Tyler was faster.

He fought for his zipper and turned, Brandy's body behind him, just as the door creaked open a scant inch.

"I hate to bother you"—a hand slid through the open doorway, holding a phone—"but you might want to get this."

Tyler reached the doorway before the man could poke his head through. "Thanks, buddy." He grabbed the phone and shoved the door closed and locked it before the man could get in so much as another word.

He glanced at the missed call and saw his brother's name blazing on the screen. A sight that drew his immediate attention despite his throbbing body.

He hit the REDIAL button and held the phone to his ear. It rang and rang before going straight to voice mail.

"Dammit," he growled a split second before he felt her soft hands at his back.

"Maybe this is a bad time."

"Just give me a minute." He worked the button on his jeans and started for the door, eager to get away from the need to say to hell with Cooper and the phone.

To hell with everything except the woman perched on the dresser, staring so lusciously back at him.

It would be so easy to turn back to her, and it was that realization itself that kept him from doing just that. Because no woman, even one as soft and warm as Brandy, was going to turn Tyler from what was really important—his family, his career, his future.

He'd worked too long and too hard to throw it all away on a woman who wouldn't do the same for him.

The thought struck and niggled at him the way it did in the dead of night when he wasn't thinking straight. When he started to contemplate that maybe, just maybe, being home wasn't so bad with Brandy here.

Crazy.

Rebel was as bad as it could ever get. It was the one place that held his shitty past and kept thrusting it into his face. The one place he wanted to leave behind and forget once and for all just as soon as he saw that Cooper was well on his way to doing the same.

Yep, he was out of here in a heartbeat, and Brandy would be the first to wave good-bye and mean it.

"I'll be back," he said, and then he left her staring after him.

"I don't think we should be doing this again," Ellie said as Duff peeled off her shirt and tossed it to the nearby floor.

They stood in the back room of the bakery, where Ellie had been about to close up for Brandy and call it a night. Until Duff had shown up and licked batter off Ellie's fingers.

"Correction," she added as his tongue flicked her thumb and she felt a zing between her legs. "I know we shouldn't be doing this."

"Damn straight, we shouldn't," he agreed, but he kept licking, sucking, ahhh . . .

"You're not my type," she blurted, trying frantically to summon her common sense.

"That's what you say, but your body says something different." He touched her nipple through the thin fabric of her bra. "I think she likes me."

"But *I* don't. I don't like you."

"I don't like you, either, and I surely don't love you. Just so we've got that clear."

"I'm not an idiot. I know good and well you don't love me, and I don't care. I mean, it's not like I love you. I don't, you know. I don't even know you so how can I love you?"

"Exactly."

"I mean I thought I might feel a little something for you because it just seems like whatever is between us is so powerful that there has to be more to it."

"Does there?" He pulled the bra cup down and under her breast, plumping the flesh so that he could lean forward and flick the tip with his thumb. Heat speared her and she caught her bottom lip. "Maybe I'm just attracted and you're just attracted, and we should just enjoy it."

"That's what I've been telling myself. What I always tell myself." And she'd had no trouble believing it until now.

Until him.

"I don't know anything about you, yet I feel more comfortable than I ever have in my entire life," Ellie told him before she could think better of it. But there was just something about him that made her say, as well as do, things she normally wouldn't. "I feel like I can talk to you."

"That's a good thing."

"That's a bad thing. It's not about talking. It's just sex. Except it's not just sex." She was rambling, she knew. So much that any man would have said to hell with it and given up on getting her naked. Men didn't like complications.

Especially freewheeling, here-today-gone-tomorrow cowboys. She knew the type. Her mother had hooked up with one after the other, a parade of men through their small house that had always ended with a box of Cracker Jack for her and a bunch of heartache for her mother.

She'd vowed to spare herself the same angst and, so far, she'd done just that. No cowboys. No getting attached. No getting hurt.

Yet here she was with this cowboy, getting attached.

Physically, she reminded herself. It didn't have to go beyond to the hurt part if she didn't let it.

"We can stop." He looked as if it was the last thing he wanted to do, but he said it anyway and she believed him. But then stopping would mean that she was scared she couldn't follow through and keep things in perspective.

Nope. She wasn't stopping.

"Let's do this," she told him, tugging at the back clasp of her bra. The cups fell open and she reached for her pants. "Let's do this right now."

He grinned and tipped the cowboy hat still sitting atop his head. "Whatever the lady wants."

"I'm no lady," she told him, stripping off her pants.

His grin widened. "I know, sugar. That's what I like most about you."

CHAPTER 28

Tyler left a dozen voice mails for Cooper before climbing into his truck and heading for the Happy Times Trailer Park.

"Is he home?"

"Who?" His mom glanced up from the reality show she was watching, the remote in one hand, a GIVE ME JAVA OR GIVE ME DEATH coffee mug in the other. The familiar stench of liquor and the leftover perm supplies sitting on the kitchen table filled the air and burned his nostrils.

"Cooper. He called me."

She didn't look half as interested as she should have. Then again, Tyler had bought her her weekly stash of cigarettes and booze, so she didn't have a reason to concern herself with Coop's disappearance. Until she ran out and needed more. That, and it was hair day. Nothing brought Ellen down when she had a fresh perm on her hair and booze in her cup. "So what did the little fucker say?"

"Nothing. I didn't get the call. It went to voice mail." He glanced at the coffee table littered with magazines, a few bottles of nail polish, and the familiar bottle of Jack. "I thought maybe he'd come home."

But then why would he?

The question echoed in his head as he stared at the run-down interior and the worn woman stretched out on the sofa. Cooper had nothing decent to come home to and now that he was eighteen, he'd made up his mind to get the hell out.

But not this way.

Tyler wanted more for his brother.

And maybe Cooper just wanted out.

The possibility followed Tyler back down the now sturdy steps of the porch and out to his truck. He was longing to head back to the rodeo arena, but he wasn't ready to give up on his brother yet.

That's what he would be doing if he went back to Brandy right now. He would be giving up on Cooper, on the chance that the boy had finally smartened up and come home, that he'd finally made the right choice.

Cooper's choice, Tyler knew.

But still.

Tyler wanted to at least talk to the kid, try to guide him down the right path.

Otherwise, while Cooper might be out of the Happy Times Trailer Park, he would never be out of Rebel for good, on his way to something better.

No, he'd be stuck, scrounging to make the next paycheck, to ace the next score.

Just the way their mother was stuck, living day-to-day, waiting for a dream that would never happen, a man that hadn't loved her or his kids enough to stick around.

Tyler couldn't let his brother do that.

He spent the next few hours combing the nearby bars, driving by Kenny Roy's, and looking for some sign of Cooper. He didn't find anything except a headache by the time he arrived back at the rodeo arena.

A headache and a mess of disappointment because Brandy Tucker was gone.

Hell's bell, son. Did you really think she'd stick around?

He hadn't, but there'd been that small hope deep in his gut. That Brandy wouldn't give up on him any more than he meant to give up on Cooper.

But she'd bailed.

And she always would.

He knew that. He'd always known that.

It just had never bothered him as much as it did at that moment. Enough to send him downstairs to the dark rodeo arena, straight to Junkyard Dog.

He'd left her.

The truth followed Brandy on the long cab ride home that night, and back to the bakery the next morning, where she mixed up enough muffins for the usual morning rush.

Wishful thinking because she opened her door to find exactly one customer waiting for her.

"I thought you'd never open up," Sheriff De-Massi told her. "We need to talk."

She smiled and tried to hide the sudden unease that stirred in the pit of her stomach. "Can I interest you in a muffin, Sheriff? I've got more than enough."

He shook his head and disappointment ricocheted through her. So much for at least one customer.

"Actually, I was hoping you could take a ride down to the station with me." His mouth drew into a taut line. "We've got a situation."

The disappointment took a nosedive straight into a pool of *uh, oh.* "Is it about my grandpa?"

"Come on. I'll tell you on the way."

Brandy swallowed her misgivings, handed over the reins to a very bleary-eyed Ellie, who looked as if she'd had exactly five seconds of sleep.

"Are you sure you can handle things?" Brandy asked the young woman.

"This I can handle. In case you haven't noticed"—Ellie eyed the empty bakery and shrugged—"we're not exactly catering to a full house."

Tell me about it. "True, but things can turn on a dime," she reminded the young woman, drawing on the last of her optimism. "Half the town could waltz through here in the next hour."

There. The well was now dry. Her career was tanking. Her bakery was shriveling up. And Tyler McCall had left her high and dry the night before.

Get used to it, her conscience reminded her.

Because that's what would eventually happen once he found Cooper. He would roll out of Rebel the way he always did.

Only this time, he wasn't coming back.

She wasn't sure why the thought struck. He'd never said a word to indicate any such thing. But there was just something about the way he touched her whenever they were together. As if memorizing every detail.

Because this is it? Our last ride, so to speak?

The thought depressed her even more than the lack of customers and fed the anxiety that blossomed in the pit of her stomach as she climbed into the passenger seat of the beige SUV.

The ride took less than five minutes and contrary to what Hunter had said, he didn't fill Brandy in on the details for her sudden trip. Instead, he spent the ride on the radio with dispatch trying to organize the monthly spaghetti dinner at the station.

"Fine," Hunter finally said. "I'll bring the garlic bread."

"And the salad," the woman told him. "Don't forget that."

"Whatever you say, Miss Gladys." He slid the mic into its holder just as he pulled into the station. "Sorry about that," he told Brandy as he climbed out of the vehicle and ushered her inside.

"The reason I brought you in today," Hunter finally said when they were seated at a conference table in a small room lined with large cabinets, "is that we made an arrest last night and you were implicated."

"*What?*"

Hunter turned and pulled the familiar mash bucket from a nearby cabinet, an evidence tag hanging from the handle. "Do you recognize this?"

"I . . ." She caught her lip, gathered her courage, and then told Hunter the entire story of how she'd come up with a new mash recipe while trying to re-create the legendary Texas Thunder, how she'd had some anonymous person run it, and how she'd been trying to run a second batch in order to get her hands on a sample for her meeting with the distillers later that day. And all because the bakery was tanking and her dream right along with it. "Who knew doughnuts would be my downfall?" she ended, her voice catching just shy of a sob.

"Moonshining is a federal offense, you know that, right?" He wiped a hand over his face. "Although you didn't technically run any moonshine, now did you? You just made mash. Still, with the intent of turning it into moonshine."

"With the intent of letting someone else turn it into moonshine." She wiped at her suddenly watery eyes. "I'm sorry, Hunter. I was just trying to do something that could help my bakery business. I wasn't trying to cause any trouble or hurt anyone."

"I know that. You're a good person, Brandy. You've always been a good person. I think you were a little off track with your thinking. You should have forfeited a sample and just tried to sell the recipe, but you didn't. So how did you hook up with Mitchell and Betty?"

"Come again?"

"Miss Betty. We found her and her grandson cooking in their garage. The neighbor smelled the fumes. Made the bust myself. When I arrived, she told me she was exercising her God-given rights, albeit using a mash she'd stolen from you."

Brandy's memory stirred and she remembered Betty's words. She also remembered the woman's trip to the bathroom a few days ago and suddenly the pieces started to fall into place. "She must have found it in my utility closet. I had it fermenting in there one minute and the next, it was gone." Because Betty had found it and told her grandson and then, together, they'd stolen it.

"Since my main concern was over them setting something on fire since they have zero experience in the actual distilling process, I'm letting them off on minor charges. Particularly since Miss Betty's eighty-seven and has a bad heart. I doubt she could handle a run at Huntsville and my own grandma would tan my hide if I even suggested it. But the grandson is actually going to do a little jail time since he's already got a record."

"And what about me?"

"I'm going to let you off with a promise to leave the mash and the moonshine to the professionals."

"That's what I want to do, but there's no chance of that now."

The sheriff seemed to think before he turned and went back to the large closet. He emerged with a small jar filled with two fingers' worth of liquor. "It's not much. Mitchell started dumping as soon as we walked in, but we did manage to confiscate one jar."

She stared at the jar he handed her. "I don't understand."

"It's really good stuff, Brandy. It seems a shame for you to miss your shot. I don't need the whole thing anyway. Mitchell and Betty confessed to everything. If I leave it here, it'll just sit in that evidence closet and collect dust. Until I come in one day and find it missing, that is. The deputies like to play cards on slow nights and sometimes they go rummaging for a little something extra to give the night a much-needed kick. Since I know you're not going to turn around and sell it, I'm going to let you have it. Good luck at your meeting today."

"You're kidding, right?" The enormity of what was happening hit her and a rush of joy went through her.

One that followed her through the next few

hours as she headed back to the bakery to check on things, print out a final copy of her refined recipe, and get ready for her meeting with Mark Edwards.

"It's really good," Mark said after his third sip. He set the jar on his desk and stared at the recipe in front of him. "I've never seen strawberries added at this point in the process. Most go in after the brew, but you're mixing it directly into the mash."

"Some people cook them and heap them in. I've seen that, but I sugar them first and cook them down so that they all but disintegrate during the fermenting process. They dissolve, but the flavor doesn't. It packs a fruity punch to the finished product. That, and the spices. It's all about the right balance in the mix."

"I can see that." He took another sip before turning to the iPad on his desk and punching in some notes. "You know that your sister hasn't decided whether or not to sell us the recipe? But even if she did, I can't imagine it could be better than this."

"What are you saying?"

"That I think we can work out a deal. We'll do an advance, of course, and then a royalty per jar."

"An advance? Really?"

"Not a big one. I mean, we'll have to test it in a few markets and see how it does. It might tank." Another sip and a smile tugged at his mouth. "But I highly doubt that." He did a few more calculations on his iPad before turning it toward her and sliding it across the desk. "This is the best we could do at this point."

Brandy stared at the amount and her heart jumped. While it was modest, it was still enough to buy her a new oven and tide her over for the next few months while she pushed her specialty cakes among the Hill Country wedding set and made a name for herself as a top wedding-cake baker.

"You've got yourself a deal," she murmured, sliding a hand toward Mark.

They spent the next few minutes signing the preliminary paperwork and talking about marketing ideas until his phone buzzed and he had to leave to catch his flight.

"I'll have our accountant draw up a check. It should be ready in a week or so once legal goes over everything and then it's a done deal."

"Thank you so much."

"Thank you. We've been trying for a good moonshine recipe ever since we got our distillers permit. This is going to take us into new markets and make us both a lot of money."

But Brandy wasn't half as concerned with the future of her recipe. She had what she needed to save her business and all was right with the world.

Except that it didn't feel so right.

Because all wasn't right. Not with Tyler's world. He was still waiting on his brother, still as frustrated as she'd been and like it or not, it bothered her. She wanted him to solve his problems, as well. To find his brother and get on with his life. To move on so that she could get back to her own life.

At least that's what she told herself.

If only the notion wasn't so freakin' depressing.

CHAPTER 29

It was Friday night and Brandy was on her third drink.

"To new ovens and lots of special orders," she said, touching the edge of her glass to Ellie's.

"New ovens," her baking assistant declared. "And hot cowboys. May they rot in hell."

Okay, so Ellie was on her sixth drink since they'd walked into the small bar where Brandy had had her encounter with bootlegger Gator Hallsey a few nights ago.

Not that she was back for another. All's well that ends well for her moonshine recipe and her newly signed contract with Foggy Bottom Distillers. She and Ellie had needed a place to celebrate, and her assistant had wanted to steer clear of the local honky-tonk and a certain calf roper who'd turned her personal life upside down.

"You think he could just come out and say it—I like you, Ellie. You like me. Let's see where this goes. But no." The woman downed the drink and signaled the bartender for another. "Instead, we're just creeping around at night. Don't get me wrong, it's fun. But I want more than fun."

"Since when?" Brandy sipped her drink and shook her head when the bartender offered her another.

"Since always I guess. With him, that is. From the first day, I knew something was off." Ellie shook her head. "I have shitty luck with men. Seriously, when I finally find a decent one, he's not the least bit interested in sticking around." She took a sip of drink number seven. "Men suck."

"Not all men." What the hell was Brandy saying? Tyler sucked. He really sucked after abandoning her the other night. Royally. "I mean, Reverend Harper is a decent enough guy. And the sheriff? He's a Grade A catch if you ask me. Super nice."

"I'm not talking about the nice guys. I'm talking the hot guys. Why do they all have to suck?"

"I wish I knew." She would love to understand what made Tyler McCall tick.

The thing was, she knew. She knew all about his past, about his dad taking off and his mother's emotional abuse. She knew that Rebel, Texas, held nothing but crappy memories for the bull rider and so it made sense that he would want to leave and never come back.

She knew and she understood. She had her own demons to contend with, her own past to outrun. As much as she wanted to brand him a jerk, she couldn't.

She related to Tyler McCall.

She liked him.

"On second thought, maybe I will have another drink." She signaled the bartender. "Hit me again."

"Somebody wants to have a good time."

Or to forget the good times she'd already had. She took a sip of drink number four and let it ease the tightening in her chest.

A feeling that lasted all of five heartbeats, before she turned to see a pair of worn jeans moving toward her. Her gaze slid higher, over trim thighs and a lean waist, to a faded denim shirt covering a broad chest . . . Speak of the sexy-as-sin devil.

A straw Resistol sat atop Tyler's dark head, tipped forward just enough to cast a slight shadow over the upper part of his face, making his gaze impossible to read in the dim light.

Until he tipped the brim back and stared at her with a hunger that burned so fiercely, she felt the scorch on her face. The neon lights cast colorful shadows across his face, illuminating the stern set to his jaw, the sensuous slant to his lips.

"Isn't it too late to still be looking for Hallsey and your mash?"

"I'm not looking for either. The sheriff found the mash." She spent the next few minutes filling him in on Betty and Mitchell and Sheriff De-Massi's show of mercy with her sample. News she should have shared earlier with him, but the need to do just that had scared her even more than the thought of him walking away and so she'd kept her mouth shut and her hands off her phone.

"So you did it," he said, his expression softening into a look of pure excitement. "You sold the recipe."

She couldn't shake the smile that tugged at her lips. "I sure did."

"That's great, Brandy. Really great."

Only it didn't feel so great. Because while things had worked out for her, they still sucked for him and for some reason that knowledge kept her from being really and truly happy.

"Have you heard anything from Cooper?"

He shook his head. "Nothing." He slid onto the bar stool next to her and signaled the bartender. "Coors Lite."

A few seconds later, he held up the bottle. "Here's to the future success of Sweet Somethings. May she take the Texas wedding cake business by storm."

"May she snag her own feature in every major wedding mag in the state," Brandy added, doing her best to ignore the awareness zipping up and down her spine as she touched her glass to Tyler's.

"And to stupid cowboys who don't know a good thing when it's right in front of them," Ellie added, holding up her own glass. "Present company excluded," she went on when Tyler arched an eyebrow. "So, um, where's your buddy tonight?" she prodded in a nonchalant tone, as if the anxious light in her eyes didn't glow as brightly as the neon green Dos Equis sign hanging over the bar.

"He was getting in a little practice at the arena when I left a little while ago." Tyler chugged another swallow of beer. "He's got one of the local guys filling in for his partner while he polishes up his own technique."

"That's nice." Ellie took a swig of her drink and seemed to think. "Actually, that's not so nice. I called him to see if he wanted to hang out, but he didn't call me back. I guess he's not interested."

"That or he was too busy tying up a calf. When we're practicing, we usually leave our phones on the sidelines."

"Don't care," Ellie said, but it was obvious the piece of info had made her think.

"You should try him again," Tyler said.

"Why? So we can hook up and then he can dump me because he doesn't know a good thing when it bites him in the ass?"

"Or don't," he added, taking another long pull on his beer. He sat his own phone on the bar and stared at the screen.

"I won't," Ellie assured them, finishing off her drink. "I think I'm going home," she announced when she slid the glass back across the bartop. "I've got an early day tomorrow."

"Me, too—" Brandy started, but Ellie waved her off.

"Don't let me put a damper on the celebration. Keep going. I'll just call a cab."

Or a cowboy, Brandy thought as she watched her friend disappear outside, her phone in hand.

"You sure she'll be all right?"

"Once your buddy gets here to pick her up, I'm sure she'll be just fine. For a little while. Until he packs up and leaves."

"Maybe he'll ask her to go with him."

"And maybe she'll tell him to go to hell. She has a life here. Besides, if he likes her that much, why doesn't he just stay?"

"There's nothing for him here."

"She's here," Brandy pointed out, a statement that stirred a long moment of silence while he sipped his beer and she finished off her glass.

"Maybe it's not that simple. He's got a life somewhere else. A good life. A successful one. He can't just give it up."

"And she can't just give up hers."

She knew they were talking about Duff and Ellie, but the wealth of meaning behind the words hit her and her stomach hollowed out.

"It's hopeless, right?"

He didn't say anything. Instead, he shook his head, giving her the answer she'd dreaded.

It *was* hopeless, not that she'd ever thought otherwise. She'd known it was doomed from the beginning.

At the same time, when she was with him, so close she could feel the heat from his body, the strength of his determination, she found herself forgetting that all-important fact. She found herself thinking that maybe, just maybe they could work something out. She found herself hoping.

And hope was a bad thing when it came to a man. At least as far as Brandy was concerned.

"I really should get going myself," she blurted, eager to kill the crazy emotion pushing and pulling at her.

Because that's all it was. Crazy. Ludicrous. Ridiculous.

Brandy Tucker and Tyler McCall? Maybe in an alternate universe. But this was the real world.

Worse, it was Rebel, Texas.

"I'll give you a ride," he offered.

"That's okay. I'll just call a cab . . ." The words faded as she turned and caught sight of the man who walked into the bar.

"I can't let you do that—"

"It's Gator," she blurted, her gaze swiveling from the doorway to Tyler. "He's here."

Tyler turned in time to see Gator Hallsey stroll into the bar, but it wasn't the sight of the bootlegger that stole the air from his lungs. It was the man hot on his heels.

"Holy hell," he muttered, staring at Cooper McCall. The young man followed Gator inside, over to the small pool table in the corner.

Tyler's baby brother had changed in the two short years since he'd been a pimple-faced kid.

The acne had cleared up and his short hair had grown even longer, to brush the tops of his shoulders. He was the spitting image of the picture that sat on his mother's nightstand of their dad when he was younger.

A carbon copy of the worthless piece of shit who'd ruined all their lives.

And Cooper was walking the same path, making the same mistakes, getting caught in all the same worthless shit.

"Wait," Brandy called, her soft hand pulling at Tyler's arm, but he'd been waiting for this moment much too long to put on the brakes now.

"Catch a cab," he growled. He motioned to the bartender. "Get her out of here, understand?"

The man nodded and Tyler shook away the one touch that had helped him through the past few days. And then he made a beeline for his brother.

CHAPTER 30

"Where the hell have you been?" Tyler demanded when he reached the pool table.

Cooper glanced up. A flicker of fear gleamed in his gaze and he stiffened. "Tyler," he murmured. "What the fuck are you doing here?"

"Looking for you. That's all I've been doing for the past week, which you damn well know." In the corner of his eye, he saw the bartender usher Brandy outside and relief welled through him for a split second before the seriousness of the situation brought his anxiety level back up to overdrive. "My turn," he growled. "What the fuck are *you* doing?"

"Playing pool," offered Gator Hallsey, who came up behind Cooper and put a hand on his shoulder. "Is there a problem here?"

"Damn straight, there's a problem," Tyler said. "My brother is here when he should be at home getting ready to leave for College Station."

"About that," Cooper started. He shook his head. "The thing is," his gaze met Tyler's, "I'm not going."

"You damn well are," Tyler said. "You're going to college and then you're going to get a job and you're going to make something of yourself."

"I already have a job."

"Running shine isn't a job. It's a felony. Don't be an asshole, Coop. You can't throw everything away to hang around here. Christ, the whole point of everything is to get out of this shithole. That's what you always wanted."

"That's what *you* always wanted. I'm doing just fine here." The eighteen-year-old pulled a wad of cash out of his pocket and set it on the edge of the table. "Leave if you want to, but I'm staying."

"You heard the man," Gator said.

"He's not a man. He's a kid," Tyler started, reaching for Cooper's arm, but Gator was faster. He stepped up, the barrel of a very lethal-looking Glock pointed at Tyler's chest.

"He wants you to leave him alone."

"He's barely legal," Tyler said. "He doesn't know what he wants."

"And you do?" Cooper turned on him. "You don't know me. You haven't known me for a long time because you're not here. You're never here. It's just me and Mom all the time."

"Coop, I can't—"

"I know, I know. You can't be in two places at one time. You have to ride, but I don't. I don't have to be someplace else. Anyplace else. I can be here. I'm okay with being here. Mom likes me here."

"She doesn't even know you're here half the time. And the other half, she doesn't care. Don't you get that?"

"Damn straight, I get it. I always did. She doesn't care, but so what? I don't need a nurse-maid. I don't need you. I don't need anybody. I'm doing just fine by myself."

"Really?" He stared at Cooper so hard that his brother actually looked away. But not before Tyler saw the rush of insecurity. The fear.

Because his brother wasn't half as afraid to stay in Rebel as he was to go. To fail.

"I'm not you," Coop said. "I'm not some big-time rodeo rider. I'm good at math. That's it. And driving. And I like driving a hell of a lot more than I like doing math."

"What's he talking about?" Gator asked.

"He was offered a scholarship to Texas A and M." Tyler expected the man to scoff, to start talking about loser geeks and how Cooper was so much better off working for him.

"You're fucking with me, right?" Gator said, his expression unreadable.

"A full ride," Tyler added. "He's a smart kid. Too smart to be involved with you."

The gun pushed into his chest a fraction more, the finger on the trigger tapping ever so lightly, and every muscle in Tyler's body went on full alert. Brandy's breath caught behind him and he damned himself for rushing over and not getting her out to safety first. But he'd been looking for Cooper for so long . . .

"Get out of here," Gator said, shoving the tip of the gun deeper into Tyler's chest for a long moment before pulling away, tucking the firearm into his waistband, and turning back to the pool table. "And take the kid with you."

"What?" Cooper turned.

"You heard me. Get the hell out of here. Both of you."

"But I thought you liked my driving."

"It isn't about that," Gator said, his gaze shifting to Cooper. "You're too smart to be so stupid, kid. A&M? Seriously?" He shook his head. "Go on and get out of here. Now."

"Let's go," Tyler told his brother. Cooper didn't look as if he wanted to comply, but then a glimmer of relief flickered in his gaze and Tyler knew that Cooper wasn't half as sure about giving up his future and sticking around to work for Gator Hallsey as he pretended to be.

"You can't tell me what to do," he told Tyler before snatching up the keys and the money on the table and heading for the door. "You're not my boss."

"You better nip that shit in the bud," Gator told Tyler once Cooper had disappeared out the doorway. "You make sure he goes to College Station, even if you have to hog-tie him and haul him up there yourself." The *clackkk* of pool balls punctuated the sentence.

"Why did you do that?" Tyler asked when the man pulled back to survey the table.

"Do what?" Gator chalked the end of his pool cue.

"Let him go like that."

The bootlegger grinned, revealing a row of straight white teeth and a smile that had probably charmed many a female into the backseat of his souped-up car. "Maybe I'm just a nice guy."

"Try again."

His grin faded. "Maybe I know what it's like to want something for somebody more than he wants it for himself." He turned then, his gaze catching Tyler's. "I had a brother once. I didn't keep near as close an eye on him as I should have. I won't get a chance to correct that mistake because he's gone. Cooper's alive and well and not a half-bad kid, and you're still in the game. Don't lose. And make sure he keeps his mouth shut about our recent business dealings. Or else."

"Thanks."

Gator didn't say anything. He just nodded, turned, and leaned over the table. The pool cue cracked again and a striped blue ball sailed into the nearest pocket.

Tyler turned, grabbed Brandy's arm, and headed for the parking lot. Cooper had already left, but Tyler had a good idea where to find him.

"You should have left when I first told you to," he said a few minutes later as he fed her into a cab.

"And let you get shot? No thanks. I dodged

one felony today. I'm not about to witness another."

"And here I thought you were worried about me," he murmured before brushing a kiss across her lips. One that lingered a little too long considering he was pissed at her and she didn't give a shit about him.

"Go easy on him," she breathed against his lips before she pulled back and signaled the driver.

The cab grumbled out of the parking lot and Tyler ignored the strange emptiness that filled him. Instead, he headed for his truck.

Twenty minutes later, he pulled through the entrance of the Happy Times Trailer Park. Just as he'd hoped, Cooper's old truck sat in the driveway, the engine still running, as if the kid wasn't half as content right here in Rebel as he wanted Tyler to think.

He killed the engine, climbed out of his truck, and walked around to the passenger side of Cooper's ride. Opening the door, he climbed in and sat there for a few long moments next to his brother as he contemplated what to say.

"I made some good money." His brother broke the silence first.

"I know you did. But it's not nearly good enough to warrant the risk. I know you think Gator and his buddies have it all figured out, but they do what they do because they have no choice. They don't have anything better waiting for them."

"What makes you think I do?"

"You have a scholarship, for Christ's sake."

"All contingent on how well I do each and every semester. Do you know if I blow it even one semester I could lose everything? If I can't keep up my grades, that's it."

"And?"

"And I'll be right back here."

"No, you won't. If you blow it, I'll pay for it." Coop shook his head. "I can't let you do that."

"Then you get a student loan. A grant. We'll figure out something. If that situation even comes up. Right now, the possibilities are endless. It's all a matter of moving forward, of trying."

"What about Mom?"

"What about her? She'll be fine. She's got enough money, and I'll make sure she doesn't go without. Beyond that, she doesn't matter, Cooper. She doesn't give a shit about us. She never did. And while I know you keep hoping for some moment of realization, some happily-ever-after where she realizes what a bitch she's been and decides to change her ways, sometimes things just don't work out that way in real life. Sometimes the best you can hope for is to change yourself, not anybody else. That's all we can do."

Cooper didn't say anything. He just killed the engine, climbed out of the truck, and walked toward the trailer.

"You're going," Tyler called after him. "And call Erin. She's been worried sick about you."

His brother still didn't turn. Instead, he paused

at the door, drew a deep breath, and then went inside. No doubt with his hopes high that maybe this time things would be different. That their mother would be different.

Fat chance.

Tyler damned the woman a thousand times and climbed out of the old truck. Walking back to his own Chevy, he climbed into the driver's seat and slammed the door.

CHAPTER 31

Tyler meant to head back to the rodeo arena.

His brother was safe and sound for now.

But the real test would come when he boarded the bus for Texas A&M in a week.

Would Cooper follow through?

The question haunted him and made him even more restless because he knew that if his brother lost his nerve and went back to Gator and his crew again, there wouldn't be a second out.

There would be nothing Tyler could do about it.

Just as he hadn't been able to keep his dad from walking out, he wasn't going to be able to keep Cooper from making the biggest mistake of his life.

The truth ate at Tyler as he hauled ass down the gravel road that led to town. But instead of turning down the main Farm Road, he found himself heading for the second turn that led away from Rebel, straight to Brandy.

She might not have gone home. Maybe she'd stopped off at the bakery. Or another bar. She could have gone someplace else to keep the party going.

She'd done it. She'd signed a deal with Foggy Bottom Distillers and now her future was set.

And his?

His shoulder ached from the last fall he'd taken on Junkyard Dog. One that Brett, himself, had witnessed and then chewed Tyler a new one about what he'd done wrong.

Too many things to count, but Brett could help.

He would help.

That was the other piece of good news.

But Tyler didn't feel so good.

He felt desperate. Uncertain. Anxious.

Was she out celebrating with another man?

While most folks might think so, Tyler knew better. He knew her. She wouldn't do that. While she might be interested in merely a good time, she wanted it with him.

He knew that much.

He felt it, and so he took the dirt road that led to the Tucker spread and the old Oldsmobile parked in the gravel driveway. Parking his truck, he climbed out and headed for the front steps. A quick knock and he waited.

She hauled open the door on the third knock. Wearing a pair of shorts and an oversized T-shirt, she looked soft and rumpled from sleep and he felt a moment's regret that he'd obviously pulled her out of bed.

Until her gaze met his and he read the raw need blazing deep in the depths of her eyes.

"What's wrong?" Concern edged out the hunger, and a strange warmth spread through him.

"I talked to Cooper," he murmured. He didn't mean to tell her. He meant to push her backward and plaster his mouth against hers, no words required. But there was just something about the way she looked at him. As if she cared what he had to say.

What he felt.

"I don't know what's gotten into him. I told him what an idiot he's being, but he won't listen. He's got a quick way to some easy money and suddenly studying for the next four years doesn't have the same appeal. He doesn't realize that what he's doing is going to get him put away for a lot longer than four years."

"He's still got a few days. He's smart. He'll wise up."

"And what if he doesn't?" He voiced the one fear that nagged at him. That his brother would really and truly throw it all away. Just like their dad.

That Tyler would bust his own ass and do the same in Cheyenne.

"He will. You just need to give it some time. Trust me, my sister has made her fair share of mistakes, but she might finally be getting her act together. Just last night she swore to break up with her latest boyfriend face-to-face and straightforward. Talk about being spared six months of stalking."

The wind trembled the bushes to her right. "And maybe not." She grabbed Tyler's arm and pulled him inside before sticking her head back out and yelling, "She's not here. She had an all-nighter at the clinic." The bushes trembled again and the sound of footsteps echoed and faded into the grumble of an engine.

"That should get rid of him for a while," she said, turning back to Tyler.

"I'm sorry I didn't make it back to the apartment that night," he heard himself say before he could think better of it. "I shouldn't have left you high and dry."

She shrugged. "You changed your mind. It's fine."

"I didn't change anything. I still want this." His gaze collided with hers. "I want you." And then he did what he'd wanted to do ever since she opened the door: He pulled her close and covered her mouth with his.

Sex, Brandy told herself, throwing herself into the single act of kissing Tyler McCall, desperate to ignore the strange feelings that had assailed her the moment she'd found him standing on her doorstep next to the old dusty swing where her parents had sat every Friday night.

One look at the rickety wood and she'd had the sudden vision of herself, barefoot and pregnant, rocking back and forth, Tyler next to her, no cakes or cookies in sight.

Like hell.

No matter how good he kissed. Or how he pulled her close and rubbed the base of her spine with his thumb until she wanted to melt onto her back and purr. Or how he held her close, his arms solid and strong and possessive, as if she actually meant more to him than a few moments of pleasure.

This wasn't about forever.

It was about this moment, this kiss, *this* . . .

For the next few moments, she drank in the taste and feel of him, ran her hands up and down his solid arms, relished the ripple of muscle as he cupped her buttocks and pulled her closer, treasured the whisper of joy because they were together one more time. One last time.

The thought fed her desperation and she held on to him tighter as he rocked her, his hardness pressing into her. Heat flowered low in her belly, spreading from one nerve ending to the next until every inch of her body burned and sizzled like a match just struck.

She moaned into his mouth, communicating her need in a way that no words could touch. Without breaking the kiss, he swung her into his arms and headed down the hall for the nearest bedroom.

A few seconds later, her feet touched down in the small room she'd shared with Callie when they were children. Her sister had moved out once their parents had died, and Brandy had repainted the lime green with a bright pink that matched the bakery boxes she used at her shop. Frilly pink curtains framed the two windows that faced the side of the house. It was an ultrafeminine room that made Tyler McCall seem that much more masculine and dangerous by comparison.

A ripple of excitement went through her and she pressed herself up against him again. Need mounted and multiplied as she clawed at his shirt. He caught her wrists and pulled back, his grin slow and wicked and dangerous.

"Easy. We've got all night, sugar."

"I've got to be at the bakery early for my apple loaves."

"Early as in six or seven?"

"Four, so you'd better start undressing." She meant to rip off her clothes and get busy, but then he touched her and her breath caught. Time seemed to stand still as he pulled her close. The hands that slid from her shoulder to her collarbone, and down, were strong and sure and possessive.

As if he were branding her his and only his.

Just as the thought struck, he touched the tip of her nipple through the soft fabric of her tee. The ripe tip throbbed in response and she barely caught the whimper that jumped to her lips.

He pressed a kiss to her lips then, coaxing them open with his tongue before delving deep for a long, heart-pounding moment. "I love every sound that you make," he murmured when he finally pulled away. "Every gasp. Every whimper. Every cry."

He pulled the shirt up and over her head, his hot fingertips grazing her skin, and she forgot everything except the need churning inside her.

Brandy closed her eyes and tilted her head back, arching her chest forward. She all but screamed at the first stroke of his callused thumb over her bare breast. The next several moments passed in a dizzying blur as he plucked and rolled her sensitive nipples, until they were red and ripe and aching for more.

He blazed a trail down her rib cage, his palms warm against her stomach. A deep male growl vibrated up his throat when his hands slid into her panties and found her wet and ready. One fingertip parted her swollen flesh and dipped inside.

She cried out, grabbing his shoulders, clutching fabric as she fought to feel his bare skin against her own.

He leaned back far enough and let her peel the material up and over his head. She tossed the T-shirt and went for his jeans, but he'd beaten her to the punch, his tanned fingers working at the zipper.

Metal grated and the jeans sagged onto his hips. He stepped back far enough to push them down and kick them free until he stood before her wearing only a pair of white briefs. He was rock-hard beneath the clingy cotton. A heartbeat later, the full length of him sprang forward, huge and greedy, as he pushed his underwear down and kicked it to the side.

But it wasn't the sight of him naked and tanned and fully aroused that took her breath away, it was the heat burning in his gaze, making his eyes brighter and even more translucent. Like a shimmering Caribbean oasis reflecting the hot sun.

And oh how she wanted to dive in headfirst and hold her breath for as long as possible. *Forever.*

"Aren't you forgetting something?" she breathed when he made no move to remove her last item of clothing—a pair of skimpy bikini panties decorated with tiny pink polka dots.

"Soon," he murmured. He cupped her, his palm warm through the thin covering.

An ache flowered low in her belly. "Soon isn't soon enough. I can't wait, Tyler. I need to feel you." Anxiety zipped up and down her spine, along with a ripple of fear. "I want to feel you."

Because she didn't *want* to want him so deeply. So desperately.

If only she didn't keep forgetting that all-important fact.

CHAPTER 32

He dipped one finger past the elastic, into the steamy heat between her legs. He stroked and teased and a sweet pressure tightened low in her belly. It was the most erotic fizzle of sensation, the most decadent, and it stalled the air in her lungs and made her body burn for something more potent than oxygen.

A few heartbeats later, he slid his finger into her slowly, tantalizingly, stirring every nerve to vibrant awareness until he was as deep as he could go, and then he withdrew at the same leisurely pace. Advance, retreat.

Until her heart pounded so hard and her breath came so fast, she thought she would hyperventilate. Or go up in flames. Or both.

She was close.

So close . . .

"Not yet," he murmured, withdrawing his hand before dropping to his knees in front of her. "I want to see if you still taste like blueberries." He touched his mouth to her navel, dipped his tongue inside, and slid his hands around to cup her bottom for a long moment before moving his mouth lower. His tongue dipped under the waistband of her panties. He licked her bare flesh before drawing back to drag his mouth over her lace-covered mound. His lips feathered a kiss over ground zero and her legs buckled. "Mmm," he murmured, "definitely blueberries."

"Too much talking, not enough tasting," she managed, her hands going to his bare shoulders to keep her from falling.

A warm chuckle sent shivers down the inside of her thighs before he lifted his head and caught the waistband of her underwear with one finger. He drew the material down, lips and teeth following the decadent path and skimming her bare flesh. Her entire body trembled by the time she stepped free.

"My turn," she managed, determined to give as good as she was getting. So good.

"I don't have any underwear on." He pushed to his feet and faced her.

"I'll figure something out." She knelt and kissed his navel, swirling her tongue and relishing the deep male groan that vibrated the air around them. She grasped him in her hand, running her palm down the length of his erection. He was hot and hard and she did what she'd been wanting to do ever since she'd seen him standing there completely nude. She took him into her mouth and laved him with her tongue. One lick. Two. Until a low hiss issued from between his lips.

He grasped her head, his fingers splaying in her hair, guiding her, urging her—

"Stop." The word was little more than a groan before he pulled her to her feet. "I want to come inside you." He urged her down onto the bed. "I need to come inside of you."

She watched as he withdrew a foil placket from his jean pocket and put on a condom in record time.

"I thought you wanted slow and easy," she said as he settled himself between her thighs, his penis pressing into her a decadent inch.

"It'll be easy," he promised, "I'm just not so sure about the *slow* part." Before she could comment, he pressed her thighs wider, grasped her hips, and slid into her with one deep thrust.

He stilled for a long moment, letting her feel every pulsing, vibrating inch of him. Her body reacted the way it always did, holding him deep, tight, massaging him in an intimate way that wrung a gasp from his lips.

But it wasn't the connection of their bodies so much as the way he stared down at her, into her, that sent a rush of warmth through her. As if he could see everything about her instead of just her reputation. No one ever looked at her like that and it touched something inside of her.

She closed her eyes, fighting back the sudden tears that threatened to overwhelm her. This was crazy. This was all about feeling good, not about *feeling*.

Sex wasn't love, and she had no intention of confusing the two. Especially with a man like Tyler. He'd said himself that he didn't want more.

"Are you okay?" His voice was soft and deep and so tender she had to fight back another wave of tears.

She swallowed and forced her voice past the lump in her throat. "Stop talking and just fuck me, cowboy."

His mouth opened at her bold words and she thought he was going to make a smart comeback, but then he dipped his head and his lips closed over her nipple. Thankfully. She needed a distraction from the strange feelings threatening to overwhelm her.

All thought faded into a wave of delicious pressure as he suckled her with enough force to wind her even tighter while his erection pulsed inside her. The sensation of him drawing on her breast while her body milked him was a double whammy and oh, so potent.

He moved, pumping into her, pushing her higher—stroke after stroke—until she cried out, her nails digging into his back as she climaxed.

Several frantic heartbeats later, her eyelids fluttered open just in time to see him throw his head back, his eyes clamped tightly shut. He thrust deep one final time and stiffened, every muscle in his body going rigid. Her name tumbled from his lips, riding a raw moan of pure male satisfaction. A burst of satisfaction rolled through her because she knew that while he might, indeed, walk away from her, he would never forget the way she made him feel.

He collapsed beside her and gathered her close, pulling her back against him in spoon fashion. His chest was solid against her back, his arms strong and powerful around her. Warmth seeped through her, lulling her heartbeat for the next several minutes as their bodies cooled.

"I think the dog likes me." His deep voice slid into Brandy's ears and she opened her eyes to see Jez standing beside the bed, her tail wagging, her tongue lolling as she stared up expectantly.

"She's not my dog. She belongs to Jenna."

"She looks mighty cozy in here not to belong to you," he said, watching as the dog trotted over to the far corner and settled on a discarded apron. She buried her nose in the pink fabric and closed her eyes.

"It's the bakery smell that attracts her. She's got a sweet tooth."

"So do I." His deep voice sent a whisper of heat along Brandy's nerve endings, but it wasn't the heat that wrapped around her and settled deep in her belly. It was a sense of contentment, and she realized in a startling instant that she liked having Tyler curled around her as much as she'd liked having him deep inside.

Maybe more.

"I really need to get dressed," she blurted, suddenly desperate for a quick exit strategy from the crazy feelings.

Before she could blink, she found herself yanked onto her back. Tyler glared down at her for a long moment as if the comment actually bothered him. Ridiculous, of course, because nothing she said or did seemed to really shake that charming, controlled demeanor.

Sure enough, his expression eased, quickly killing her theory as a slow, sensual smile crept across his lips.

"Not until I get one more sugar fix." He slid down her body, his large hands going to the inside of her thighs. He spread her legs wide and scorched her with a heated glance before leaning in to press his lips against her pussy. Slow. Sensuous. Tender.

She didn't want tender. She wanted wild and wicked and hot, and over. That's what she really wanted. To be done with him. To move on.

The trouble was, she wasn't done with him. Not yet, anyhow.

And so she relaxed back against the pillows, closed her eyes, and let him love her with his mouth. For just a little while, anyhow.

CHAPTER 33

Time's up!

Tyler's days in Rebel were almost over.

He knew that, but he couldn't make himself leave just yet.

Not when he had Brett Sawyer himself giving him pointers and helping him on his ride. That, and he fully intended to be there on Monday when Cooper boarded that bus for Texas A&M.

And Brandy?

With each day that passed, Tyler was finding it harder and harder to remember that this was just sex. Temporary.

Because it felt more permanent than anything else in his life. More right. He found himself looking forward to the little things. Counting on them. Seeing her smile when he kissed the tip of her nose. Holding her until the crack of dawn. Listening to her off-key singing in the shower. *Liking* her off-key singing in the shower.

Brandy Tucker was the last woman he needed to fall in love with. She'd made it clear that she didn't want anything beyond a physical relationship. She'd made no false promises, left no room for maybe. She was a Tucker and he was a Sawyer and while her older sister had defied the odds, Brandy had no desire to do the same.

She was all about her business. Her future.

And he couldn't blame her. Heaven to hell, but he felt the same.

If only he could shake the crazy feelings pushing and pulling inside of him. He needed to switch them off and simply enjoy whatever time they had left together.

But damned if he didn't want her to feel the same riot of emotion. To miss him when he climbed out of bed in the morning, to look forward to his company every night, to want to see him in a capacity that didn't involve getting naked.

Hell, maybe she already did.

The thing was, there was no way to really know because the sex was muddying the waters. She might already like the little things as much as he did. She might like him.

Enough to thumb her nose at a one-hundred-year-old feud?

He wasn't sure, but there was only one way to find out.

"This isn't part of the deal." Brandy stood in the kitchen of her bakery and fed flour into her giant mixer. "Since when do you want to know how to bake?"

"Since I'm on the road most of the time and it

might be nice to whip up something in the motel kitchenette that doesn't come frozen in a box with a set of heating instructions. I happen to like apple pie and you happen to make the best in town, so I figured you could help me out." He'd pulled his shirttails free of his jeans and unfastened the top buttons of his western shirt. The vee afforded her a glimpse of silky chest hair and tanned skin.

Her stomach tingled and her nipples tightened and all was right with her world.

Sex.

That's all it was between them. It wasn't as if she liked standing next to him, working side by side, as a slow, twangy country song drifted from the radio sitting atop a nearby shelf. It was all about the heat that raged between them. The intense lust. The overwhelming physical attraction. About packing as much punch as they could into their short time together so that she could work out all her frustrations and get her mind back on her business.

She held tight to the thought as she retrieved several cold chunks of butter from the large stainless-steel refrigerator. Thankfully, she could feel his eyes following her as she reached for a pastry cutter and chopped up the butter before tossing it into the flour. Her skin prickled with awareness as he moved next to her and added half a cup of the ice water sitting nearby. Her nipples tingled. Her tummy quivered.

He turned and his arm brushed against her

breast. A tiny thrill of excitement zipped up her spine. He stared deep into her eyes and for a split second, she felt him lean forward. His warm breath brushed her lips and she closed her eyes. This was more like it. They could forget all this domestic crap and get to the really good stuff. He was going to kiss her—

"Oops, I think I left my cell phone in the car," he murmured before planting a kiss on the tip of her nose. "Don't add anything else until I get back."

Her nose. He'd kissed her nose, of all things.

Her skin tingled and a strange warmth stole through her. Okay, so it was nice, but still. It wasn't what she'd expected.

The sound of his footsteps drew her from the emotional push–pull. Her eyes popped open in time to see him disappear into the front of the bakery. The bell jingled on the front door as he headed outside and she found herself alone.

Her chest hitched at the thought. A ridiculous reaction because the solitude gave her a few minutes to pull herself together and remember that she wasn't here for *nice*.

She drew a deep, shaky breath and hit the on button on the mixer. The machine grumbled, incorporating the ingredients together until a ball of dough started to form.

She focused her complete attention on adding a tiny bit more flour until the dough reached the perfect consistency to work with.

"It looks good."

The deep voice stirred the hair on the back of her neck and sent a jolt of awareness through her. Her hands trembled and the flour pitched forward into the mixer. The beaters stirred and a cloud of white dust hit her in the face.

Tyler's deep chuckle sent tingled through her body. "I didn't realize a faceful of flour was part of the recipe for a good crust." He reached out and wiped a smudge from one cheek. The feel of his skin against hers sent a jolt of heat straight to her nipples.

"Very funny." She turned and reached for a dish towel. "Do you always sneak up on people?" After wiping at her face, she slapped at the sprinkle of white clouding her apron.

His eyes twinkled and his sensuous mouth crooked. "So." He glanced around. "Where did you learn how to do all of this?"

"My mom." The words were out before she could stop them. This wasn't about having a conversation. It was about getting to the good stuff. The physical stuff. "She loved to bake. She won a bunch of contests when she was young. She even placed in the national Pillsbury Bake-Off. She could have gone on to have her own bakery. That was the plan, at least. But then she met my dad and started having kids and she got too busy raising us to even think of opening her own place. She still baked at home and she taught me, and now I'm living the dream for the both of us." She caught his stare. "What about you? How did you get into bull riding?"

He shrugged. "I used to hang out at the arena and watch my cousin Brett. He made it look so easy and I figured why not try?" He shook his head.

"Easy, huh?"

"Okay, so maybe he just made it look appealing. He was the king when he was on top of that bull. A Sawyer through and through, and I guess I wanted to prove that I was just as much a Sawyer as he was."

"But you *are* a Sawyer."

"And you're a Tucker." His grin was slow and wicked and her heart skipped a beat. "Hey, maybe I should get my shotgun."

Before she could stop herself, she popped him with the dish towel and his grin faded into a look of pure shock. "What was that for?"

"In case you haven't heard, we Tuckers don't like you Sawyers all that much," she said, turning back to wipe the sides of the mixer. She finished up and set the dish towel aside before hitting the ON button again. "You're the enemy," she said with a wealth of conviction. He was the enemy. But not because of his last name.

Rather, he threatened her peace of mind. Her future.

She turned then and her gaze caught his. Understanding gleamed so hot and bright in his eyes and a sudden rush of warmth went through her. A feeling that had nothing to do with the lust that burned between them and everything to do with the fact that while Tyler McCall might be her enemy, and she was his, as well, he still felt more for her than he wanted to admit, and it scared him.

Yeah, right.

She tossed the dough onto a slice of plastic wrap and secured the edges before popping it into the refrigerator to chill. "So we're doing apple, huh?" she asked as she turned back to him.

He arched an eyebrow and his mouth hinted at a grin. "Is there any other kind of pie?"

His expression was infectious and she couldn't help but smile. "Oh, I don't know. I'm a big chocolate fan, myself." She grabbed the bowl of Granny Smiths and started to core and peel.

"Chocolate's good. But warm, gooey, spiced apples?" He made a *mmm-mmm* sound. "There's nothing better."

"Nothing, huh?"

"Well, maybe one thing," Tyler's deep voice whispered into her ears as he came up behind her. "I do have a hankering for blueberries, too." One hand slid around her waist while the other closed over hers.

"You don't have to do this." *What the hell?* a voice whispered. This was exactly what he needed to do. To get them off the topic of baking and bull riding, and back onto the real reason they'd agreed to spend time together—sex.

She knew that. But her heart beat double time anyway, as if there was much more at stake than getting busy in her kitchen.

The fingertips that held her frantic grip on the apple peeler slid down until his thumb massaged the inside of her palm. The heat started at the tips of her toes, traveling upward until her cheeks burned. Air lodged in her chest and she couldn't seem to catch her breath.

"It's nice, smooth strokes, right?" Tyler murmured, the words little more than a breathless whisper against the sensitive shell of her ear. He held her hand as he slid the peeler over the edge of the Granny Smith in one fluid motion. "Like this?"

She wanted to say yes, but she couldn't seem to find the words.

She became instantly aware of his hard male body flush against hers, her bottom nestled in the cradle of his thighs. His erection pressed into her, leaving no doubt that he was turned on.

Extremely so.

Her mouth tingled and she had the insane urge to turn into the warm lips nuzzling her ear.

A perfectly natural reaction given the situation. A perfectly physical reaction.

Yet there was more at stake at the moment.

She felt it in the double tap of her heart. In the strange fluttering in the pit of her stomach. Both physical reactions.

The thing was, she'd never felt either with any man before. She'd never wanted to feel anything. To turn into her mother.

To lose her dream. Herself.

No man was worth that.

Not even *this* man.

Her man.

The thought struck and before she could drop-kick it out of her mind, she turned.

And then she wasn't just thinking about kissing him, she was actually leaning forward, sliding her arms around his neck, and pressing her lips to his.

CHAPTER 34

She was kissing him.

Tyler felt a split second of panic as her lips parted. Her tongue touched, swirled, and teased. She didn't hold anything back.

Which meant he should have taken the lead and put on the brakes right then and there. This wasn't about sex. It was about like. About spending time together and figuring out if she felt even half of what he did. Just for his own peace of mind. To fill up those long, lonely nights when he was far, far away from Rebel.

At the same time, there was something desperate about her touch. As if this kiss meant more than all the others they'd shared over the past few days.

The thought intoxicated him even more than the sweet taste of her lips. He planted one hand on the back of her head, tilted her face to the side, and kissed her thoroughly. Deeply.

He nibbled her bottom lip and explored the interior of her mouth. When he couldn't breathe, he slid his lips across her cheek and along her jaw. His mouth slipped to the side of her neck and he pushed her hair down her back. She smelled of apples and sugar, and warm, feminine skin. He breathed her in for a long, heart-pounding moment and closed his eyes. He thought of all the things he wanted to do with her.

Everything.

He ached to see her soapy and wet in his shower. Naked and panting against his sheets. Smiling and laughing across the breakfast table—

He killed the last thought and concentrated on the lust that rolled through him like a ball of fire that dive-bombed straight to his dick. He edged her sideways until they were clear of the apples and pie fixings, then bent her back over the countertop and captured her lips again.

He fed off her mouth for several long moments, tasting and savoring, before nibbling his way down the sexy column of her throat.

His cock throbbed, and it was all he could do to keep from shoving his zipper down, parting her legs, and plunging fast and deep inside her hot, tight body.

Now. Right. Friggin'. *Now.*

He wouldn't.

He didn't want just sex anymore. He wanted to know that she felt something more.

Love?

Hell, he was the last person to even know what love was. He'd never been in love. He'd spent his younger years barely surviving, and his teenage years trying to do more than just survive. He'd never had time for anything more than sex.

He didn't have time for it now.

But he wanted it.

Not that he wanted her to fall madly in love with him or anything bat-shit crazy like that. He just wanted to know that she at least felt *something* for him. Something that might make her as reluctant to see him leave as he was to go.

Not mind-changing or anything that extreme. Just a little regretful. And that meant slowing down enough to give her time to feel. To think. To long for him the way he longed for her.

He stiffened against the desire slamming through him and concentrated on the small cry that bubbled from her lips when he licked her pulse beat. He liked pleasing her, so he held tight to his control and paced himself. With each touch of his lips, she made some sort of sound. A sigh. A gasp. A cry that fed the need whirling through him and cheered him on.

When he reached the neckline of her shirt, he traced the edge where her skin met the material with his tongue. Her breathy moan was his reward and he smiled against her flushed skin. He unfastened the apron tied around her neck. The material gave and slipped to her waist until she was wearing nothing but the signature hot-pink T-shirt of Sweet Somethings. He trailed his fingertips over the soft fabric, tracing the goodies underneath—her rib cage, the undersides of her luscious breasts, the indentation of her belly button.

He slid his hands down, tugging the ends of the cotton free of her shorts and plunging underneath until he felt bare skin. Heat zapped him like a live wire and his pulse jumped. He touched the lace of her bra, tracing a path to the luscious plumpness of her breasts at the edge. A quick tug on the front clasp and her breasts spilled free.

Grabbing her sweet round ass, he lifted her, hoisting her onto the countertop. He stepped between her legs, pulled the T-shirt up and over her head, and caught one ripe nipple between his lips. He suckled her and she arched against him.

He pushed her back down, still sucking as he tugged at the button of her shorts and shoved the zipper down. She wiggled and the shorts sagged on her thighs.

He slid a finger inside the edge of her panties, straight into her slick folds, and her body bucked. He plunged another finger inside, wiggling and teasing and testing.

He wanted to feel every steamy secret. Even more, he wanted to taste her.

Tearing his mouth from hers, he worked his way down, kissing and teasing and tasting until he reached her hot-pink panties. He glanced up and his gaze caught hers for a brief moment as he pushed the panties down her hips, her legs, until the shorts hit the ground and the scrap of lace soon followed. Then he dipped his head.

He licked the very tip of her clit with his tongue and she shuddered. She opened wider, an invitation that he couldn't resist. He trailed his tongue over her clit and down the slit before dipping it inside.

She was warm and sweet and more addictive than her prize-winning apple pie. Hunger gripped him hard and fast. He sucked on the swollen nub and plunged his tongue inside until her entire body went stiff.

"Come on, baby," he murmured. He gripped her thighs and held her tight. "Let go."

A few more licks and she did just that.

A cry rumbled from her throat and tremors racked her body. He drank her in, savoring her essence until her body stilled.

He pulled away and stared down at her.

"Please. Just do it. Do it now," she murmured, her eyes closed, her face flushed. Her chest rose and fell to a frantic rhythm that made his groin throb and his entire body ache. She was so beautiful. So damn sweet. He wanted her more than he'd ever wanted any woman.

But even more, he wanted her to want him more than she'd ever wanted any other man.

He needed the truth of that to warm him on all the cold nights to come.

"I think the apples are turning brown."

Her eyelids fluttered open. "What?"

He took a huge drink of oxygen and forced his hands away from her. "The peeled apples. We need to do something with them before they turn brown."

"Apples? You're worried about the pie?" Her gaze swiveled toward the forgotten fruit.

"Oh, no." Her cheeks fired a brighter red as she reached for her T-shirt.

She dressed at the speed of light and then disappeared into the storage room as if she couldn't get away from him fast enough.

As if she'd just realized she'd made a big, big mistake.

"We really should let the dough chill for at least an hour and I need to pick up a few things at the Piggly Wiggly before they close," she said when she walked out, her expression unreadable, her purse in hand. "We should do this another time."

"Sure thing."

"I know I said we could do it now, but I really am running low on sugar and—what did you just say?"

He winked. "If you have to leave, you have to leave."

"That's okay with you?"

"I'd rather you stay and finish the pie, but duty calls." He arched an eyebrow. "You can wait, can't you?"

"Um, yeah. Of course." She turned and snatched up her keys perched on a nearby hook. "I'll just head out then."

"Later, sugar," he called after her.

"Don't bet on it," she muttered under her

breath, and a rush of satisfaction went through Tyler. He'd won this battle. He'd given her just enough to make her think.

Now if he could only win the war.

They weren't having sex.

It had been several days since the pie disaster on Saturday morning and other than a few hot kisses and some heavy petting, she wasn't any closer to working Tyler McCall out of her system. She needed the real deal for that. At least that's what she was telling herself.

Meanwhile, the clock was ticking.

All the more reason she needed him inside of her and her wrapped around him and an orgasm. A major, mind-blowing orgasm during the actual deed. The preliminary stuff . . . It was working her up too much and she needed to work off some steam. To shed her anxiety.

Her worry.

Because Tyler would put his brother on a bus on Monday—in exactly four days—and then his very reason for being in Rebel would be gone, headed to College Station and the rest of his life.

And she would go back to being alone.

Lonely.

Real sex.

That was all she needed to relieve the tension in her shoulders and ease the anxiety knotting her stomach. She held tight to the truth as he ended the heavy-duty petting session that had started the minute she'd arrived on his doorstep late Thursday night, after a long day at the bakery and a phone call from Sheriff DeMassi telling her he wanted yet another look at her grandpa's room.

All the more reason she should have headed home to get a good night's sleep before he came calling first thing in the morning to pick through all the boxes yet again.

But Brandy wanted more. She wanted to see Tyler, to touch him, to prove to herself that he was still real and here and that he did, indeed, want her as much as she wanted him, and so she'd headed to the rodeo arena.

And straight into his bed.

For about fifteen minutes, she felt convinced her dry spell was about to end. But then he pulled away, kissed her one last time with enough passion to make her hormones literally cry, and rolled over to go to sleep.

Sleep.

Seriously?

She tossed and turned and did everything she could to keep him up, but then he slid an arm around her and pulled her back flush against his body. Her hopes soared one last time, but then she heard the deep snore directly in her ear.

"You can't be serious?" she muttered, barely resisting the urge to pinch the hell out of his arm.

But the solid muscle wrapped around her did feel good and she found herself relaxing a little.

Enough to stop contemplating revenge plots and actually close her eyes for a few moments.

It *had* been a long day and this was sort of nice, too.

Not that she was falling sleep.

She had an early morning with the sheriff, then she had an elaborate wedding cake to finish up at the bakery, delivery at noon. She didn't need this tonight.

No relaxing. No sleep. *No.*

CHAPTER 35

Brandy fell asleep.

The truth sank in several hours later when her eyes finally popped open and she realized that it was almost five o'clock in the morning.

She'd fallen hard and fast, but he hadn't.

Her gaze went to the empty stretch of sheets beside her. Obviously he'd been the one to beat a hasty retreat this time and now she was all by her lonesome.

All the better.

She needed to leave anyhow.

She certainly wasn't going to lie there and wonder where in the world he'd run off to at five o'clock in the morning. Probably some early-morning training session. Or some powwow with his brother. Or maybe he was out helping Duff with something.

Not that she cared.

She rolled onto her right side and punched the pillow a few more times before snuggling back down. There. She was going to close her eyes and she wasn't going to remember the happiness in his eyes when he'd opened the door to her. As if she'd just turned on the light after a long, dark night.

As if.

She sat up and climbed out of the bed. A few steps and she managed to retrieve her clothes. She pulled on everything and gathered up her purse.

"Can't sleep?" The deep, husky timbre met her the minute she stepped outside the door and started down the stairs toward the dark rodeo arena.

She found Tyler standing in the shadows at the bottom. The sight of him wearing nothing but a pair of snug, faded jeans stalled her heart for a long moment. Soft denim molded to his lean hips and strong thighs, and cupped his crotch.

He had the hard, well-defined physique of a rough-and-tough bull rider. Broad shoulders. Muscular arms. Dark hair sprinkled his chest from nipple to nipple before narrowing into a thin line that bisected his six-pack abs and disappeared into the waistband of his jeans. Her gaze riveted on the hard bulge beneath his zipper for several fast, furious heartbeats before shifting north.

"Hungry?" he asked.

She swallowed. "You have no idea."

"Me, too." He glanced past her at the stairwell leading to the apartment. "I was thinking I could grab a shirt and we could go for pancakes or something."

The mention of the word made her stomach grumble and he grinned.

"The diner is already open if you want some." She didn't miss the heat that simmered in the aqua depths of his eyes, which made her all the more confused as to why he'd stopped before the main event last night.

He obviously wanted her.

She could see it.

Feel it.

But then his gaze darkened and he stiffened, as if he'd just remembered some all-important fact.

"Just give me a few minutes." He moved past her, up the stairs, and into the apartment while she stood there, her heart aching for something she couldn't quite name.

Pancakes. Sex. *Love.* Luckily, he hauled open the door at that moment, a shirt stretched tight over his broad shoulders, and she didn't have to think too hard about that last thought. Instead, her stomach grumbled again, helping her to hit rewind until the only thing on her brain was scarfing down some breakfast.

"Let's go." He took her hand and she followed him to his truck.

Half an hour later, they were seated across from each other at the diner, a stack of pancakes between them.

The first breakfast of many over the next few days as Monday loomed ahead of her like a black cloud.

"Looks like we're early," Tyler said as he pulled the truck to a stop outside the bus station early

Monday morning and noted the empty seats inside. He glanced at his watch. "Looks like we've got an extra half hour." He eyed his brother. "You hungry?"

Cooper shook his head and stared at the window.

"Thirsty?"

Another shake and his brother caught his stare. "I'm still not sure about this."

"About what? Making something of yourself? That's the one thing you should be one hundred percent sure of. You can do this, Cooper. I know you can. It won't be easy, but nothing worthwhile ever is."

Not bull riding.

Or falling in love.

The last thought struck and Brandy's image danced in his head. But he didn't see her stretched out on the bed in front of him. Not this time. Instead, he saw her sitting in the car that first night, her hands sticky with chocolate shake, a smile curving her full lips. And again at the diner, her mouth stuffed with pancakes, syrup dribbling down her chin. She was as beautiful out of bed as she was in it.

Breathtaking.

"You earned the scholarship. College is going to be a piece of cake."

"But what if it's not? What if I wind up right back here?"

And there it was. The fear that haunted his brother.

The same fear that haunted Tyler himself.

The notion that he would bust his ass in Cheyenne, that he would break an arm or a leg and wind up stuck back in Rebel, holed up in the two-bit trailer that held so many bad memories.

He was terrified to wind up back here, but he was even more afraid not to leave in the first place. To at least try.

To never know if maybe, just maybe he might have been something.

"So what if you do go off to college and fail? What if you wind up right back here? You're no worse off than if you say to hell with it right now and just stay. At least if you go, there's a chance at more. But there's no chance if you don't get on that bus, little brother. No chance in hell."

"You really think I can do this?"

"I know you can, but even if you don't, you're still my brother and I'll always love you."

Just as he would still love Brandy whether she loved him back or not.

The truth vibrated through him. Yep, he loved her, all right. Not that it changed anything. He was still going. She was still staying.

That's the way it had to be.

He wanted her to be happy, and if that meant her staying here, then he would let her when the time came.

He just wanted to know how she felt before then. To at least feel it for a little while.

Until Tyler packed his bags and left Rebel, Texas, for the last time.

Because no way was he coming back this time.

"You can do this," he said again. "I know you can and so does she." He motioned to the petite brunette sitting off to the side in the bus station, a small suitcase next to her. Erin stared around, her gaze searching and finding Cooper in that next instant. A smile touched her face and just like that, Cooper didn't look quite as scared.

"She chewed me a new one last night when I told her I still hadn't made up my mind."

"Because she knows how important this is."

"That, and she doesn't want to do it alone."

"So go and play the hero. Help her out. You can't let her go off all by herself."

"We did promise each other we would do this together."

"A man's only as good as his word."

Cooper nodded and gathered up his duffel. "You're right." He reached for the door handle. "I still might fall on my ass."

"It's okay if you do," Tyler told him and he realized in that instant, that it was. If Cooper failed miserably, Erin would still care about him.

And if Tyler himself failed?

Brandy would still care.

At least he thought so. But there was only one way to be sure.

CHAPTER 36

They were three weeks shy of the wedding and Callie still couldn't make up her mind.

Brandy fought down the urge to scream and took off the powder-blue dress before stuffing it back onto the hanger and reaching for the hot-pink number sitting nearby.

Her twenty-ninth dress.

Seriously.

She slipped it on and tugged the bodice up over her breasts but it wasn't about to fit. Not when the dress was made to fit a twig with zero figure.

She was just about to shove it back down when she heard the deep, husky voice.

"Not bad."

Excitement rushed through her for several fast and furious heartbeats before two all-important facts registered.

First, she wasn't doing fast and furious with Tyler McCall. Not anymore. Not since fast and furious led to long and slow and, well, she couldn't go there with him any more. She wouldn't.

That's why he'd spent Sunday night alone while she'd walked the floors at home all by herself.

Actually, she hadn't walked so much as she'd moved. All of the boxes from her grandpa's room out onto the front porch. With the exception of the one box containing a few pairs of shoes, James Harlin's grandmother's old Bible, and three belts that Sheriff DeMassi had confiscated on Saturday morning. The rest Brandy had transferred to the front porch to wait for the church van to pick up the donation.

She'd finally decided on the church when she'd come to realize that it really didn't matter which one she picked, just as it didn't matter if her grandfather had really and truly loved her—or not. It was something she might never know and she had to be okay with that.

She was, she told herself for the countless time. So what if he hadn't given her the time of day? He'd eaten a cookie or two in his time, so she knew he'd at least noticed her.

And that would have to do. She accepted it, just as Tyler had been forced to accept that their booty calls were officially a thing of the past.

She blinked, praying that he would disappear. He wasn't real. This was just a figment of her imagination. Another fantasy to add to the long list that had haunted her each night as she waited for Tyler to ride out of town and leave her like he always did.

He didn't disappear.

The curtains swished closed behind him and he simply stood there. He looked so tall, dark, and delicious in his white button-down, his shirt-sleeves rolled up to reveal tanned forearms, his faded Wranglers worn and snug in all the right places. He'd left his hat behind and so there was nothing except a thick fringe of black lashes shadowing the intense aqua of his gaze.

He eyed her, his attention sweeping from her head to her toes and back up again.

Her heart thundered and goose bumps chased up and down her bare arms. Bare, as in naked. She was naked in front of him. Again.

When she'd vowed to keep her clothes on.

Hello? You're wearing underwear. Granted, it's a pair of skimpy bikini briefs, but still.

The last thought killed some of the panic she was feeling and she drew a deep, calming breath. She wasn't completely nude, and she certainly wasn't going to forget everything she'd worked so hard for. She wasn't giving up the bakery and he wasn't giving up his career, and so they were at a standstill.

On opposite sides of the spectrum.

Hopeless.

She reached for the straps on the dress and pulled it up, eager to cover up as much as possible.

"You look good in that," he said as he took a step toward her.

"It doesn't fit," she responded. "It's too small."

"That's why I like it." He took another step.

"I can't go prancing around in front of everyone like this."

"Not everyone. Just me." The deep, husky words slid into her ears and thrummed the length of her spine. He stood even closer now, his body so hard and warm and tempting in the frigid air-conditioning of the dressing room.

He stepped up behind her, his chest kissing her shoulder blades.

The scent of him surrounded her and his hard warmth teased her shoulder blades. When she felt his large, callused fingers at her waist, her own grasp went limp. The straps of the dress slid from her desperate grip. Her head snapped up and her gaze collided with his in the mirror.

His aqua-blue eyes glittered back at her, bright and hot and mesmerizing. "You're really something, you know that?"

"I . . ." She swallowed. "You shouldn't be in here."

"Maybe I shouldn't, but I couldn't help myself. I can't stop thinking about you and that photographer your sister tried to set you up with. You can't go out with him."

She hadn't meant to tell him, but the subject of Callie and the wedding had come up over pancakes and, well, she'd needed to talk to someone. Especially since she was dreading the blind date.

"Says who?" she countered.

"Please don't go out with him." He shook his head, a strange light glimmering in his gaze.

"When I think about the two of you . . . about him touching you." His hand slid around her waist and trailed down her abdomen to her panties. His fingers skimmed the pink silk triangle covering her sex. "About him touching you *here*—" His voice caught. "It's driving me crazy."

"I . . ." she started, but his intimate touch stalled her frantic thoughts before she could come up with something coherent. Reason fled in the face of so much sensation, and the only thing she could do was feel.

His fingertips burning through the thin material of her panties. His hard pelvis pressed against her buttocks. His strong arms surrounding her. His warm breath ruffling the hair at her temple.

"You're mine, Brandy. You've always been mine."

"You're leaving," she pointed out. "Cooper got on the bus this morning. Duff told Ellie."

"It doesn't change anything. I still don't want you to see anybody else."

Because he loved her? Because he wanted her?

The questions rolled through her head and she waited, her breath stalled, to hear the words.

Not that it would matter.

That's what she told herself.

"I love you, Brandy. I don't know what the hell to do about it. I just know that I always have and I always will," he murmured once more and then he walked away.

It doesn't matter.

She repeated the mantra to herself, but as he

walked away, she couldn't shake the crazy rush of joy that went through her, followed by an emptiness so profound that Brandy found herself blinking frantically when Callie and Jenna threw open the curtain and walked in from the opposite room.

Because it did matter.

"What's wrong with you?"

Brandy sniffled and shook her head and did the only thing she could—she played off her rush of emotion as dress-inspired. "It's just so beautiful," she cried, motioning to the latest disaster.

Callie smiled as Jenna fought back a look of horror. "I think we've got ourselves a winner."

CHAPTER 37

I love you.

The words echoed through Brandy's head throughout Tuesday morning, taunting her as she tried to concentrate on pulling a batch of blueberry muffins from the oven. She had to get back on track and forget all about Tyler and the fact that he loved her.

Just where did he get off loving her? He wasn't supposed to love her and she wasn't supposed to love him.

Her heart pounded double time and tears burned the backs of her eyes as she tried to concentrate on refilling another muffin tin.

One scoop per tin. Top off with crumbles. Extra blueberries on top.

Just the way Tyler liked them.

Not that he was going to get a taste. Not this time. He was leaving in a matter of hours, regardless that he loved her.

Regardless that she loved him.

She did.

Denial rushed through her. No, she didn't *love*

love him. She was close . . . Dangerously so. That's why she'd barricaded herself in her kitchen and left Ellie and the others to handle the front business. Because she needed to keep busy, to work and not think.

Because she wasn't falling all the way, not head over heels, body, heart, and soul, in love with Tyler McCall. Love required sacrifice, and as much as she wanted to, she just couldn't sacrifice everything she'd worked so hard for.

She wouldn't.

She wouldn't do something so self-destructive as to fall in love with any man. She wouldn't give up everything.

If only everything didn't seem like nothing at all without Tyler McCall.

"What do you mean you can't see me?" Tyler demanded when he stomped into the bakery later that afternoon, after a very heated phone conversation. He'd called to ask to see her, no doubt to discuss the bomb he'd dropped the night before and tell her he still had to leave. Of course, she'd turned him down.

And turned him down again when he'd called back the second time.

And the third time.

Now here was Tyler himself, standing on the other side of the counter, wearing a black T-shirt that read IT'S ALL ABOUT THE RIDE and faded jeans and an intense look that made her pulse leap.

"Let me rephrase that, I don't want to see you." There. She'd said it, despite the fact that she was inhaling the all-too-familiar and terribly sexy scent of warm male and leather and him. Her nostrils flared and her lungs filled, and Brandy damned herself for being so weak.

She wasn't weak. She was holding her own, keeping up her defenses, until Tyler made a run for the hills and she could let her guard down again. And, more important, before she gave in to the hunger inside her and begged him to stay.

"We need to talk—"

"—you're leaving," she cut in. "I know. It's no big deal. I know you didn't mean what you said the other day. You were worked up and so was I and you didn't mean to say what you said."

"Oh, I meant it, all right—"

"Oh, wow, would you look at the time? I've got a birthday cake due over at the church for Maureen O'Reilly's eightieth. I promised to deliver it myself and I'm late," she said, untying her apron and hanging it on the nearest hook. "Look, you just run along and don't worry that I'm making more out of it than you meant. We all get a little crazed in the heat of the moment. Chemistry is a powerful thing. People mistake lust for love all the time. Just look at the divorce rate. Lust," she rushed on before he could say anything to shake her determination. "The other night was just a bad case of lust, but now it's sated and—"

"Is it?" he cut in, his gaze deep and searching,

as if he struggled to see everything she was trying so hard to deny.

"Yes," she declared with as much bravado as she could muster considering he smelled so good and she had this insane urge to press her head to his chest just to hear if his heart was beating as fast as hers. "It's definitely sated."

He eyed her for a long, breathless moment, and she knew he was going to argue with her. That, or throw her over his shoulder and tote her back to the rodeo arena and make love to her over and over until she developed such a craving for him that she couldn't keep from loving him back. And damned if a small part of her didn't want him to do just that. To take the decision out of her hands so that she didn't have to think, to worry, to be afraid of what she felt for him.

What she *almost* felt, she reminded herself. She wasn't there yet. She wasn't in love. Not with him. She *wasn't*.

As if he sensed the turmoil inside her, his fierce expression eased into his usual charming grin—which made her that much more wary.

"It was fun," she blurted, "and now it's over. Let's not make more of it than what it was. You go your way and I go mine."

"Lust, huh? Just lust?"

"Exactly."

He nodded. "And it's over, right?"

"Right."

"Good. Then I don't have to worry about you

jumping my bones while I walk you over to the VFW Hall. I need to say a few good-byes." He shrugged. "You're going and I'm going. We might as well walk together."

"No." She shook her head. "I can't." She put her purse back down beside her.

"So you're not going?"

"Of course, I am. Later. After lunch." She eyed the half-eaten hamburger in front of her. "You just run along and do your business and I'll stop off later. I think that would work much better. I mean, our time together *is* over. Business concluded. You really should get on with your life, and I'm already zooming right ahead with mine."

He eyed her for a long moment. "You're stubborn, you know that?"

"I'm confident, not stubborn. I just know what I want out of life, that's all."

"Let's hope." He winked before turning toward the door.

She drew a deep, steady breath and sent up a silent thank-you. The good-bye was over. Now he would leave and she could get back to work and all would be right with the world again. Rationally, she knew that.

It was the irrational urge to run after him and throw herself into his arms that scared the crap out of her, and made her all the more determined *not* to love Tyler McCall.

She loved him.

With any other woman, Tyler might have had

his doubts. After all, she'd ditched him last night and given him the brush-off just now. Talk about rejection.

But this was Brandy.

Bold, sassy, sexy as hell, and scared.

Business concluded, she'd said.

He might have believed her, except that he'd seen the wariness in her eyes, heard the desperation in her voice. There'd been none of the cool confidence of a woman completely uninvolved, none of the nonchalance of someone ready to turn her back and walk away because she didn't feel anything for him.

Yep, she loved him all right, and so Tyler had backed off when he'd wanted nothing more than to pull her close and never let go. He didn't want her to feel pressured or anxious or afraid.

He wanted her willing, sure, certain-beyond-a-doubt.

That meant she had to come to terms with her feelings in her own time, and so he decided then and there that he wasn't going to press or push.

Not too much, that is.

He certainly wasn't going to hide away and bide his time and simply hope that she came to her senses. Tyler had never been a patient man when it came to something he wanted, and he really wanted Brandy Tucker.

And she wanted him back.

She just needed a little help admitting it.

CHAPTER 38

"There's a word for this, you know," Brandy said nearly a week after Tyler's declaration when she opened her front door to find him standing on the stoop.

Still in Rebel even though the Cheyenne rodeo was happening in less than a week.

The devil danced in his eyes as he grinned. "Dating?"

She ignored the thumping of her heart and glared. "Harassment. You've shown up every night this week." Every night at exactly the same time. So punctual she could have set her clock by him.

As if his presence, so tall and sexy and reliable, wasn't bad enough, he'd come bearing gifts. The first night, he'd shown up with a dozen pink roses. The second, he'd brought a box of chocolate-covered strawberries. The third had been a gallon of ice cream from the local Baskin Robbins. Today?

She eyed the starched Wranglers and pressed

western shirt. He'd traded the frayed straw cowboy hat for a sleek black one, his boots shiny and polished. He handed her a clear florist's box with a wrist corsage nestled inside.

"What's this for?"

"The Elks are having their monthly dinner and dance, and I thought you might want to get out."

"Shouldn't you be training?"

"I'm done for the day. Besides, this is more important."

You're more important.

That's what his gaze said even though the words never left his lips.

Wishful thinking, she told herself.

"Come on. You need to get out. Have a little fun."

Like hell. That's what she wanted to say, but truthfully she'd never felt so idle in her entire life. She'd finished up all her prep for tomorrow and the only thing that loomed ahead was a lonely night watching *Shark Tank* reruns with Jez the dog. "If I go, you have to promise me that this is strictly platonic. Just two friends having a night out. Promise me." Her heart pounded for several long seconds as she held his gaze. "Please," she finally added.

As if he sensed her desperation, his expression faded and he nodded. "Just friends."

"This is my friend, Brandy Tucker." Tyler introduced Brandy for the umpteenth time to one of the elderly couples standing near the punch table and she did her best not to frown.

They were just friends, she reminded herself.

Which meant it shouldn't bother her when he said the word. Or left her sitting alone to dance with Mrs. Meyers, the chairperson for the event. Or Mrs. Davenport, wife of the head Elk. Or Mrs. Carlisle, newly widowed and president of the senior ladies crochet circle.

She watched Tyler lead the small, round woman around the dance floor. Her silver hair piled high on top of her head in a monstrous beehive. Bright-orange lipstick matched the blinding shades of her flower-print dress, and her white patent-leather shoes gleamed in the dim lighting. With every turn, Brandy glimpsed the top edge of her knee-high panty hose just below her hemline. On top of that, the woman was three times his age.

It's not like Brandy had anything to be jealous of even if they had been more than friends.

Which they weren't.

"Where's the domino group?" she asked the minute he walked back to their table. "The band's playing so they should be out back by now, right?" She pushed to her feet. "I think I'd like to sit in on a hand."

"I promised Miss Earline I'd dance with her first."

"Then point me in the right direction and you can go dance with Miss Earline."

He eyed her for a long moment, and a light

twinkled in the depths of his eyes. "If I didn't know better, I'd say you're jealous. But then that would mean that you actually do care, and you've been hellbent on making it clear that you don't."

"I'm not jealous, I'm just anxious. I have to be up early tomorrow. They're bringing in my new second oven."

"Don't worry. I'll get you home in plenty of time for a good night's sleep. But first things first, let's have a dance."

Two hours later, Brandy stood on her doorstep, her feet aching from all the dancing and her face sore from smiling so much.

She stared at the man who walked her to her door.

"Thanks for tonight." She stuck out her hand to shake his, desperate to keep the distance between them and end the evening before she surrendered to the push–pull of emotion inside her and planted one smack-dab on his lips. "I wouldn't have even known about the dinner dance if it weren't for you and I want you to know that I really appreciate everything. It was more fun than I expected."

He stared at her, into her. "I don't want your thanks."

Her hand fell away. "Please, Tyler. Don't—"

"I want you."

"It could never work. I live here and you don't. And even if you did, I can't get involved with someone right now. It's too much." And then she turned and walked away from him, because after years of clinging to her dreams, of fighting to make them happen, she didn't know if she had the strength or the courage to let go.

Not that she wanted to. She was happy just the way she was.

Wasn't she?

She *was* happy.

That's what she told herself the next day as she fed half a dozen loaves of apple cinnamon bread into the oven and tried to forget Tyler and all the ways he'd made love to her since he'd rolled back into town this last time. The way he'd tried his best to woo her the past few days. The way he'd put his foot down at the thought of her going out with Mike the photographer.

As if he had a leg to stand on.

They didn't owe each other anything.

No explanation. No responsibilities. No expectations.

Which was why she did her best to look the other way when he showed up at the Bingo Hall on Friday night with a date.

She was already there, setting up the platters of coffee cake that the bingo coordinator had ordered, in addition to the dozens of boxed doughnuts from her competition.

She watched him steer the young woman to a nearby table and pure longing shot through her.

Because she wanted to be that woman.

She wanted Tyler beside her, smiling at her, loving her.

And he wanted someone else.

She reached for one of the habanera jelly-filled doughnuts and took a big bite.

Mmm . . . Okay, so they were really good. Better, in fact, than she'd hoped. She took another bite and tried not to look at Tyler and his lady friend.

Walk away. That's what she should have done.

But it wasn't what she wanted to do.

She wanted Tyler. More than anything. She always had, which was why she'd been so scared.

She'd been so afraid of falling for a man who made her feel so much—to the point that there was no room left for anything else. Not her hopes. Her dreams.

Herself.

But she wasn't her mother. She'd already made her dreams come true. She was doing it right now and while she wanted to believe there was no room for anything else, she'd spent far too many sleepless nights to keep fooling herself.

She wanted Tyler every bit as much as she wanted her bakery. More, even.

And as much as that frightened her, what scared her more than anything was her sudden notion that he might leave town and she might never have the chance to tell him how she felt.

The third bite of jelly doughnut lodged in her throat and panic bolted through her. She crossed the room in a few heartbeats and grabbed his arm.

"I really need to talk to you," she blurted "I need to tell you something. I love you," she rushed on before she lost her courage. "I always have, I just didn't want to admit it because I was afraid that I would have to choose. I'm still afraid because you're leaving and I'm not and, well, I have no idea how this could possibly work out, but I don't want to blow it off without even trying. I want to work it out. I want to love you and I want you to love me."

He arched an eyebrow at her. "Is that a proposal?"

"What?"

"Are you asking me to marry you?"

"No. Yes. I don't know. I just know that I don't want you to give up on me and start dating someone else. "

"He's not on a date." The woman sitting nearby gave her a horrified look. "Hells bells, I wouldn't date the likes of Tyler McCall. He's just dropping me off on account of my granddaddy's here and he can't see well enough to read his own Bingo cards."

"She works at the rodeo arena with the barrel racers. She asked if I could drop her off. Since I heard from Duff who heard from Ellie that you were delivering desserts, I thought I'd stop by." Tyler wasn't the only one sticking around Rebel. Duff had decided to lease a small house on the outskirts of town and stick around long enough to see where things with Ellie might lead.

So far it had led to the two of them living together and an engagement ring. Obviously Duff's declaration of love had been the real thing even though neither had wanted to admit it. But the cat was out of the bag and Ellie oozed happiness.

Enough to make Brandy want a little for herself.

But not to the extent that she was going to trade her common sense for a piece of the pie. "Let me get this straight." Her gaze swiveled back to Tyler as realization hit. "You mean I rushed over here and made a fool of myself for nothing?"

"You rushed over here and made a fool of yourself because you love me and I love you. I do, you know. I have since the moment I saw you standing outside the locker room. You were a sight for sore eyes back then and you make me feel just as good now. Better because I know what it feels like to kiss you and touch you and love you." His grin faded and a serious light gleamed in his eyes. "I know and I can't forget, Brandy. I don't want to forget." She saw the sincerity in his gaze, and felt it in her heart, and she knew. She gave in to the longing inside and threw herself into his embrace. Strong arms wrapped around her and held her tight.

"I love you so much," he murmured into her hair. "I don't know what the hell I'm going to do about it, I just know that if you love me it's worth figuring out."

She pulled back and stared up at him, tears streaming down her face, happiness overflowing her heart. "You could stay here."

"And you could go with me."

Warmth coursed through her and she smiled. "Yes," she blurted.

"Yes, what?"

"Yes, I'm proposing to you. I mean, sort of. I'm declaring my intentions. I want marriage and babies and a future, and I want it all with you. Only you. I don't care where we live. If I have to follow you around the country—"

"I won't let you do that."

"If that's what it takes to make it work."

"All it takes is you and me. We can make it work through this season."

"And then?"

"And then we can make it work right here. I'm coming back to Rebel, Brandy. I'm going to buy a little spread near the rodeo arena and train there in between rodeos. I'll hang on and hopefully win a championship or two and then I'll come back here and help with the younger guys the way Brett is trying to help me."

"But you hate it here."

"I hate the memories here, which means it's time to make new ones. Better ones. It's not this place that I hate. I used to think so, but I know now it's the way it always made me feel. But you changed all that. When I'm with you I feel good. Better. Hopeful. It's not so much about getting away from the past as getting over it."

She knew how he felt. She'd cried when the boxes had been loaded into the church van. She'd cried and she'd let go of the past.

And now it was time to get on with the future.

"I love you," she murmured, and then she pressed her lips to his and showed him just how much.

EPILOGUE

"And the first-place ride goes to . . ." The anticipation inside the Las Vegas hotel reached fever pitch as the crowd waited to hear the identity of the new PBR champion. "Archie Wolznak from Quebec, Canada!"

The cheers erupted and Tyler held tight to the second-place buckle in his hand. He waited for the rush of disappointment, but it didn't come.

The only thing he felt at that moment was a sense of excitement thanks to the woman standing next to him.

"I'm so sorry," Brandy murmured, holding tight to his free hand. "It should have been you."

"No, it shouldn't have. I was a long shot. Reaching second place after being number thirty-five in the ranks? That in itself is a miracle."

And how, he realized over the next few hours as the reporters came at him left and right. Everyone wanted a chance to talk to the dark horse who'd shocked the world by climbing the leader board to a solid second. Tyler McCall was the hottest interview ticket behind the scenes and it took several firm refusals to finally shut down the circus.

But Tyler was done talking about the past few hours. He wanted to think about the night to come and the woman standing next to him.

"What do you say we call it a night and head back to the hotel?"

"If I didn't know better, I'd say my fiancé missed me these past few months." Brandy and Tyler had been going back and forth since the ride in Cheyenne. She would join him on the circuit every other weekend, while he flew back to Rebel when he wasn't riding.

It had been hectic and stressful, and the best three months of his life.

Because of her.

Because being with her was worth the plane rides, and the dread driving by the Happy Times Trailer Park. She made everything seem better. Doable.

Especially since she'd agreed to be his wife.

While she'd set up the groundwork with her declaration at the VFW Hall about wanting kids and a future enough to pop the question, he'd wanted to do things right. Traditional. And so he'd dropped down on one knee and popped the question smack-dab in the middle of a Saturday at the bakery.

Brandy had cried. The few customers had applauded. And the gossip had started. Another Sawyer tying the knot with another Tucker. Talk about shameful.

But Tyler didn't give a lick what people said, and neither did Brandy. Just as her older sister had bucked tradition and married Brett Sawyer, Brandy was more than happy to face the critics and declare her love for the enemy.

Callie and Brett's wedding had been the biggest event to hit Rebel in a long, long time and folks were still talking about how lavish and extravagant it was.

And they were still talking about Brandy and her elaborate cake creation. One that had landed her on the Home page of the Hill Country Happily Ever Afters wedding site and a steady stream of cake orders throughout the next year.

Brandy was in cake heaven, and Tyler was just in heaven. Despite the recent news that had just surfaced.

Sheriff Hunter DeMassi had just announced that he was officially reopening the investigation into Brandy's grandfather's murder based on new evidence that put him at Big Jimmy's still just a few short nights before the explosion. And even more DNA confirmation that someone else had been at the scene of the explosion.

Big Jimmy's DNA had turned up just outside the blast site and Sheriff DeMassi was busy trying to pin a murder rap on the man.

But there were still many unanswered questions, and so the investigation would continue.

The news had stirred even more questions about Brandy's grandfather and her lack of relationship with him—all of which she'd shared with Tyler. And while he couldn't change her past any more than he could change his own, he could make the future so bright it overshadowed everything else.

He loved her and he intended to spend the rest of his life making her happy.

"Has anyone ever told you that you look good in a cowboy hat?" he asked as he sat his on top of her head and stared into her brilliant green eyes.

"No, but I seem to recall someone who likes to see me in boots and little else."

"Now, there's an idea, sugar," he murmured. "Only this time we'll try it with the boots and the hat. I already had my ride." His gaze caught and held hers. "It's time for you to climb into the saddle."

"Lead the way, cowboy. Lead the way."

Coming soon . . .

Look for the next Rebel Moonshine novel by
Kimberly Raye

TEMPTING TEXAS

Available in November 2016
from St. Martin's Paperbacks